TRIAL BY FIRE

SHADOWS OF LONDON #3

ARIANA NASH

Trial by Fire, Shadows of London #3

Ariana Nash ~ *Dark Fantasy Author*

Subscribe to Ariana's mailing list & get the exclusive story 'Sealed with a Kiss' free.

Join the Ariana Nash Facebook group for all the news, as it happens.

Edited by No Stone Unturned Editing.

Proofread by Marked and Read.

Cover design by Natasha Snow.

Warning: The unauthorized reproduction or distribution of this copyrighted work is illegal. Criminal copyright infringement, including infringement without monetary gain, is investigated by the FBI and is punishable by up to five years in federal prison and a fine of $250,000.

Alexander

Thomas Montgomery shook my hand with gleeful force. "Alexander Kempthorne! What an absolute pleasure it is to meet with you." He cupped my hand in both of his and squeezed. His pale, almost slate-blue, eyes narrowed, then widened again, freezing and thawing in the space of a second. "We have met before, although I doubt you recall. You were a plucky young man then. Shall we sit?"

Plucky? Hm, I didn't recall being plucky. More troubled, tortured, alienated. "Please do." I wasn't sure I recalled much of this man either, although he was familiar.

I took my hand from his and resisted the urge to wipe my palm on my thigh. As we both made ourselves comfortable at the restaurant table, I stole a few surreptitious glances to read the man whom Robin had arranged for me to meet. Thomas Montgomery's tweed jacket, thick sweater, and corduroy trousers suggested an old-fashioned taste in clothing. Wiry grey hair continued down bushy sideburns into a trimmed salt and pepper beard. The overall affect was neat and well kept. Quick smiles and rapid gestures suggested an approachable friendliness. The kind of man who would hold open doors for the elderly and pet puppies. Unfortunately, the off-kilter resonance of his trick cut through all the outward deception and revealed this man was potentially one of the most dangerous latents in London.

"I must say," Montgomery went on. "You're a hard man to get hold of." He chuckled, picking up the lunch menu.

"My assistant can be somewhat aggressive in fielding my calls." The smile on my lips wasn't as genuine as it could have been. When I'd agreed to this meeting, I hadn't expected Montgomery to be a latent, nor had I expected his trick to undulate and throb in a way I'd never seen before. We had met before, I was sure of it, sometime during my early academy days, perhaps. Days I didn't like to dwell on.

Absorbers, such as myself, can spot a latent even when they're not wielding their trick. Normally, a trick manifests as a slight aura. Most tricks radiated hues on the white and yellow spectrum. Montgomery's was purple and black. Most tricks rippled softly, as rhythmic as breathing. His twitched and sparked, as though pinned and desperate to flee. I'd never seen anything like it.

Considering his age and the fact latents had only begun to emerge in the seventies, he had to be one of the first, predating the IRL's register. That made us both powerful, and both unregistered. Interesting.

We ordered lunch, then coffee, and exchanged typical small talk regarding the weather, stocks, and London traffic. All the while, I fought not to stare at his trick or lose my thoughts in what its painful beat meant. What kind of latent was he? Could he see my trick? If he was an absorber, he could. But if he had any sense of the power I carried, he didn't show it.

With the coffee cups almost drained and the small talk all but exhausted, Montgomery's jovial tone hardened. "Forgive my bluntness, but the real reason I asked for us to meet is to offer you a proposition. I'd like to invest in your agency." He took a sip of his coffee, set his cup down, and leaned back in his chair, fixing his unnerving attention on me. "You're consistent in closing cases. A team of three with your success ratio? Remarkable, really."

"Four."

"Sorry?"

"A team of four. Five, if you're including Mr Mitchell?"

"Ah, of course, the recent addition of *the American*." He'd said *the American* as though he'd had something stuck in his teeth. "How is the case for John Domenici's innocence coming along?"

Montgomery was well-informed. Suspiciously so. "It's coming," I hedged.

"I wish I could help." He spread his hands and applied a sad smile. "He's in Wordsworth?"

"Temporarily." I picked up my coffee, diverting my gaze from the man and his distracting trick, and buying myself valuable time to mask my expressions. "I'm sorry

to disappoint you, Mr Montgomery, but Kempthorne &
Co has no need of a business partner. We're quite
comfortable, financially."

He laughed with such abandon several other restaurant guests looked over. "Of course you are. The
Kempthornes didn't leave you wanting, dear boy, did
they."

Too late, I'd narrowed my eyes, and some of my real
thoughts likely bled through my sociable mask. What did
this man know of my parents' situation, and mine? He
smiled and said all the right things and appeared to be
mostly harmless, but at the mention of my parents, some
of the kindness had left his eyes. This was... interesting.
He knew far more than he was letting on. He believed he
had something over me. Perhaps he did. My parents'
activities went far beyond my own personal experiences
and the pieces of information I'd scraped together on
them. Montgomery was of their generation, before the
IRL, when *things* were done very differently. Such as
experimenting on latent children in search of the source
and ultimate power.

He leaned forward and lowered his voice. "It's not
money I want to invest. You obviously have no need of
that."

"Then what are you offering?" I measured my breathing, careful to keep my heart rate from spiking. Any
increase in blood flow would risk my trick responding,
and if he could see me, as I saw him, he'd know my
current smile was shallow.

"Knowledge." Slate-blue eyes sparkled.

He had an angle, but I couldn't see it, and there was

little I hated more than finding myself on the back foot. "How so?"

"Unlike the other agencies, yours tries to help latents. I do the same." He produced a business card from inside his tweed jacket and set it down on the table.

Thomas Montgomery.

Latent Studies & Neutralization.

Wordsworth Psychic Correctional.

"I believe they can be... freed of their affliction." He pushed the card across the table and gave it a tap.

I kept my gaze on it, careful to buy myself a few heartbeats to maintain a flat expression. Wordsworth. Was that why he'd mentioned Dom? Was this a precursor to some kind of bribe? *Let me into the agency and I'll see Dom receives fair treatment?* Wearing my smile again, I set down my coffee and met his sharp gaze. "Do *you* want to be freed, Mr Montgomery?"

Now he knew I'd *seen* him. Seen his trick, seen what he was. Seen his truth. All the humor vanished from his eyes and his lips thinned. I found myself looking at the real man behind the jolly, friendly persona. We all had masks, and I'd taken a peek beneath his.

"We're alike, Alex," he said coolly. "We should help each other."

"You're employed at Wordsworth?" I picked up the card and examined it. It was certainly going on my murder wall. Despite my best efforts not to call my montage at Ravenscourt a murder wall, the title had stuck. Although, Dom couldn't have known how accurate his assessment was.

Montgomery stared, unblinking. As a latent in a position of power within Wordsworth's walls, Montgomery was someone to be revered. He knew about me, about my family, about latents. He'd brought up Dom's incarceration. This was more than a luncheon meeting. He was here to read me, as I was reading him. He knew more than I did. That was the glint in his eye—*knowledge* indeed.

Had Thomas Montgomery somehow maneuvred Dom into Wordsworth so that Montgomery and I might be seated here, discussing our futures, or was that too much of a stretch? Max—the unstable latent who had targeted Dom—had recently been released from Wordsworth, and with a convenient dirty artifact whispering in his ear, no less. The kind of dirty artifact bought from illegal auctions. Max had also had a list of latents who needed to be *removed*. The list, the artifact, Max—I'd pinned them to my wall, and all those loose threads led back to Wordsworth.

Back to Thomas Montgomery.

Coincidences were also facts.

Thomas Montgomery...

M?

Surely not?

Multiple threads wove together, pieces from my wall falling into place.

M... the figure who had been one step ahead of me for years, the man who had tried to deter Dom and me from looking too close at his workings, the man who had given Dom the dirty pen. But why? As a test? To see what Dom could handle?

"I don't trust easily, Mr Montgomery. And I feel there are a great many things you're not telling me." His eyes shone with knowing. He knew I was an absorber. I knew he was M. Historic tension crackled between us. "Perhaps, if you truly wanted to offer me something of worth, you could release my agent, John Domenici? There are no lawful grounds for his incarceration. He's been legally cleared. It's nothing short of abduction. Help me, and perhaps we can talk some more about your interest in my agency?"

His smile turned artificially sad. "My position at Wordsworth is merely in research." A lie. His trick churned, haloing the man in angry psychic energy. "I can't release John."

It wasn't that he couldn't. He didn't want to. He wanted something from me. Possibly my agency, but my gut told me it was more than that. It was personal. I had to get back to my murder wall, to join the threads and discover if Thomas Montgomery was M, and what that meant for me, for Dom, and for Kempthorne & Co.

I raised my hand, catching the eye of a passing server. "Free John and we'll talk," I told Montgomery, using Dom's real name, then to the server said, "The bill, please."

Montgomery breathed in through his nose and shifted sideways in his chair. He scanned the restaurant, the crowd, and all the softness stiffened, turning his edges hard. "You see them," he said. "You can't stop seeing them. You see them moments before you fall asleep, you see them when you walk down the street, you see them on every corner, in every room. They're everywhere. They want you. They want power. And it's getting worse. What if I told you it's not latents becoming unstable, but the source itself?"

My heart beat its way up my throat. He spoke of shadows. *My* shadows. As though their rising was somehow my fault. "I really don't know what you're referring to."

The server arrived with the card machine and Montgomery watched in polite silence as I settled the bill. The server had barely left when Montgomery said, "You're not a boy any longer, Alex. Your lies won't wash with me like they did your parents."

I exhaled hard and forced a chuckle. I needed to get away from this man and his knowledge before the itch to set the trick free became too powerful to ignore. "You know what I am, Mister Montgomery?"

He cocked his head, curious. The curiosity of a decades old so-called *Academy* and its self-professed members—my parents, and probably Montgomery, among them.

I stood, threw on my jacket and flashed Montgomery a frivolous smile. "I'm the one who got away."

2

Montgomery had won that round. But not without sacrifice. After years of games, M had shown his hand. It was progress. Concerning—he was not what I'd expected—but definitely progress.

I had to get to the murder wall to see how it all fit together. If Dom were with me now, in the new Aston, he'd have theories, he'd pull threads and tie them together. His mind had a way of rummaging around in the dirt to dig up diamonds. But he wasn't with me, because I'd let him down.

I leaned my right foot on the Aston Martin's accelerator pedal, weaving the car through M23 traffic.

Thomas Montgomery was M. I needed Robin on this, immediately. I dialed the office with hands-free.

"*Kempthorne & Co,*" Robin said, picking up.

"I need you to look up everything you can find on Thomas Montgomery. His career, his family, where he lives—*everything.*"

"That will take some time. Gina's out on a tracking case and the shop—"

"Shut the shop. This takes precedence."

"I can't do that, Kempthorne, and you know why. The charity event is at four."

My runaway thoughts slowed. I was due back at Cecil Court by three to host some kind of wine and nibbles thing that included donning a suit, chinking glasses, and eating hors d'oeuvres. A few celebrity authors were due to arrive. We had stacks of books around the shop for them to sign. Tickets had been sold, with the proceeds going to Latent Children in Care. And I had more important things to be doing, such as getting Dom out of Wordsworth. I could tell Robin I wasn't up to it—

"Don't you dare back out."

She knew me too well. "The last thing I need to be doing is schmoozing with —"

"That's exactly what you need to be doing. You know it's for a good cause. And the journalist will be there— what's-her-name? The one who fancies you. She knows the mayor, who knows Wordsworth's governor. You asked me to organize it to get her here. Turn the car around—"

I made a disgusted sound that hopefully Robin didn't hear, checked the car's on-screen map for the next exit, and grumbled, "I was already on my way."

"No you weren't, you were going to Ravenscourt."

"Robin, which one of us is psychic?"

"I know you." She huffed. "And I understand—we all want him back, even me. Schmoozing will help with that. I promise. I'll research a little on Montgomery now and continue after the event. It's called multitasking. You should look it up."

She understood I wanted Dom back, but she didn't understand how I didn't want to go back to London. I didn't want to be Alexander Kempthorne, the man with the perfect life. He didn't exist. What I wanted was to go to Ravenscourt, pin a picture of Montgomery on the murder wall, and see how he fit inside the web that was my real work, my real life. If he was M, and Dom was trapped inside Wordsworth with him... I had to know what that meant. Instead, I was about to spend too many hours smiling until my face ached and my soul was hollow.

"Fine," I surrendered.

"Did you manage to see Dom this morning?" Robin asked softly.

Another sigh. "I arrived at Wordsworth at the allotted appointment time, but he was suddenly unavailable. Apparently."

"I don't believe that."

"Neither do I."

He'd been unavailable a lot lately.

I flicked the car's indicators on and slipped the Aston out of the southbound traffic. Robin stayed on the line, quiet and contemplative. She hadn't always been on Dom's side, but a great deal of her reticence was her protective nature and Dom being an *unknown* at Cecil Court. She knew Dom now. Knew his quick wit, his quick laugh, and his quick hands, with those fiery cards of his. She knew he stole the custard creams, and she knew I liked him in ways that went beyond the professional, ways that consumed my thoughts like a fever. "We must get him out of there," I muttered.

"We will."

She thought I needed him out for personal reasons, because of what she'd seen between us. A rushed kiss, interrupted. And I did want him free for that. But there was more to it. As well as being irresistible, in multiple ways, Dom was a walking weapon. A highly trained, highly tuned latent. In the wrong hands, he could be used to summon an enormous amount of trick and wielded with deadly precision. With us, at Cecil Court, he'd been safe. I'd made sure of it. But somehow, despite my best efforts, I'd failed him.

I couldn't lose him—not another agent, another friend, another someone I cared about.

If anything happened to him...

A liquid glow spilled around my fingers and over the Aston's steering wheel—the trick spilling free, creeping outward, so hungry—

"Your suit is dry-cleaned and waiting."

"I'll be there." I hung up, got my trick under control, and drove toward London and a life that had never felt like mine.

3

Cecil Court in winter shimmered and twinkled like a scene out of a Dickensian novel. Cobbled streets and strings of fairy lights lit up the old bay windows, trailing over rare books or curiosities. The atmosphere of the tiny book-lovers street was partly what had charmed me into buying a slice of it from a retiring gentleman and using it as my London bolthole. The books had been a bonus. From a young age, I'd always lost myself in reading. The countless worlds between their pages were more welcoming than reality. I'd read every book on Cecil Court's shelves, from floor to ceiling and tucked into every corner and alcove. Some I'd discovered to be artifacts, and those I'd set aside in the basement, hidden away—until the basement collection had become too loud and too dangerous to ignore.

"Oh, Alex! I'm early, I hope you don't mind." Rebecca Stevens from *London Today* thrust a champagne flute into my hand the moment I stepped into the shop. With her stout figure poured into a flower-print dress, she filled the narrow aisle, both in personality and physicality.

With no choice but to take the glass, I lifted it and scooted between her and the shelving, trying not to brush too *closely* to either. "A delight, Becky, as always."

At the back of the store, near the till and already in conversation with guests, Robin peered through her glasses, unimpressed by my tardiness. She wore a stunning bottle-green dress, cut above the knee, with her red hair pinned high. Many had underestimated her over the years, assuming her to be my beautiful, ditzy assistant. That was usually the last mistake they ever made. If either of us was prone to daftness, it was me.

"Nice of you to make an appearance," she beamed, cutting off her companion's conversation.

"Sorry. Traffic. My suit?"

"Upstairs." She took the champagne from me and nodded toward the door, where more guests had begun to file in. The shop bubbled with life and laughter, its ambience warming. It was a shame Dom wasn't here to see it—as an authenticator, he'd feel and see how the old building hummed with pleasure.

"I'll be right back."

I slipped through the crowd, sprinkling in a few more polite greetings— "Ah, Mrs Kumar, how are the dogs and children—how lovely,"—and hurried upstairs, passing the agency rooms on the second floor, where most of the Kempthorne & Co work happened, and climbing to my loft apartment.

After spilling off my jacket, I slung it over one of the kitchen island chairs and unhooked my cufflinks. The suit lay on the couch. No time for a shower. I tossed the cufflinks onto the dining table and paused. Various folders and notes from my latent research that hadn't yet made it to Ravenscourt covered the table—I liked them that way. And everything almost looked as it should. I knew every slip of paper, every post-it note, and every photograph. And I knew exactly where they should be. Chaos to the casual observer, but it was organized chaos. My organized chaos.

A note was out of its proper place.

Someone had been here. Not Robin. She knew never to touch.

I might have blamed Dom, had he been free to snoop. He was rather good at it.

Someone else had been inside my apartment.

Someone uninvited.

A guest, an accident, they'd gotten turned around searching for the bathroom? Or someone else? Someone with a motive?

The door hadn't been locked. I hadn't thought it necessary, but I'd forgotten about the event.

A quick scan of the loft revealed nothing else amiss. Whoever had taken themselves on a tour of my apartment would be downstairs. I merely had to ascertain who and what they'd wanted.

I donned the fresh suit, reapplied the cufflinks, ignored my reflection in the mirror, and left the apartment, locking the door behind me. If Dom were here, he'd question the guests and blunder his way into discovering the truth. Without him, the charade I descended the stairs into felt a great deal more suffocating.

Robin caught my eye. Her eyes narrowed and she moved as though to make her way over. I shook my head, caught the eye of an approaching guest, and slammed my barriers down behind my smile—thus began the dance.

I lived two lives. Two halves. The half everyone saw and assumed was real, and the half I kept to myself. The damaged, neurotic, paranoid half. The real me beneath the suits, the expensive watches, the fast cars, and the dazzling smiles. I walked the line between the two with every breath. Dom had seen the real me. Robin had too. There had been others, over the years, but they were gone now.

I spotted a couple standing by the window—a fake couple—and while avoiding Rebecca's attempts to catch my eye, I maneuvered through the crowd to reach the handsome pair.

"Alex, how are you?" Annie's presence was welcome, but the man standing beside her tempered some of my familiarity with her.

"Good evening, Annie. You're a delight." She did look stunning in a blue dress and heels. "Kage," I greeted him, losing any friendliness. "How long have you been here?"

He straightened, shoulders and chin lifting. "I just arrived," he drawled, American accent thick. "Why?" Dark eyes tried to read my face. I'd seen the way Dom gazed at him, drinking in his classically lean stance and too-long hair, right now tied back in a short ponytail that no man older than nineteen years had any business wearing. Accusations rested on my tongue. All of them, so close to the surface. *What were you doing in my apartment?* I knew who he was, who he worked for, why he was here, and I knew he'd fucked Dom, when secretly, I'd wanted *exactly that*. He'd waltzed into our lives—with his gun, his coat, and his Wild West attitude—and seduced the one bloody thing in London I couldn't have. A better man than me would have let it go. Dom had made his choice. But, I'd have liked nothing more than to shove Kage Mitchell through the shop window.

"You just arrived?" I echoed.

"Literally... just now." He snorted.

"Is everything all right?" Annie asked, tuning in to my unease. Her latent aura was a pleasant golden hue, making her glow a little. She was the kind of person who would have glowed even without a trick. One of the good ones.

"Yes. Fine." I turned away from the pair and eyed the crowd, seeking a new target.

We'd sold sixty exclusive tickets. There had to be at least fifty people piled into the shop's narrow aisles. More chatted outside the shop, content to gather on the street. In theory, someone could slip in and out without my seeing them. But the trespasser wouldn't leave, that would rouse too much suspicion. They'd stay, play at being a guest. They were still here...

I caught Rebecca's eye. She smiled and waved me over.

Behind her Robin bobbed her head, urging me forward to begin the real reason for this event. I wasn't going to be able to root out whoever had helped themselves into my apartment, which left sweet-talking Rebecca into asking the mayor to call me so I might have an introduction to Wordsworth's prison governor. So convoluted, so shallow. Good lord, when would this evening end?

Robin placed a glass of wine in my hand. "All good?" she asked.

"Will be." I gulped a mouthful.

Rebecca had zeroed her sights on me and bumped and excused her way over. She greeted me with the usual polite nonsense, complimenting me on the charity event. I remarked on her dress and gave her a few pull-quotes she could print the next day, keeping her happy.

"Darling, you make these events look effortless." Her thin laugh tinkled.

"This is my team's doing. They do all the hard work. I just make an appearance and look rather nice in a suit, like an ornament."

She tittered and rested her hand on my arm. "Well, you're rather more than an ornament, Alex." Her beaming smile lost some of its brightness and she shuffled closer. "I haven't apologized enough for John's unfortunate circumstances and my part in them. I do hope you can forgive me?"

I plucked a fresh glass of wine from a nearby tray and switched her empty glass out. "We all make mistakes."

Her mistakes had cost Dom his freedom, but who cared about one unfortunate latent put away? Not Rebecca or her readers. Things would be so much easier without unstable latents to contend with on the daily commute.

"I heard the man John saved corroborated his story. Still, John has such a terrible past." She tutted, trying to sound sympathetic. "You know what they say, there's no smoke without fire."

I'd never met a single latent who hadn't had a terrible past. And there most certainly could be smoke without fire. They were two very different things. I downed my glass of wine. "Did you ever get around to printing that retraction?"

"Oh yes, of course. I'm afraid it only made it to page five, but it was in there."

Which was better than nothing. Still, the damage had been done. Dom's past, both in the military and with organized crime, had become public knowledge.

"Rebecca, the damage you did with that article can never be repaired." I rested an arm against the bookcase beside her, leaning in, creating a little bubble of privacy. I'd learned, over the years, there was a fine line between threatening and charming, and it really was very easy to switch between the two in a blink.

She lifted her gaze. Her smile began to fall away. "I am sorry."

"I need a favor. Will you do something for me?"

"Well, that depends, Alex."

"We've always had a good relationship, no? Until that article. When you hurt my team, Becky, you hurt me."

"Gosh, I am sorry, Alex—"

"Why don't you help me get John out of Wordsworth? That will go a long way to fixing"—I flicked my fingers between us—"us."

Her eyes widened and her makeup-coated cheeks colored. "I'm not sure what I can do."

"Call the mayor. Have him call me. An injustice was done. John is innocent."

Rebecca laughed dryly. "He's hardly that. Some of the information given to me was too graphic to print. He's an extremely dangerous individual who should be exactly where he is—"

I chuckled, when what I really wanted to do was

backhand her drink from her grasp and demand she leave. "Hm, your racism is showing. It's not a good look."

She flustered. "I didn't mean... It's just... You clearly like John, but perhaps you don't know all the facts about him? His father was... well—"

"I sincerely hope you're not suggesting I don't do my due diligence on my staff?"

Rebecca reached her tipping point and her fluster became anger. "You do realize he's a thug! I have evidence of his crimes going back long before he joined the military. He was Marco Domenici's enforcer. You know the name, I assume, as you've done your due diligence. The things he did—"

"The things he's *alleged* to have done. Were you there?"

"Well, no, of course not!"

"People change."

"Do they though?"

I held her pointed gaze. "No, actually. You're right. They don't. But they can try. Dom has been trying. He's a valuable member of Kempthorne & Co and a dear friend. Do you think I would befriend a criminal, Becky?"

"It's almost, Alex—" She sipped her drink. "—as though your interest goes beyond the professional."

I switched my empty glass for a new one from a nearby table, giving me an excuse to break away from her glare. "What are you suggesting?"

"I think it's obvious, don't you? Women sense certain things." Her eyes raked over me.

It would've been easier on her ego if I was gay—a convenient excuse as to how I'd resisted her advances for so long—and it would sell a great deal of newspapers.

She knew Dom had had past relationships with men; she also knew I was trying to rescue him. Then there was the fact I hadn't dated and appeared to have no interest in the opposite sex at all. You didn't need much of an imagination to put two and two together. Journalists regularly printed facts with less evidence.

"Can you sense the lawsuit coming your way if you print baseless gossip?" I asked, keeping my smile.

"Between you and me, then?" She continued to push, layering on the charm. "Tell me the truth, and I'll get you your call with the mayor."

Two halves. One life. I'd hidden parts of me for so long I sometimes wasn't sure what was real and what was pretend. But this was real. My feelings for Dom were real. Did that make me gay? Labels were so limiting. But it would sell her papers and get me a phone call. "Ask the question."

"Are you and John an item?"

"Wrong question." I smiled into my glass, sipped wine, and wondered what Dom would make of all this. I'd kissed him. And not in a gentle, undecided way. More of a thorough, fuck-me-now way.

"Are you gay, Alex?"

She would print my answer. Tomorrow it would be splashed across her front page. The phone wouldn't stop ringing. Robin would moan about all the extra work. Chaos, drama, accusations. Sometimes it was worth it. Sometimes I wanted to throw the cat among the pigeons just for the hell of it. I had many secrets. Being gay was the least of them. She could have it. Print it. Do whatever she bloody liked with it. Just so long as she helped free Dom from Wordsworth.

"It has never occurred to me that I might be something other than exactly who I am supposed to be," I said. "I am generally not an intimate person, Rebecca. Intimate relationships rarely feature in my day-to-day. But for the sake of your question, yes, I am occasionally attracted to men." It didn't feel terrible saying it aloud. If anything, it felt right. Dom would call that rightness sensation a luxury. Privilege brought with it freedoms few others had. What did I lose by coming out? Nothing. Dom would say that was a privilege too.

"Well," Rebecca said with a sigh. "That's the sound of a thousand female hearts breaking."

I wasn't fool enough to think Rebecca a friend, or that this was anything but a business transaction. But we each knew where we stood. "Help me get Dom out of Wordsworth," I said with more feeling behind it than I'd wanted to reveal.

Rebecca heard it. She was too astute not to. "I will. I owe you both that."

If she did, then this event would be a success, just as Robin had assured me. I searched for her among the crowd just as a tremor ran through the floor, shifting the floorboards beneath my feet. I steadied myself against the bookshelf. How many glasses of wine had I had?

Then the roaring came.

It rolled through me like a physical force—surged upwards through my legs, into my chest. The bookshelf rattled, either from the force of whatever this was or my stumbling into it. Someone screamed. A glass smashed. But all of that was happening on the outside. Inside, my trick twisted me in knots, tightening with every breath. *Too much.* I couldn't control it, couldn't hold it. But I had to. If I let it slip here, in front of all these people, they'd know. Or worse. My uncontrolled trick could level the entire theatre district.

The surge beat hotter, rippling in waves from far below. Had to control it. Push it back down. Not let anyone see it.

"Alex?" someone asked. But I couldn't look up. Had to keep it inside. Stop it breaking out. I was on my hands and knees now, staring between my fingers at the dusty floor. The ground trembled and growled, as though it were alive and about to swallow me. Panic threw my heart against my ribs.

The people here would know... So many people. But they weren't looking, not all of them, because someone else was suffering.

Annie had bent double too. Her latent glow fizzled in my vision, then sparked, growing brighter and hotter. Kage's arms went around her. She fought like I did. He held her close, said something in her ear, recognizing the signs of a spiraling latent.

Nobody held me. Nobody ever had. I'd always been alone. It had to be that way.

As suddenly as the surge had come, its thunderous, earthbound trembling stopped.

"Alex?" Robin. She reached down. I caught her arm, clinging on as though she were a life raft and my only hope. People. I was surrounded by people, and they'd seen. They must have. Did they know? No, my hands weren't glowing, my body wasn't ablaze with trick. I'd kept it hidden, kept it controlled. They'd just seen me have some kind of episode, that was all.

"What happened?" she asked.

Something alive, I wanted to tell her. I could taste it on my tongue, hear it in my head, like a thousand screams boiling up from below us.

The shop phone rang.

I glanced through the staring crowd toward Annie. She had her face buried in Kage's chest. Kage's narrowed gaze caught mine. He had seen. If he hadn't known I was a latent before, he suspected now.

The office phone upstairs rang, joining the incessant ring from the shop phone.

My mobile chirped in my pocket. Robin's bleated. The guests' mobiles began to chirp and chime and ring.

Something had happened. Not just here, but all over London. I knew it in my blood, my bones, my trick. Something fundamental had changed. The source had reached out and touched us all.

"Are you all right?" Robin whispered, trying to meet my gaze. "Talk to me."

"I have to get to Dom."

4

The charity event had been wound down, the shop closed, and now I paced in Cecil Court's small kitchen while Robin called Wordsworth and tried to reach anyone there who could confirm Dom was safe.

Robin shook her head, ended the call, and tried another number. Wordsworth wasn't answering their phones. The prison was in lockdown after latents all over London had simultaneously turned unstable, losing their control. Twenty-three dead, that we knew of, with multiple injuries to anyone who had the misfortune of being near them. Two Wordsworth inmates had succumbed.

I could only hope one of them hadn't been Dom.

The last time I'd seen him, weeks ago in the visitors' room, he'd been clinging to reason and hope. His pride had stopped him begging me to save him, but it had been in his eyes, and since then I'd barely done a bloody thing to get him out. Calls, favors, bribes, threats.

Nothing had worked. Nobody could get to him. Montgomery had been the closest I'd come, despite his denials he could do anything. That man—M—could free him. I just had to give Montgomery whatever he wanted in return.

"What the hell happened out there?" Gina entered the kitchen. She'd been busy with call-outs, mopping up what was left after latents had been overcome.

"A surge," Robin explained, phone to her ear, still trying to reach someone at Wordsworth. "Every latent in London felt it." Someone answered her call and she put on her official-sounding telephone voice for Kempthorne & Co, using the company name to open doors. A few minutes had ticked by when Robin met my gaze and nodded. Speaking into the phone she said, "So, he's all right? Thank you. That's very helpful." She hung up and sighed. "Apparently, he's fine."

He wasn't fine, but he *was* alive. I was his next-of-kin —something he'd laughed about when he'd joined the agency over two years ago. 'I'll put you,' he'd joked, 'There isn't anyone else.' Wordsworth was legally obliged to tell me if he'd died. I let out a breath. He was alive, but he would have felt the surge, it would have been difficult for him—especially alone.

Gina fixed her stare on me, holding nothing back. She blamed me for Dom's incarceration, and she wasn't wrong. By the thunder on her face, she blamed me for the surge too. "Tea?" I asked.

She narrowed her eyes.

"Right." I had to do something. The surge had left me jittery in a way I experienced after absorbing a dirty arti-fact. The psychic blast had been the same, but amplified, coming from *underneath*. All psychic energy originated from below. It was one of the many mysteries of latency.

I boiled the kettle, dropped three tea bags into three cups, and opened a cupboard above the counter. A packet of custard creams sat on the shelf, unopened.

'I ate all her custard creams', Dom had told me. A confession filled with humor and fear. Because he didn't believe Robin liked him; he didn't think himself worthy.

Clutching the counter's edge, I bowed my head and *breathed*. To think of him, in *that* place. Wordsworth Psychic Correctional. It hadn't always been called that. A different name, but the walls still had eyes, and the rat maze of corridors still echoed with shadows.

He was going through hell, and I couldn't bloody well get to him.

"I er... I wasn't sure if you'd want me here."

Kage's American accent grated on my frayed nerves. I hadn't heard him climb the stairs or enter the kitchen.

Did I want him here? No. Could he help? That remained to be seen. "Tea?" I asked without turning around.

"D'yah have coffee?"

It took every ounce of my frayed restraint to make his coffee and set it down in front of him on the table without sneering. Gina scooped up her tea and hung back, keeping her distance, like she had since she'd learned I was a latent. I reached for the custard creams.

"No," Robin snapped. "They stay there. Until he's back."

Leaving the biscuits safe inside the cupboard, I closed the door, picked up my tea, and leaned against the counter. Robin. Gina. Kage. Each was silent, each had their own thoughts. We all cared about Dom in a way he didn't know. "I have Rebecca Stevens making contact with the mayor on my behalf, but after the surge, Dom's well-being is paramount and we can't wait. Does anyone have any more immediate ideas on how to free him?"

The kitchen clock ticked.

"Can we break him out?" Gina asked, eyebrows raised.

Kage twisted in his chair to frown back at her. "It's a prison."

She spread her hands. "You think of something, then."

"Dom has military connections." Kage faced me. "Perhaps his old CO could apply for—"

"No," I said. "They have *history*. His CO is a git who wants Dom behind bars for personal reasons."

Kage fell silent.

"His er..." Robin adjusted her glasses. "*East End* connections? They might have someone inside who can get to him."

"Good." Yes. Promising. "Get on that. At this point, I'll take anything just to know he's all right." All faces turned toward me. "The same as I'd do for any of you, of course." I sipped my tea. The wall clock ticked some more. Only Robin knew the depth of my feelings. Gina perhaps suspected. Kage... *I'd rather not think about him.* "Right, anyway. Gina and Kage, I need you on the phones until the fallout from the surge settles."

"I'd like to help with contacting Dom." Kage lifted sheepish eyes. "I..." He cleared his throat and shifted in his chair. "I said some things to him. And I don't... wanna leave it. Like that, I mean."

I flashed him my classic smile. Exactly what had been said between them? Did he confess to poisoning Dom? I hoped so. "Then how does some light surveillance sound?"

He glanced at Gina for help but she shrugged. "I... okay?"

I pushed from the counter and headed for the kitchen door. "Robin, email me everything you discovered about Thomas Montgomery. Kage and I are going to pay the man a visit."

"Who?" he asked.

"Get your coat." I hammered down the stairs, grabbed a jacket and scarf from the hook by the main entrance, and muttered, "It's going to be a long night."

Thomas Montgomery's house was a modest end-of-terrace house in Brentford, with a postage stamp of a front garden and a Ford Focus in the driveway.

Parked across the street in the Lexus, Kage and I blended in well enough. It was late, and as long as we didn't stay too long, we wouldn't be noticed.

"Why are we here?" Kage asked after fifteen minutes of silence.

"You tell me."

He snorted a humorless laugh. "I have no idea. I don't even know where *here* is."

"Hm." I kept my eyes on the end-of-terrace and the occasional movement behind the closed blinds. Despite the late hour, someone was awake inside.

My mobile rang. *Robin.*

"Hi."

"Okay, so… it took some doing but I managed to track down Dom's friend Renick, at a snooker club in Hackney. He says he can get a note to Dom tomorrow. But he wants something from you."

"Of course he does," I sighed. I hadn't officially met Renick, but I knew him. The nasty piece of work had ordered his people to bind and gag me in a grotty little flat as leverage against Dom. Vicious and surprisingly wily, according to Gina's police contact, Renick was dangerous, but predictable. "If it's money, pay it."

"Not money. He wants to meet you."

"He could have *met me* when he had his people kidnap me. Fine, but tell him I want more than a note inside, I want a note out from Dom too."

"All right. I'll let you know how it goes."

"Thank you."

"We'll get him."

"I hope so." I hung up and felt the weight of Kage's gaze. In the gloom of the quiet car with only a nearby streetlight to illuminate us, Kage's stillness and low-level thrum of general distaste matched my own. On paper, he was my agent. But we both knew the reason for his employment was a lot more complicated. I wanted answers.

We had fallen silent again. The shadows moved behind Montgomery's drapes—normal shadows, not the sentient kind. Those I hadn't seen up close since Dom's incarceration. Just flickers here and there, the sensation of being watched in the dark. The same as I'd always dealt with, at least, since my parents had… changed me.

"Dom accused me of poisoning him," Kage said.

"Good lord, how terrible. Perhaps you shouldn't have then."

He dry-laughed again. "You made up your mind about me months ago. As soon as we met at that dinner in Chelsea, you decided I was your enemy."

"'Enemy' is a strong word." I kept my eyes on the house, aware of Kage's burning stare.

"I don't know what your problem is, but you should let Dom make his own decisions instead of dragging him into your delusions."

I faced Kage. "You spent the night together. The next morning, while you were conveniently elsewhere, Dom experiences an episode that almost saw him level half of Victoria Docks. The only reason he didn't was because of your miraculous reappearance and your bullet in his arm, shocking him out of his downward spiral. I know him like you never will. I know his limits and his control. He's military-trained to control his trick. He doesn't just *go off* in public. He *was* drugged. Please, go ahead and explain that to me."

Kage's cheek twitched. "I don't know, okay? I was walking to the tube, like I told him, and I just... I knew something was wrong, so I went back, and I saw him on the dockside. I know it sounds like bullshit but it's true. I didn't poison him. I..."

I narrowed my eyes. "You what?"

"I care about him. I wouldn't hurt him or put him at risk like that."

"You *care* about him?"

He stared out of the windscreen at the house and sighed through his nose. "More than care, all right? We had a good thing and I think I maybe ruined it the last time I saw him."

I turned my face away from Kage, no longer able to hide the distaste in my expression. I'd never wished I hadn't saved someone quite as much as I did right then. He'd lain bleeding on Cecil Court's kitchen floor, would have died in minutes. I could have watched him die. I'd watched friends die to protect my secrets. I'd done worse. Much worse. But for some reason, I'd pressed my hands on him, charged up the trick, and saved him. For Dom. Because Dom liked Kage, and Kage liked Dom, and it sickened me to think of how bloody perfect they were for each other. Dom's smile when Kage entered the room had made it worth it.

"I don't understand you. You keep me on, but you don't want me here. You try and turn Dom against me—"

"It's not about you," I snapped. "None of this is about you, or me, or Dom. That man..." I pointed at the house across the street. "He's been buying vast quantities of dirty artifacts at auctions for years. He sits in a powerful position at a latent prison and he's part of the original academy that ran experiments on latent children." I choked, but hurried on, hoping Kage missed it. "The experiments conducted at that academy sought a way to harness the source, or in the words of the late Olivia Barns, a god-like entity residing beneath London. A source that recently surged, simultaneously killing over twenty latents in seconds. Wordsworth is at the center of something far worse than any of us has faced, and that man—*M*—is at the heart of Wordsworth."

"M?"

"Thomas Montgomery."

"The man in that house is M?"

"I believe so, yes."

He straightened in the seat, dark eyes fixed dead ahead, then flicked his gaze to me as I watched him. He'd suddenly become invested, when moments before he'd have preferred to have been anywhere else. Because he knew all about M. The single letter had been in his notes.

"You work for the Latent Observation Agency, not the FBI, but close enough. They want you here, either for Dom or for Montgomery—" He tried to laugh me off, but I continued. "Perhaps you do care for Dom, in which case I don't envy you because the US government won't care about your feelings when they order you to stop observing and either kill him or bring him in."

He tried to keep his cocky smile, to laugh me off, but his lips twitched and the laughter in his eyes dulled.

Kage Mitchell met my gaze and took a deep breath. "You don't know the half of it."

"Perhaps not, but I know enough." I was right. Neither of us was happy about it, but I was bloody well right. "I can be your enemy or your friend, that's up to you. But if you put Dom in harm's way, you will quickly discover how easy it is to make a man disappear in London."

"Damn, are you threatening me?" He laughed.

"I'll be more explicit, for the sake of clarity. Jeopardize my operation or my agents in any way and the problem that is Kage Mitchell goes away. I've done it before. Don't think I won't do it again."

He opened his mouth to offer some sort of retort but movement at the house caught my eye. Thomas Montgomery carried a large golf bag to the boot of his car and lifted its considerable weight inside.

"What do you think he has in there?" Kage asked. "A body?"

"There are easier and less incriminating ways to dispose of a body."

Montgomery gave the bag a final shove and slammed the boot lid.

"I was joking," Kage said tightly.

"So was I," I added. It wouldn't hurt to keep him guessing.

Montgomery opened the car door and climbed in. The headlights flickered on, and he pulled away. I gave it a few seconds, hit the Lexus's start button, and followed. "You want information on M as much as I do?" I asked.

"I have orders, yeah." At least he wasn't denying it.

"To bring him in or observe?"

"Observe." Kage's amber eyes—so rare a color— flicked to me and then back to Montgomery's car ahead. "For now."

"Then our interests align. We don't have to be enemies."

"'For now,'" he repeated.

Tightening my hold on the steering wheel, I smiled to myself and followed the Ford's red taillights through Brentford's quiet, late-night streets. Kage was LOA. He'd admitted it. He was, by his nature, an enemy to latents. He had better tell Dom before I did.

"I won't hurt Dom," Kage said softly, his thoughts finding their way to Dom like mine always seemed to.

You already did.

5

Montgomery pulled his car into a sprawling industrial estate lined with high metal fences, CCTV, and floodlights, and stopped outside a rectangular building, single level, wrapped in corrugated metal sheeting. There was nothing to differentiate it from the vast Amazon distribution center next door. No logo, no company name. The Ford Focus pulled up to the gates, waited for the number plate recognition camera to log the car, and when the gates glided open, Montgomery drove inside.

Kage and I watched from the Lexus, parked a few hundred meters away behind a few trees, until the Focus swept around the building, out of sight.

"Looks like a professional set-up," Kage said.

I cruised the Lexus under bright streetlights, taking a right to keep the metal box of a building in my line of sight. The same high fences glittered all the way around. They couldn't be scaled, and even if someone did try to climb them, the cameras dotted about the grounds would record it all. Were they manned cameras or remote?

After completing a loop around the building, I pulled the car to a stop a few hundred meters away from the entrance and switched off the engine. Cloned number plates would get me in. The entrance gate wasn't manned. But sourcing plates would have to wait until tomorrow. Right now, all we could do was wait outside and see what Montgomery brought back out.

"What do you know about M?" I asked.

Kage stared ahead through the windscreen, probably wondering how much to reveal. He leaned an arm against the door and flicked his gaze to me, checking I was still watching. "M recently became a person of interest."

"To the LOA? The agency you work for?"

He scratched his neck. "Before two years ago, 'M' didn't feature on the government radar. But the LOA techs spotted his name in association with the purchase of high-value artifacts—artifacts smuggled to the US. Anyone buying up artifacts is of interest to the LOA. Including you. There's no good reason to hoard dangerous weapons."

"I'm keeping them out of the general population."

"I'm sure Montgomery tells himself that too."

So Kage was tarring me with the same brush as Montgomery. A villain until proven otherwise. He was half right.

"Is he a latent?" Kage asked.

I feigned ignorance. "How would I know?"

His eyebrow arched. "Don't you?"

I could admire anyone who tried to get the measure of me. Kage had been watching me closely for months now. How much had he asked Dom, and how much had Dom told him? Dom was careful, but also smitten, putting him at a disadvantage. "Thomas Montgomery is a latent, yes."

"That's what we thought," he muttered. "An absorber?"

"That I don't know."

"They're the most dangerous."

Kage knew his latents. I was impressed. "How so?"

"As the head of Kempthorne & Co, you should already know."

But he hadn't accused me of being one. I gave him a flat smile. "Humor me."

Sighing, he reeled off, "Absorbers are walking batteries for psychic energy. Dom's trick ebbs and flows, he pulls it from the source and generally keeps a steady charge unless he's spiraling, but absorbers hoard it, potentially amassing immense power. It makes them highly dangerous. Especially if they're unstable."

"You're not just a pretty face."

"The looks help." His perfect smile flashed.

"Did you seduce Dom to get closer to me?"

Kage snorted. "That's some A-grade paranoia you've got there."

"Perhaps." I stared out of the window. A light drizzle had begun to fall, haloing the floodlights around the metal box of a building. What would Dom make of all this? Of Montgomery being M and the LOA observing us, along with the UK military, who—despite my writing them a large check,—had never relinquished full control of Dom.

Our kiss had been the last moment we'd been alone.

I'd been drained from our encounter with the shadows and he'd glowed like a beacon of all things power and light and sex, oblivious to how alluring he was. I'd wanted nothing more than to drink him all the way down, body and soul. I'd wanted him with every fiber of my heart and mind. *Want* was too soft a word. I'd *needed* him, to the point where I'd felt myself beginning to unravel. That was why a kiss was all it could ever be. If it became any more, I'd hurt him, drain him like Olivia did, only worse. Maybe... kill him.

Something about Dom, his trick, the man, flicked all my switches to on in a way I didn't fully understand. But wanted to. I'd wanted to create a murder wall just for him, with all its pins and strings and photographs. Thankfully, I'd held off, or he'd have seen it in Ravenscourt and realise how far my obsession went.

"I didn't *seduce* him," Kage said quietly, now slumped against the door. "I didn't expect to like him like I do. He was supposed to be a target. Nothing more."

"Undercover basics. *Don't believe your lie.*"

He glanced over. "Do much undercover work, do you?"

My whole life was undercover. "I know lies."

"Why am I not surprised." He straightened and glared without blinking. "The posh Englishman act is bullshit, isn't it? That's not you at all. You play to it because it's what everyone expects." He shifted closer. "Who are you really, Kempthorne?"

Movement behind the gate caught my eye. I turned my head away from Kage as a black Transit van rolled out from behind the building, to the gateway. "Just someone looking for answers." The gates opened and the van pulled to the road then waited, engine burbling. Two gloomy figures sat in the front. "Something tells me we've outstayed our welcome."

"Maybe they haven't seen us."

The van trundled off the curb, turning right, toward us. Headlights swept the fences and briefly skipped over the Lexus.

"Get your phone out."

Kage plucked his phone from inside his coat.

"Bring up maps. Quickly."

He thumbed the device as the van pulled to a halt beside us. I hit the button to lower the window. The van's tinted window rolled down, revealing two men who wouldn't have looked out of place guarding nightclub doorways. "You boys need to park somewhere else."

I gave the driver my daftest smile. "We got lost looking for Costa. Google maps brought us here."

Kage raised his phone, showing them the maps, and did a grand job of adding a sheepish smile.

"Does this look like a fucking coffee shop, mate?" the driver's pal suggested, leaning over to get a look through the window. Whatever he saw, his snarl suggested he didn't like it. "Leave."

"This is a public road, you have no—"

"No, it ain't. It's private property. Now piss off. Don't make me get out the van."

"Sorry." I started the car. "There's no signs. We didn't realize. We'll just turn around."

"Yeah, you do that, eh."

With the window up, I pulled the Lexus away from the curb and turned the car in the road. The van glinted all black against the curb as we cruised by, waiting for us to leave. When we pulled up at the junction, headlights flashed behind us. The van was approaching, and as I squinted into the reflection of their high beam, it came to a stop a few inches from our rear.

"Guess we have an escort," Kage said with a flicker of concern.

"Not subtle, are they?" I made a right. The van followed, headlights lighting up my mirrors.

After we'd turned onto the main road, the streetlights ended, plunging us into tree-lined darkness. "Oh bugger."

"'Oh bugger'?" Kage echoed.

"I should have turned left." I wasn't familiar with this area of outer London and didn't know the roads. Trees crowded outside the tunnel my car's headlights made. The white central line snaked, heading deeper into the countryside. The map in the center of the dash wasn't helpful, just showing green either side of a road with no exits.

The van's high beams bounced back off the mirrors, blinding me. "I'm beginning to take this personally."

A wide section of road opened up ahead. I dropped a gear and leaned on the throttle. The Lexus growled, rev needle climbing.

The black Transit stuck fast to our arse.

"I think they've made their point—"

The Transit rammed us. Metal screeched. The car—moving too fast—jolted and tried to snatch its wheel free of my grip. I clung on, fighting to stay in control. All right, this *was* personal. The road ahead appeared to twitch right. I planted the throttle and threw the car around the bend. The Transit backed off, but not for long. As soon as the road straightened, it loomed, then pulled up alongside. Black panels gleamed.

The van slammed into the side of the Lexus. Metal-on-metal screamed again. Glass windows popped, raining shattered fragments. Kage swore and grabbed for the handle. And all the while, I fought to keep us rooted on the road and not buried in a hedge.

Kage suddenly had a gun in his hand. I wasn't sure what was more alarming, the fact two thugs were trying to run us off the road or seeing a firearm thrust in front of my eyes. "Why do you have a gun!?"

"Because I'm in a car with you!"

"I hardly think I warrant a firear—"

The van slammed into us. The Lexus bucked. Its steering wheel tore free of my grasp, and the car's back end fishtailed, sliding sideways. I caught a silvery glimmer of tree trunks sweeping through the Lexus's headlights, knew we shouldn't be facing those, and yanked the wheel back, lurching the car with it. We were going to hit *something*. We had to. The road was only two lanes wide, and we were sideways.

The Lexus's slide rocked to a halt amid a waft of tire smoke and Kage's swearing.

He flung open the car door and was gone, probably to shoot something or someone.

The van's taillights blinked red and vanished, too, its occupants escaping unscathed.

I dropped my head back and sighed.

Kage's, "Goddammit!" echoed outside.

The van had gone, its driver's message clear: Don't come back.

6

We made it back to Cecil Court by 1am. Kage crashed on the sofa while I rattled around my apartment. Chasing sleep was hopeless. Instead, I turned over what I'd discovered so far. I'd learned more about M and also Kage's real motives, but it wasn't enough. None of that got me closer to Dom, or closer to understanding what M was planning.

I waited until the more reasonable hour of 7a.m., showered, and ventured down to the kitchen to find Robin already there, sipping tea and looking thoughtful. Her fluffy green slippers diluted the impact of her hard scowl.

"Good morning."

"Why didn't you tell me?" she asked.

There were multiple possible answers to that. Despite trusting her with most things, there was much she still didn't know. So, what exactly hadn't I told her about? "I..."

She shoved a cup of a tea across the counter toward

me and placed a folded newspaper next to it. The headline read: *LATENT UNREST*, which was sensational but nothing new.

"Page four," she prompted.

I turned the pages and caught sight of my own photograph, taken a year ago at a dinner in some glitzy bar. The headline read: *ALEXANDER KEMPTHORNE'S SECRET REVEALED*. Icy panic clutched my heart until I saw the byline and its author. *Heartthrob Billionaire Reveals He's Gay. Exclusive by Rebecca Stevens.* I arched an eyebrow at Robin. "I would have thought it obvious from what you saw with Dom."

"Not *that*." She rolled her eyes. "The fact you told Rebecca *now*. I'm going to have half of London's gossip columnists calling when I'm trying to do real work, not fielding your superfans."

"'Superfans'?"

"Oh my God. You're impossible." The tone was harsh, but her smile wasn't. She snatched the newspaper out of my hands and harrumphed. "Good for you."

"Why on Earth my sexual preference warrants any attention is beyond me, but it convinced Rebecca to help us and cost me nothing."

"You *came out* for Dom? That's not nothing, Kempthorne." Her glare thawed some more, turning almost soft, in a soppy way that was rare for her. "It's sweet."

"Sweet?" Good lord. I scooped up my tea. "It's really not important. Last night, Kage and I followed—"

A squeal alerted us to Gina's arrival. She flew across the kitchen, as though launching an attack. I tensed, expecting something hideous, like a hug, but she pulled up short and grinned instead, then took the hand not holding my tea and shook it. "This is so awesome." She beamed.

What was?

"If Dom were here, he'd totally lose his *shit*." Moving like a whirlwind, she threw a teabag into a mug that said *Princess* and poured hot water from the kettle. "In a good way, I mean. I cannot wait to tell him!"

"I'm fairly certain Dom already knows," Robin mumbled into her cup.

And apparently, we were still on the tabloid revelation. "Can we focus on work? As I was saying, last night, Kage and I followed Montgomery—"

Kage sauntered into the kitchen, looking like something warmed too many times in the microwave. "Congratulations," he drawled, "on coming out."

"Is there some kind of worldwide announcement?" I exclaimed. "Sky writing perhaps? A full page spread in *The Times*?"

"It's all over Facebook." Kage yawned and dropped into a kitchen chair. "You have a fan group. I joined up a while back for... you know, research. Must be nice." He yawned again. "No more livin' the lie."

I leaned a hip against the counter and breathed in. The irony in his tone wasn't all directed at me, even if his cocky smile said it was. Robin and Gina heard the complicated layers too, and now the kitchen had become exceedingly small. "As I was saying, Kage and I were almost run off the road last night by Montgomery's security. I managed to limp the Lexus home, but it's out of commission for now. Montgomery is up to something he really doesn't want us seeing. Robin, I need some number plates made up for the Aston. I've emailed you the details. Kage and I will return to the warehouse tonight."

Kage nodded, thankfully on board with the plan. "Won't an Aston Martin be too conspicuous?"

"It's the only vehicle I have available and the gates weren't manned. It will have to do."

"I need your note for Dom too," Robin said. "Renick's guy is coming by at ten to pick it up."

"Yes. Right. The note." What I was going to say in that note was another matter I hadn't dwelled on. It wasn't as though I had any good news to tell him. A curiously awkward sensation nibbled on my nerves and had me focusing on my tea.

"You can get a note to him?" Kage asked. Gina had passed him a coffee. He cradled it now. With his hair flopped over his eyes and his clothes all askew, he looked downtrodden and exhausted. I was reminded of the man who had almost died in this kitchen and the reason I'd saved him. For Dom. What was I going to say in a note anyway? *Don't trust Montgomery. Keep your chin up, we're coming for you.* I didn't know how to write the things I felt. Half the time, I didn't understand them myself.

"Do you want to write something?" I asked Kage.

He shrugged and clutched the back of his neck. "Yeah, sure, I guess."

Robin frowned, but I wasn't looking at her and her judgmental expression. Kage could make better use of a note. "Just mention in it to be careful of Montgomery and that he can reply and we'll get it," I said, while the squirming sensation inside got worse, but I couldn't withdraw the offer now. "Assume it will be read, so keep it vague."

"Renick will want to meet you tomorrow," Robin said.

"Set it up for *after* we get a reply from Dom and I'll be there."

"Do you mind if I get cleaned up here?" Kage asked. "I don't think I can face going back to the Docklands apartment."

"Go ahead. Use Dom's room."

"Thanks." He carried his coffee from the kitchen.

I listened to his footfalls echoing down the short hall. The second I heard the sound of the door closing, I turned to Robin and Gina. "He works for the LOA, a US government agency that has a habit of making latents disappear. He will turn Dom in, if he's ordered to."

Robin wasn't surprised. I'd already discussed my suspicions with her, but Gina's eyes widened. "He confirmed it?"

"Yes."

"Son of a bitch!" she hissed under her breath. "I knew there was something off about him. Nobody is that sexy *and* nice."

I snorted a laugh. "I do believe he genuinely cares for Dom though, so there's that angle we need to be aware of."

"Better not tell him you kissed Dom then," Robin said.

Gina sucked in a breath, held it, then exploded. "Oh my God, *why am I just finding out about this now?!* Am I the last to know everything? You kissed Dom?" Her eyes went big and strangely glassy, as though she might cry. If that happened, I'd have to leave.

"If you must know—which clearly you do if we're

ever going to get any work done," I whispered, "Dom kissed me. And it was just a moment. Nothing more."

"Yeah, no." Robin grinned. "That's not what it looked like from where I was standing. And I got an eyeful."

Gina slumped against the counter. "I never get the gossip anymore," she whined. "I miss Dom. We have to get him out."

"I'll get those number plates organized," Robin said, her voice back to business. "And you should write the note, Kempthorne. As much as Dom likes Kage, in that place, it's you he'll want to hear from."

He would? But I couldn't take the offer back now without Kage wondering if there was more to my relationship with Dom than employer and employee, and we really did need Kage on our side. If he learned Dom and I were... something... there was no knowing how Kage might react.

7

The Aston, with cloned plates to match Montgomery's car, burbled to a halt outside the shiny, metal gates and the number plate recognition camera scanned the front of the car. We'd get inside, I wasn't worried, but once inside, the rest was unknown.

My senses itched here like they did at Wordsworth. I had to know more, and fast. Besides, Montgomery had ignored my calls since our luncheon, so he'd left me with little choice.

As the gates rumbled open, my thoughts drifted to Kage beside me, and the note he'd written for Dom. I hadn't read it, despite wanting to. I already knew what it must have said: *Kage was sorry for whatever he'd done. There were some 'other' things he wanted to tell Dom. He hadn't been straight with him, but he had good reasons. He'd tell Dom he cared and missed him.* An idiot could see that much.

I could have told Dom those things. I should have written a bloody note.

"We'd better be quick," Kage remarked, eyeing the perimeter fence and cameras.

The gates clunked all the way open and in we drove.

"We will be."

Montgomery was at home, I had Gina watching his house for any movement, and the rest of the parking lot around the warehouse appeared to be empty. By the time anyone noticed the Aston Martin wasn't Thomas Montgomery's Ford Focus, we'd have seen all we needed to and we'd be done.

I cruised the Aston around the back of the warehouse and pulled her into one of the bays. Cameras clocked us the whole way, but I was gambling on them being unmanned.

Kage tossed me the ski mask and did the slick, Hollywood action of loading a round into his gun's chamber. Dom hadn't been wrong with the nickname. "For the record," he said. "Going into that building blind is a terrible idea."

"Not if it works."

"All right," he huffed. "Let's do this." With a spontaneous burst of enthusiasm, he tugged his mask over his head and climbed from the car.

My mask fit well and smelled faintly of cheap chemicals. I'd dressed down for the occasion, in black jeans and a black sweater. Everything chafed and pinched. Savile Row, the clothes were not. Still, I wouldn't be recognized. There wasn't a soul alive who had ever witnessed me wearing jeans.

I fell into step alongside Kage and the both of us kept

to the shadows along the south side of the squat building. The lack of windows made getting a peek inside an interesting challenge, but there were multiple doors and several fire exits. I'd spotted a potential fire exit during our first drive-by the night before. It was nearby and had a small window. A good place to take a peek.

My gaze dropped to Kage's gun. It hadn't escaped my notice that he could aim it at my head and eliminate me in seconds. "I hope you don't plan on shooting anyone with that."

"I'll wave it around menacingly. Is that British enough for you?" I couldn't see his smile behind the mask, but heard it in his voice, and laughed. Then cut the laugh off. I could not warm to Kage Mitchell.

Kage stopped at the foot of a small set of metal steps and nodded for me to climb. I got to the top and peered through the wire-meshed window. A gloomy corridor stretched into the dark, with doorways leading off it. To see more, I had to get inside.

"Anything?" Kage whispered.

"Can't see." I touched the handle. Locked. As expected. But there was a way to *unlock* it, just a touch of trick should do.

He climbed the steps and peered inside, apparently not believing my assessment.

"Try the handle?" I suggested.

He snorted. "Like it's going to be"—the door clunked open—"unlocked?"

"The English." I tutted, hiding my trick-warmed, tingling hand behind my back. "We never lock our back doors."

With no time to question how the door had become

unlocked, he headed inside and I followed, preferring to keep the man with the gun where I could see him. A low-level thrum vibrated through the hallway floor, like the drone of air conditioning, but it touched the part of me I'd long ago buried deep inside. "Do you hear that?"

"Huh? Hear what?"

There was psychic resonance here. "Never mind."

The corridor fed us straight into the heart of the warehouse, and considering all the cameras on the outside, we hadn't seen any inside. Someone didn't want whatever happened here to be observed.

A vast door barred the way, thick and made of shining metal, like a refrigerated safe. The background droning thrummed louder from behind it. I hadn't been here before, but the door and its thumping beat emanating from behind were familiar.

Kage reached for the handle.

A thrumming sound turned to hissing, growing louder. Whispering. Or bees. A warning. The latent part of me prickled, stirring awake, crackling to my fingers. I knew what it was because I had a similar set up at home, in my study. An overabundance of psychic burn. "Wait, don't—"

Kage cracked the seal on the door.

Air *whooshed* between the gap and silence flooded the corridor, pouring into my ears. My thudding pulse beat like a racing drum in my head. Kage pushed the door open and stepped into bright white light. All of him blurred inside the glare, turning to smoke. Or so it seemed. I gasped, trying to gulp air that wouldn't come. Kage said something, but the silence muffled it, trying to snuff him out. I moved, driven forward toward rows of shining examination tables by a sickening sense of dread and a terrible need to know. A boy's screams echoed from my past. I'd been smaller back then. Weaker. But the tables... the tables were the same.

Two rows of examination tables shimmered under harsh lights. They were empty, but in my head, a boy lay on every one, pulling at the restraints holding him down, begging them to stop. Muddles of tubing hung suspended above each table. Empty now, but they were designed to carry liquid—

Tears are for the weak.

I choked on air that wouldn't come.

Hush, Alexander, it will be over soon.

The room spun. I couldn't breathe. Why couldn't I breathe? I reached for one of the tables, needing it to prop me up, but the second my fingers touched it, the psychic burn lashed out, surging into my fingers and up my arm, diving like an arrow straight to my heart. I wasn't prepared. The psychic blast hit hard, driving me to my knees. All the voices, sensing weakness, came at once. A hundred latents who had been through this room and screamed as they'd carried the weight of a power none of us understood.

Trick bubbled from my fingers and bled across the table. I had to get it back, but my body wouldn't respond. I couldn't bloody breathe, think, move. I was tied down again, fighting uselessly for escape. And when I couldn't get free, I'd begged, until they'd covered my mouth with

—can't breathe.

Fingers dug into my shoulder. "Kempthorne... Can you hear me?"

All around the voices screamed. Mine was among

them, from so long ago. A boy on a table. It hurt. Why wouldn't they stop?

I choked on the memory and pried my grip from the table, falling on my hands in the next breath. Shadows swam in my vision. Real or imagined, I couldn't tell. They couldn't have me, damn them. Nobody could have me again!

I had to get out of this room.

"Get out!" I snarled.

Kage caught my hand and hauled me upright. The room spun again, my feet going out from under me. Too much. It was too much. Like the study in Ravenscourt, the study I never went into, with its dirty table and horrible memories. And the ghost of my sister. The one person who had tried to help.

Kage slammed me against the corridor wall. I blinked wetness from my eyes and panted. Sensation spilled back into my limbs and the screams faded. The door was still there, hanging ajar behind Kage, holding back the horror that was that room. But I was out, I could breathe. I was me again, refilling my own skin.

"You all right?" Kage asked, propping me up with a hand on my chest.

"Not at all." I brushed him off and staggered into motion. "We have to leave. *Now*."

"What is that back there?" He hurried close behind. "What's goin' on?"

"It's where they flood latents." The exit door beckoned, the *FIRE EXIT* sign aglow. Air. I needed air, and some whiskey. A lot of whiskey and a roaring fire and Ravenscourt, and the murder wall, where things began to make sense again. *Put a pin in it, line up the clues, organize the chaos.*

My phone rang, chirping in my pocket.

"Meaning?" Kage asked.

"Torture. It's industrial torture." Saliva pooled around my tongue. I grabbed my phone. Gina: (6 missed calls) Text: *MONTGOMERY LEFT!* The phone's signal had dropped out twenty minutes ago. Didn't matter. We were leaving. I stumbled out of the door, almost falling down the steps. Get away, get home, before Kage saw how weak I was, how insane, how outright dangerous I was.

"Alexander Kempthorne," a familiar voice boomed.

I staggered to a stop in front of a line of black-clad security guards with the corduroy-clad Thomas Montgomery at their centre.

"Hello, dear boy." He chuckled. "It's terribly late for trespassing."

Well, we were well and truly caught. I yanked off the mask and *breathed*, filling my lungs. The mask hadn't helped with the memories. But then I hadn't expected to be assaulted by the past inside such an innocuous-looking building. "How did you know it was me?"

He gestured at the Aston parked just behind Kage and me. "Not many burglars drive Aston Martins."

"I told you it was too conspicuous," Kage muttered, pulling off his mask too.

"Yes, thank you. I heard you the first time."

"Kage Mitchell." Montgomery smirked but there was nothing kind about it. "Your snooping leaves me with something of a dilemma." He started forward and spread his hands, like a lecturer presenting to his class. "You see, it would be understandable for Alexander Kempthorne to take a sabbatical from the public eye, after his recent revelation in the press, but if the American agent working for him were to vanish, too, making him the third Kempthorne & Co agent to disappear, it all gets rather messy." Montgomery stopped in front of Kage. He smiled, but it was full of thin resentment. "I do despise the LOA."

Kage pressed his gun to the side of Montgomery's head. "Tell your men to back off."

Montgomery sighed. "Are you going to execute an unarmed man in full view of multiple cameras, Mr Mitchell?"

"You're not unarmed." Kage's finger twitched over the trigger. "You're a latent."

"Well, that's difficult to prove, especially from prison."

"Put the gun down, Kage." I sighed. There was no use in him getting arrested. Although having him deported had some merit.

Reluctantly, Kage lowered the gun.

"What do you want?" I asked Montgomery.

"It's simple really. *You.*" Montgomery nodded at his men, and they moved in. "I must say, you've made it surprisingly easy."

Montgomery's trick churned around him. If Montgomery lashed out, there was no knowing what his tainted trick might do. His thugs standing behind him weren't latents, just cannon fodder. I glanced at Kage. If I was ever going to trust him, now was a good time to start. He glanced back and nodded.

Cameras watched us from multiple angles. If I did this, my life would change forever. But I was never going to be strapped down to one of those tables again, not for as long as I breathed and my heart continued to beat.

I exhaled, easing the tension in my shoulders, and brought my hands around, clasping them together in front of me.

"I do not advise that, Alexander," Montgomery warned. His trick sparked, tainted energy building around him.

I loosened the hold on my trick and exhaled, letting it *flow*. Like always, it twitched and surged and snapped, trying to burst free. It had never been soothing, not like I'd heard it was with most latents. Mine was either on or off—a switch flicked and the floodgates opened. I knew I glowed, knew it rippled off me. It reflected in the wide eyes of the security guards and the unblinking cameras. *Beautiful*, my absorber mother had said. Right before tearing it out of me. It was the only time she'd cared.

Kage aimed his gun again, said something clever, and then Montgomery unleashed whatever his trick was—it leaked out of him like oil over honey. It looked wrong, tasted wrong in the air, like the shadows, but rippled and danced, turning into a substance that sizzled the asphalt around him.

It always felt so bloody good to let go. As though all the lies had fallen away and this was my truest self. *More*. I barely had to call it now, it just came, waves of it—too much.

"Don't force my hand, Alexander," Montgomery warned. "I don't want to hurt you."

"Then let us leave." My voice sounded thin.

"What good will that do? You'll go back to a life that doesn't fit and pretend you're something you're not until all that power one day unravels? No, Alexander." My name on his lips soothed some of the trick's sparks. "You know I'm right." He lifted a hand and the black coils extended beyond his fingers, reaching for me. "You belong with me. You always did."

With us... the shadows said, emerging from hidden corners, under the Aston, from around the gathered guards. They spilled from every crack in the ground, every hidden nook, rushing in, combining, building.

"I'm afraid I'll have to decline." I thrust the trick out, sending it lashing toward Montgomery in a great arc that should have thrown him off his feet. But instead, it splashed against him—*into* him—and the man just smiled from ear to ear.

I'd made a terrible mistake.

Thomas Montgomery was an absorber, and a lot more powerful than me.

"Kempthorne?" Kage muttered, concern showing on his face for the first time.

I licked my lips and stared at the man Olivia Barnes had called my opposite, and I understood. I couldn't beat him. "Run."

Kage, of course, didn't move.

Montgomery laughed, lifting his hand, and his trick lashed out, striking the nearby cameras, bursting them apart like electronic balloons. Debris rained. Montgomery's men began to close their net, moving in. I wasn't Dom. I didn't have combat training. I just knew how to lash out and hope for the best. "Shoot him," I growled under my breath.

Kage swung his gun up and fired. The round flashed through a barrier of Montgomery's churning trick, cutting a wake through oil, *slowing* it.

Montgomery chuckled. "Americans and their guns."

"Shit," Kage cursed.

Montgomery's trick twitched and recoiled, narrowing into a whip-like weapon extending from his right hand.

"You won't watch another agent die, Alexander."

Fear turned my veins to ice. Montgomery's trick glowed in the man's eyes and spilled from his fingers, focused on Kage. Unfortunately, I'd already seen how this ended. Kage wasn't prepared for a latent like Montgomery. He'd fight and he'd die. I'd already saved Kage once. I was about to save him again.

Montgomery's trick lashed toward Kage. The American lifted his arm, as though trying to protect himself. Montgomery's trick would burn through him, and Dom would never forgive me if I let it happen. Without much direction, I flung everything I had between Montgomery and Kage, surging trick outward in a narrow arc. Montgomery's trick and mine clashed, and like two electrical currents shorting, the tricks snapped, blasting outward. Light and heat flashed over us all. I turned my face away, and in the seconds it took the sparks to fall from the air, Kage had bolted toward the Aston.

Montgomery's men staggered, dazed. Montgomery, however, had noticed the shadows rushing across the parking lot, heading straight for him and his power. Proof his power outshone mine.

I dashed for the Aston and I threw myself into the driver's seat.

"Goddamn!" Kage fell into the passenger seat. With his door still open, I jabbed the car's start button, revved her engine, and flung her into reverse, almost toppling Kage out. He clung to the grab-handle and glared, assuming I'd meant to spill him from the car.

"Hang on!"

Golden and black threads of trick splashed over the Aston's windscreen. The car shuddered, its engine coughed. I reversed her, spinning the rear tires, and launched her forward in what I hoped was the general direction of the gates. The wipers came on, trying to slosh the trick off. They didn't work.

"We can't see!" Kage yelled.

"It's fine." I changed gears, powered on. The Aston roared. All I had to do was break through the trick wrapped around the car. Montgomery had the shadows to contend with. He couldn't blind us for long.

Gold and black threads slithered through the car's air vents.

Kage jerked back in the seat. "What the fuck!"

"Oh." That was unexpected.

All of this was rather unexpected.

"Hold on!" The Aston jolted, its front right wheel hitting something, hopefully Montgomery.

The trick let go, slipping off as though we'd splashed through a rainstorm. The huge metal gates loomed.

Kage tensed. "No."

"Yes." I dropped the clutch, slammed the car into a lower gear, lurched her forward, and prayed my insurance would cover what happened next. We hit the gates, the Aston nose first. Metal sparked and twisted, some of it snapping, threatening to come through the windscreen. By some miracle it didn't. The Aston screeched, bumped, and slid onto the road. I fought with the car, trying to keep it straight, and plowed away from the warehouse.

"Fuck!" Kage glared out the rear window. "They're not following."

Half an hour later, with the first hint of red skies and dawn creeping over London's skyline, I rolled the battered Aston to a halt outside Kage's Docklands apartment building and climbed out to assess the damage. It seemed I couldn't keep a car unscathed.

Kage frowned at the Aston's scratches and dents.

I winced, feeling every scratch as though it was my own.

"It might buff out," Kage said.

It most certainly would *not* buff out. We hadn't spoken since the warehouse. Not a single word. He knew I was a latent, he'd seen my trick with his own eyes. He also couldn't fail to have noticed I'd helped keep him alive when his gun had proven ineffective.

With a heavy sigh, he said, "We have to get Dom out of Wordsworth." And with that startling piece of obviousness, he strode away.

8

D^{om}

I danced my fingers on the wall beside my pillow. Music played in my head. Lady Gaga and some guy, a fancy duet I'd heard a few times, catchy and moody. Someone intelligent with letters before their name had studied how singing could stave off depression, or something. I wasn't depressed, but for every day I was stuck in Wordsworth, pieces of my mind fell away. The song helped. I whispered it, mumbled the words, and hummed the tune whenever I wasn't being watched.

I whispered the lyrics now, twirling my fingers, imagining I was anywhere else but in a white jumpsuit, in a white room, staring at white walls.

The light above buzzed.

I'd thrown my boot at the last one and shattered it,

only for it to be fixed by the next night. It still had the buzz though. Or maybe the buzzing was in my head, too, joining the voices crying out for help and the whoosh of the Thames, sounding so close, like blood rushing through the veins.

I stopped humming and rolled onto my back, blinking at the ceiling and that bloody light. I knew this moment was real because I was in it. But there were other moments that blurred, stuck between the real and unreal. I'd wake from those with the ghosts of restraints around my wrists and my throat hoarse. I'd been *somewhere* else during those moments. My body knew it, but my mind had checked out. The not knowing was the worst of it. At least if I knew what they did to me, I wouldn't have to think up the nightmare fuel. Sometimes I woke from those episodes feeling fine, and other times, as though my soul had been drained from my body, leaving me an empty shell.

I wasn't human here.

I was a rat in a maze. Trapped with other dull-eyed rats. We took the meds and ate the food and were taken for testing, and that was my life now.

Fuck.

But I had a plan.

I'd routinely tucked their meds under my tongue. I couldn't avoid the injected concoction muffling my trick, but the tablet shit went under the tongue and down the drain in my cell. Which meant I was more alert than the rest of the inmates. And because I wasn't drugged up to my eyeballs, I tracked the guards' movements—watched their shift rotations, looking for weaknesses. And I'd found one. Guard Glen hated his job and, like me, he wanted to be anywhere else but Wordsworth, guarding a bunch of zombie latents. Glen was bored, and being bored meant his smoking habit plagued him. When the supervisor wasn't around, he nipped out the back for a fag, leaving the door ajar so he didn't have to sign in and out.

Glen was going to be my new best friend, and my ticket to freedom.

As for that light I'd smashed? I'd kept some broken pieces back, which meant Glen was also about to find out his £9.50 an hour wasn't worth getting shivved in the back for.

I had a plan. I just needed Glen to be on shift, dying for a fag, and for the timing to be perfect, when I wasn't coming down off one of my blackout sessions. Easy.

Once I got out, though, that was where things would be difficult. Go back to the East End or Kempthorne? I should go back to the East End. It was safer, for everyone. I'd disappear and nobody at Kempthorne & Co would get hurt. That was the right answer—the right thing to do. But I didn't want that. I wanted custard creams and glitter-filled nights out with Gina, painted fingernails, unicorn cakes, and cosy mornings in Cecil Court's kitchen, where I felt as though I belonged. Where I was happy. I wanted *that* life. But latents didn't get nice things and if I went back there, the IRL, Wordsworth, and Montgomery would follow me right to Alexander Kempthorne.

I'd been here months. Maybe?

I didn't know how long for sure—the days blurred together—but I'd lost weight and the light from all the whiteness no longer hurt my eyes.

Months like a rat, trapped in a maze.

Gina and Kempthorne and Robin weren't coming for me.

But that was okay.

I hadn't expected anyone to.

The door lock thunked and swung open. "Dinner," a guard grumbled.

And like a good, docile latent, I went.

The line for food shuffled forward. The dinner people served sticky, wet slop, suspiciously like mushed cat food, and nobody said a word. I hated this place, hated the way all the inmates' faces were grey and hollow, hated the smell of the food and the squeak of shoes on polished vinyl. Hated the way my hands shook when I held out my tray. But at least I could feel something. Everyone else had become shadows in their own skins.

I drifted forward, resigned to eating cat food again, when someone brushed my arse, sending a startled jolt through me. I tensed and glanced behind me, catching a young woman's eye. Half her shoulder length hair was pink, the other half cropped so short it hugged the outline of her skull. She dipped her chin and played the dull-eyed inmate to perfection. I blinked at her. Her lips seemed to be hitched into a small, permanent snarl. Had she felt me up? Kinda weird, and not what I was into.

The line moved forward and so did I, keeping up the pretense of obedience.

Pink Girl dropped her hand and tapped her arse as a

signal. She'd tucked something into my pocket. I could feel it there now, a cool lump in my back jumpsuit pocket.

I took my dinner, sat, and ate mechanically, wishing the seconds away so I could get back to my white cell and find out what Pink had planted.

The women inmates filed out, heading to the female wing, and I lost sight of the girl's flash of pink hair among the others.

The guards collected the men and delivered us back to our cells. Alone again, and to the sounds of slamming doors, I sank my hand into my pocket and pulled a folded envelope free. No name. I tore open the flap. A King of Hearts playing card fluttered to the floor.

Renick.

That wanker.

Shit.

But the playing card wasn't all. Sitting on the bed, I unfolded a note, hands trembling:

Dom, the team is doing everything they can to get you out. They all miss you. So do I. I don't blame you. I left things all wrong. Whoever gave you this note can bring one back. If you can write, please let me know you're okay. I'm here, waiting. ~ Kage.

I didn't fucking care how we'd left things. I could hear his voice in the written words and closed my eyes, imagining the cocky American beside me, his hand on my shoulder.

I wasn't alone.

They hadn't forgotten me.

They were still trying to get me out, still thinking about me, and Kage... Kage had somehow reached out to

Renick and managed to get a note inside. Kage hadn't walked away.

Fucking Renick. Always had to find an angle. Although, this time, it was worth it.

Hollywood missed me.

I swallowed the lump in my throat.

The door lock *thunked* again. I shoved the note under my pillow and stood facing the door as it swung outward. Three guards piled in. The big guy at the front held out thick, heat-resistant cuffs. "You know the routine."

I raised my wrists—so fucking compliant—and swallowed the acidic anger on my tongue.

"Goin' on a road trip tonight, mate." The guard ratcheted the cuffs into place.

I was leaving Wordsworth? He looked up, maybe realizing he'd said something he shouldn't have, and I met his eyes. They were ordered not to talk to us, not to humanize us, but the pity in his eyes was all human. Where the fuck were they taking me?

"Wait—"

"Sorry, man." He knew this was something bad. Maybe the latents he took away didn't come back. The other two manhandled me between them and shoved me out of the door.

Were they sending me to die? But I'd just had Kage's note. They were still trying to get me out. I had to hang on. "Wait—you don't have to do this." I twisted, trying to break free.

"Someone's not been taking their meds," one of the other guards grumbled. "We'll soon fix that."

The prick in my neck was there and gone again in a pinch. Ice-water spilled down my spine. I gasped, my trick flickered, trying and failing to come to my fingers, and then I fell.

Whatever they'd done to me came back in broken pieces, needling into my head: a cold, metal table, cold things in my veins, cold in my chest. They'd turned me to ice, then set my blood ablaze, burning me up. The world had burned and I'd trembled with it. It had been my trick, only vast, like a biblical flood and I was the dam. I'd tried to hold it back and failed.

Everything hurt.

My skin was broken glass, my head a pile of bricks. I blinked at a ceiling that wasn't my room's and raised a hand to rub my face. An IV drip dangled from my wrist and looped up to a suspended transparent bag. Whatever it was supposed to be feeding me had run dry. The bag was empty.

That was why I was awake.

Unfamiliar voices grew louder, then faded again, passing outside a closed door.

The clues fell into place slowly. A different room, a different place. The drug had run dry and I wasn't restrained.

This was good, this was important. If I could just get my head straight...

The door opened.

I fell back and closed my eyes, playing asleep. Someone shuffled about. A few instruments *blipped*. The sloshing sound of liquid in plastic signaled the IV bag was being changed, then the door clicked closed. I opened my eyes. Yup, the person had left, and the bag was full and feeding shiny shit into my veins. I grabbed the needle and tape and tore the IV free. Blood dribbled. I cupped my wrist, stemming the flow.

My heart thumped. Every beat, every breath rebuilt reality and my place in it.

I hadn't heard a lock.

If that door was unlocked, I was so fucking out of here. I swung my legs off the table and breathed around a wave of dizziness. They'd taken my clothes, leaving me in just white pants and a hospital gown. If I got out of this room, I'd have to stay out of sight.

Just get out of the room.

I took a step. The floor tipped. "Shit." The table held me, for now, but my useless legs weren't cooperating.

This was my shot at escape. I had to make this count. I might not get another chance.

I'd been on the table a while. Tubes dangled from above like transparent tentacles. But I wasn't thinking about that. I stared at the door. The door was my only enemy in the world. *Get through the door.*

My next step held. Then the next. I wobbled, staggered, but made it across the room and clutched the handle, listening for anyone outside. As soon as I opened the door, it was all or nothing. Running was going to be a challenge but I'd bloody crawl out if I had to.

I cracked the door and peeked outside into an empty corridor with more closed doors. There were latents behind those doors. I knew it like I knew my own name. Didn't matter. I couldn't do anything for them. I inched the door open, avoiding any creaks, checked both ways, spotted what appeared to be a fire door at the end, and figured it was the better option than running into the un-fucking-known.

I loped into the corridor, using the wall to keep me upright, and willed the fire exit door to be unlocked. They had to be unlocked, for health and safety? But an alarm would sound the second I opened it. I didn't give a shit. Let the alarms go off. I needed out. And out was right there, getting closer with every step.

My trick tingled and sparked at the ends of my fingers, pins and needles. I shook it off, but the movement upset my wavering balance. I fell, slumped against the wall, and breathed. Dizziness rolled over me. The trick burned now, dripping from my fingers. "Fuck." I shook it off, or tried to, but it clung like glue. "Unstable. I get it. But not right now." Where I'd brushed the wall, golden handprints glowed, like a bloody neon sign pointing *this way to the escaping latent!*

I needed to get my head straight and my balance under control, or I'd never make it—

A door slammed. Something buzzed, like an alarm. "Shit." I opened a random door beside me and ducked inside, closing it softly. Voices echoed. I pressed my hot forehead to the cold door and begged whatever god was listening that whoever was outside walked right on by.

Don't pick this room.

Don't pick this room.

Don't pick this room.

The people outside chatted about the *Great British Bake Off* final and whether Paul Hollywood's blue eye color was real. Their voices faded. A door closed.

I sighed hard, almost whimpered. No, wait, the whimpering wasn't me. I turned. A bed. Like mine. Tubes hung from the ceiling, all looped and tangled like octopus legs, and filled with golden, glowing liquid. *Trick*. The tubes fed into a girl. A thin white sheet covered her, up to her chin. Messy blonde hair stuck out at all angles. Eyes closed, but her chest lifted and fell.

My stupid legs wobbled as I ventured closer, not sure if what I was seeing was real.

I knew her.

Penny. Penny from Olivia's off-the-rails adventure when she'd tried to abduct a bunch of latents. I'd helped Penny escape from the shipping container, thought she was safe at home with her parents...

Christ... I grabbed my head. Memories shifted.

Wait... Penny, Penny... her surname...

Think.

Her surname? It meant something. Penny *Montgomery*.

Montgomery: The smiling old guy in his plush office with his thick sweaters and kind eyes.

Oh fuck.

Was Penny related to the Thomas Montgomery who'd grabbed my hand and ripped out my trick, all the while smiling as though he was my best mate's uncle? And if she was related, how had Penny gotten to be here, in this bed, fixed to these machines and drugged up to the eyeballs just like I'd been?

The tubes pulsed. Golden liquid shimmered. Trick. So much of it.

"Hey! What are you doing in here?"

I spun. A nurse or technician or whatever the staff were called blinked, then glowered as she took in my dishevelled state. She reached for the radio at her hip.

I lunged, shoved her against the wall, and wrapped my glowing fingers around her throat. Her eyes widened, her mouth gaped, and my trick crept over her skin like glittering honey.

Boil her...

No, no, don't want that.

I only knew a fraction of what they did here, but as an authenticator, I felt the rest. This place was Hell. This nurse was a part of it, and I knew behind all these doors were latents just like me and Penny, silently screaming for help. I also knew I had about three seconds before my legs gave out. I could flood the nurse with trick and make a run for it, but the thudding in my head had turned to drums and the hot blood racing through my veins was now lead.

I wasn't making it out of here.

I slumped against the nurse, trying to cling to scraps of consciousness. "I need to go..." I told her. Her eyebrows dug in and maybe she'd been scared of me before, but she wasn't now. We both knew, even if I'd had the strength, I wouldn't have hurt her.

"I think someone wasn't given a high enough dose," she said.

"No." I shoved off, staggered, and reached for Penny's bed, needing it to hold me up. It rattled when I fell against it. Penny didn't stir. She was sleeping. Maybe that was for the best because if she knew she was in this place, she'd be scared, like I was. The tubes sucked trick from her, pumping it into the ceiling somewhere. It flowed like shimmering honey. They were taking pieces of her away. This wasn't right. They'd done this to me... bled my trick like this.

"Can I get some help in Room Twenty-Six-B? AWOL patient," the nurse said into her radio. Approaching me, she smiled. "Come on, let's get you back to your room."

"No, stop." I pressed myself against Penny's bed. They'd taken my trick, siphoned it off, harvested it, like absorbers did, but on an industrial scale. "No. I can't fucking be here. Don't!" But it was already too late. The nurse reached for me, the room spun, the drums beat in time with my heart, and I fell without hitting the floor.

Dom

I had to escape.

Whatever they'd done the last time I'd gone under had wrecked me. Days I'd been holed up in bed, shivering, sickly, a metallic taste on my tongue that wouldn't go away no matter how much I drank. I'd had something rammed down my throat. A tube maybe. It seemed like I should remember, but whenever I tried, the scraps fled, leaving my thoughts flailing.

Cold. Everything was cold. All the bloody time.

Couldn't wait for Hollywood to save me, or Kempthorne.

My new best mate Glen was my way out.

Today.

It had to be today.

I was stronger, back on my feet. At breakfast, I'd slipped the pills under my tongue and afterward, flushed them. Today was Glen's early evening shift. It coincided with dinner. He'd want a smoke. That was my window and maybe my last chance because if they took me away again, I might never come back.

It had to be today, while I could still think.

Dinner came around, and just like always, the guards ushered me into line and we were all driven to the dinner like obedient lambs. I kept my head down and one eye on Glen, positioned across the canteen. Bored, the big guy leaned against the wall, his dull eyes skimming the crowd but not really seeing. None of the inmates ever did anything; they were all too drugged to care.

My gaze snagged another's—Pink glared, her eyes like twin laser beams, her lip cocked in that forever-snarl, like she knew I was planning something. Shit. Why wasn't she half asleep like the rest?

I swallowed and stared at my lasagna while poking it around my plate. When I looked up, she was still staring. The guards would notice, if she wasn't careful. I glowered back. Her eyebrows pinched and she mouthed a few words. I screwed up my nose, and she tried again, silently shaping the words with her lips, *What. Are. You. Doing?*

I shrugged.

She made a face, not buying it.

The sounds of the guards' squeaking shoes approached. I ducked my head and stabbed a meaty bit on my plate. "Hey," I croaked, laying the slur on thick. "That girl... keeps staring."

Pink shot me a death-stare before her eyes locked on

the guards now approaching her. She lifted her hands. "Wait... He's just as bad!"

Glen, bless him, had vanished for his fag and had left the door ajar. I didn't think, didn't hesitate—while Pink provided a distraction, I dashed between the tables, then out of the door. No shouts rose up, nobody had seen, and now I was in the corridor and getting the fuck out. Nothing could stop me now.

Glen sauntered away from me in the corridor ahead, fag in-hand, heading for what I assumed to be a door leading outside so he didn't fill the corridors with cigarette smoke. Putting on a burst of speed, I dropped the jagged piece of lightbulb glass from my sleeve, into my hand, and flung an arm around Glen's neck from behind. "Nice and quiet, mate, and this blade you're feeling in your back doesn't have to get any more personal than it already is."

"Ughgfuck."

"Now you're getting it. Keep walking."

Glen did as he was told. Up ahead, a metal security door barred our way.

"Slowly, use your keycard."

"They'll find you," Glen grouched.

"That ain't your problem."

Glen fumbled his card on its stretchy cord and the door clunked open into another corridor. Two guards loitered near the next door.

Glen sucked in a breath, maybe to shout for help. I gave him a reminder jab in the back and growled, "It ain't worth it." I shifted alongside Glen, with my makeshift blade still at his back. "You're just taking me to see the boss. Don't fuck this up Glen an' you and me can stay friends."

He gulped so loud I was sure the guards heard.

"The boss ain't that way," Glen mumbled. Sweat beaded on his forehead.

"Then make some shit up and make it believable or you're gonna discover exactly how desperate I am, and I guaran-fuckin'-tee you won't be walkin' away from that. Nod if we're still friends."

He nodded. Good Glen.

"Inmates aren't allowed beyond this point," Guard A grumbled. Big guy. All shoulders, no neck. Possibly ex-military from his stance. He thumbed over his shoulder at the sign on the wall: *Inmates Prohibited Beyond This Point.*

"I got orders to take him to C-wing," Glen said.

"Why?" No-Neck frowned and glanced at B, who was the scrawny one and had a stern look about him that suggested he outranked No-Neck.

"Boss's orders," Glen said. "They don't pay me to ask questions."

I got the full-on suspicious glare from both of them and stared dull-eyed ahead, adding a slack jaw for the hell of it.

"Look, I'm gonna be late. Let me through or he's your problem," Glen improvised, going up in my estimation.

A grumble, and the pair stepped aside. The door lock clunked under Glen's card and through we went. The air was cooler in the next corridor, and the lighting softer. If freedom had a smell, it smelled like tarmac after the rain, and I was so bloody close I could taste it in the air.

Glen shifted uneasily. "I'm gonna lose my job."

I dug the glass against his lower back. "Be grateful you're not losing a kidney. And spare a thought for the latents you're guarding."

"Why? The scags all fuckin' deserve it."

"Oh, Glen. And we were just startin' to get along—"

Glen twisted, moving bloody fast for a heavy guy. I skipped back and his elbow skimmed my middle. Glen recovered and came at me like a snarling bear. I swung a right hook, making it fast and tight, and cracked my knuckles against this jaw. Fiery pain shot up my arm. Glen reeled. I followed through with another right, grabbed his uniform with my left, and landed a few more right hooks, throwing them fast and repeatedly, until he fell like a sack of bricks. He'd had it coming. Ignoring the burn in my bruised hand, I unclipped his keycard, left him groaning, and breezed through the next few doors until finally spilling outside.

Freedom hit me like a slap in the face. Cold wind swirled. Streetlights glowed. I staggered, gasped.

Traffic hummed behind a line of trees and a chain-link fence. I was out, but not yet free. The fence was just a plain old fence topped in coils of razor wire. I dashed across a patch of weedy grass, keeping low, found a few overhanging tree branches, and scaled the fence until reaching the foliage, then clambered into the tree and used the wood and leaves to avoid the razor wire.

An alarm screeched.

"Shit."

Another alarm joined the first, filling the evening air with sirens.

I dropped, landing too-hard on my ankle, but I was up and moving in the next second. No way was a sprained ankle slowing me down. I legged it toward an area of darkness among glinting streetlights. Skidding down a short bank dropped me by a gloomy canal side. I bolted down the towpath, under a bridge, and kept right on running until everything hurt and the alarms were a distant flicker behind the grumble of traffic.

10

D^{om}

Go back to the sparkling, Dickensian dream that was Cecil Court and the gang, or the rough-around-the-edges life I'd grown up in? In reality, I had no choice at all.

A black AMG Mercedes idled against the curb, across the road from where I loitered in the shadows, head down, trying not to look like an escaped convict in my all-white overalls.

Privacy glass hid the car's occupants. *I could still walk away.* And go where? The military? Where they'd screw me up even more?

A gap opened in the traffic, and keeping my head down, I jogged across the road and jumped into the back of the Mercedes, sliding onto smooth leather seats.

I wasn't alone in the back. Renick grinned, flashing

his black neck tats and gaudy rings. "Knew you'd be back," he drawled, eyeing my prison clothes as though he could somehow crawl under my skin and take me apart, piece by piece.

"Fuck off."

Chuckling, he tapped the front seat and the driver crawled the Mercedes into traffic.

Renick tossed me a bunch of clothes. I hid how my scratched hands trembled, and stripped off, dressing in jeans and a branded black-hooded top. The adrenaline come down was doing a number on my nerves, chattering my teeth. I folded my arms, trying to squeeze out the shakes.

"Thanks," I grumbled, hating that it had to be said, but I'd needed a save, and after a call from a petrol station phone, he'd come. He'd make me pay for it, but at least I was out.

He gripped my shoulder. "We're family, right, Domenici?"

"Yeah." A different kind of family. Cecil Court had been a different kind of family too. On the lamb, I couldn't go back to Kempthorne. If I went anywhere near him, my shit would drag him down with me. It was better for everyone if I stayed away. The East End was where I belonged. I'd been fighting the tide this whole time. The stint in the military, my time at Kempthorne & Co, it had just delayed the inevitable.

I was back on the street—*Domenici's boy*—where I belonged.

I flipped my hood up and hunkered down, surrounded by soft leather and wealth built off the backs of abused latents, class A drugs, and whatever else

Renick was selling these days. I hated the prick. Hated who I was here. But at least I could disappear in my old life and everyone I cared about would be safe.

"Hey man, sorry about that psycho, Max. I had no idea he was a fuckin' nutter." Renick ranted about unstable latents, forgetting I was one. Ignoring him, I stared out of the car window at the streetlights blurring past. Max had been a victim. I knew that much. Montgomery was to blame for the kid's downward spiral. Montgomery was at the center of *everything*. But Kempthorne would deal with it. He'd have a plan. He always did. It was nothing to do with me, not anymore. It couldn't be.

This was a clean break. I couldn't go back. To Kempthorne. To... Kage.

That life wasn't me. Even if I'd wanted it to be.

"After you get cleaned up, come by the Snooker Room, eh?" Renick said. "I got a job for you."

"Whatever." I wasn't even back ten minutes and had a *job*. It would be something brutal, something illegal. Something John Domenici did all the time because that was all I was good for. This was how it was going to be from now on.

This was how it *had* to be.

Saving latents and London was Kempthorne's destiny, not mine.

East End latent kids on the run from the law didn't get happy endings.

11

A lexander

After our narrow escape at Montgomery's laboratory, I retreated to Ravenscourt. Robin postponed all my appointments and Googled my name to see if any mention of my latent status had emerged. But nothing did. Kage went wherever Kage goes when he wasn't with us, probably to report on everything he'd learned, and the Kempthorne & Co phone kept on ringing. Gina and Robin took the incoming artifact and latent cases while I stewed in Ravenscourt and stared at my montage as though the answer would jump from the wall and into my lap.

In that warehouse, Montgomery had been syphoning off friction resonance—the trick. But why? He could only want it for two reasons: To sell the technology to the highest bidder or to keep it for himself, but what did a middle-aged man want with that much trick?

The IRL existed to stop any latent from amassing too much power. They sent latents *to* Wordsworth, where the unregistered latent Montgomery sat waiting, like a spider in his web. Montgomery was as diabolical as he was clever.

If I started rattling cages about Thomas Montgomery being latent, he'd use the CCTV of my trick to point the finger at me. If I went down, so did he. But I had no proof.

"Bugger it." I should have been more careful.

I'd been in such a bloody hurry to get to Dom, I'd made careless mistakes. Now Montgomery had leverage. "If he takes me down, I'll drag him with me," I told my wall, then continued to sip my whiskey and pace. Montgomery's picture watched my every step. So did Kage Mitchell's. Dom's was there, too, buttoned up in his military uniform. Distracted, I stopped pacing and stared at Dom's soft eyes. The photo had been taken before his deployment to Syria and after he'd killed his father. I knew what he'd done... I'd always known. Dom and I... He and I were the same.

I skimmed my fingers over the photo, touched his face, and wished he were here, saying something smart about my murder wall, making a joke about all of this, making things seem less... insurmountable.

Kage Mitchell's photo peered out from my montage. His picture had been taken on the sly after I'd hired an associate to track his movements. He had shorter hair then. But the same perfect smile and rich amber eyes. I grabbed a sticky note, scribbled *LOA* on it, and stuck it beneath his photo.

Kage had sent the letter to Wordsworth but nothing had come back from Dom.

What did that mean? Maybe Dom couldn't reply. Perhaps he hadn't received the note and Renick had lied about his capabilities.

I had to know.

I pulled my phone from my pocket and hovered my thumb over Robin's number, then hit call. "Set up a meeting with Renick tonight."

"Tonight?"

"Unless there's been word from Dom?"

"No, nothing, but—"

"I'm not waiting any longer."

"You shouldn't rush into this. Renick has a reputation. You meeting with him will send multiple signals to the wrong people."

As she spoke, my patience thinned and frayed. She wasn't wrong. Meeting with Renick would open a door that would be difficult to close again, but I couldn't stand around doing nothing for another day, like a bloody butler at a dining table. "We need eyes inside Wordsworth. Renick has them. Montgomery is planning something. Dom is in danger. I *do* have to do this. If I have to get in bed with a mob boss to get him out of there, I will—" I heard the desperation in my voice and winced. "Robin, please. I have to do this."

"All right. I'll call him."

I hung up, finished my whiskey, and refilled it. Was meeting with Renick a good idea? No, not at all. But he could get to Dom. I just needed to know Dom was alive, that he wasn't... *strapped to a table.*

Nobody deserved that. Certainly not Dom.

I pressed the cool whiskey glass to my cheek and closed my eyes, shutting off the view of the murder wall and all the threads and clues and dead-ends, and years of researching why and who and how. For so long it had been all I could think about. My obsession. Dom had been right about that. But now something else occupied my mind, distracted my thoughts. An authenticator, who despite having a shitty life, or maybe because of it, managed to smile at the little things, and do good and *be good*. He made *me* want to be good, and that was its own small miracle.

My phone rang. Robin said, "Charles Renick will meet you for dinner at Oblix West, at eight."

Oblix was a well-known restaurant on the 32nd floor of the Shard, serving a certain type of clientele. Formal attire. It was public, and my arrival with the so-called King of Hearts would spark gossip, which was obviously Renick's intention. "Fine."

"Kempthorne?"

"Yes?"

"Be careful."

I hung up and summoned Jordan by text. After a few whiskies, I was in no state to drive and probably not in the best of conditions to face a mob boss, but I needed answers and he'd have them, or a way to get them.

His picture was pinned to the wall like all the others. A string stretched between him and Dom. Renick, the man Dom had grown up with. A surrogate brother from a world very different to mine. Dom despised him, and I trusted Dom's judgment.

Renick would underestimate me. My enemies always did.

London sparkled like a bejeweled crown outside the Shard's all-glass walls. Oblix was always busy, but never raucous. Diamond-encrusted jewelry sparkled, glasses chinked, and feint laughter peppered the warm ambience.

Renick was late. Likely, deliberately. He breezed in at 8.30 p.m., his stride full of arrogant swagger. The server showed him to our table, and Charles Renick poured himself into the chair. Tattoos blackened his neck and wrists, peeking out from behind a crisp white shirt worn under an expensive suit. His Rolex was real. There was good money in being bad. His smile said as much.

"Alexander Kempthorne." He thrust out his hand between our wine glasses.

I gave his hand a shake and wore my soft smile. "Charles Renick. We meet at last."

He shrugged, laughed a little at our surroundings, and danced his gaze, soaking up the Oblix atmosphere. "I guessed this would be more to your liking than Burger King."

"How kind of you."

He heard the irony behind my smile and grinned right back.

The server poured wine and we did the usual tasting song and dance. Renick let me choose the wine, clearly enjoying himself. He ordered lobster. I ordered steak. And now the formalities were out of the way, it was just the two of us, albeit surrounded by people, half of whom had probably recognized me. Considering my recent revelation, did they wonder whether Renick was my date?

Rebecca Stevens would have kittens if she learned I was dating a crime boss.

"Something amusing?" Renick enquired, some of his loose tone tightening.

"Not at all."

"How are things in the artifact hunting business?"

"Busy."

He still smirked. The sideways smile appeared to be a constant fixture.

"How's the crime business?" I asked.

"Profitable."

We raised our glassed and toasted. "To profit," I said.

He chuckled and gulped the expensive wine as though it were lemonade. The cool London air had cleared my head of whiskey, but now I was back inside in the warmth, it wouldn't take much wine to tip me over the edge into careless territory.

"So..." He rested both arms on the table and leaned closer. "My people got your note inside. Did you hear back from our John?"

Our John? Our suggested ownership, and to my knowledge, Renick and Dom were as far apart as enemies could be. "No luck, I'm afraid. I wanted to ask you about that. We've had nothing back, so I find myself wondering if the note arrived at all."

His left eyebrow twitched. "It did. I keep my word."

"And I should just... trust you?"

"Well, yeah."

"Gentleman to gentleman?" I swirled my wine. "You see, I'd like to. But I met some of your associates recently, and considering our conversation ended in restraints, I'm not as inclined to trust you as perhaps I could be, had your associates been less... enthusiastic."

He waved the comment away. "Water under the bridge, mate. That was then, this is now. Your man got the note." He grinned, leaning toward me. Something oily and dangerous flickered in his eyes. "And you probably didn't get one back because he ain't in Wordsworth no more."

He saw the shock on my face before I had a chance to hide it. If Dom wasn't in Wordsworth, I'd have known. Robin would have known. But Wordsworth had fallen quiet of late. Robin had been stonewalled. There was a slim chance our intelligence was out of date.

I didn't reply, turning the new information over in my head as Renick watched, waiting for my reaction.

Dom hadn't been freed. We'd have been informed.

Our food arrived and Renick wasted no time in picking up his cutlery and diving in.

Assuming I believed this man, and Dom wasn't in Wordsworth, why hadn't he contacted me?

"Ain't you gonna ask me where he is?" Renick asked, my silence having gone on too long.

"I assume he's with you." Dom's options were limited. If he wasn't with me, or the military, he might vanish altogether, but he was more likely to go home, where he knew how things worked and had some advantage. And Renick's hideous grin was confirmation enough.

Renick shoved a forkful of lobster between his lips while barely able to sit still from excitement.

Whatever pissing contest was going on here, I was done playing. "What do you want?"

He put down his fork, grabbed a napkin and wiped

his mouth, then levelled his glare and lost his smile. "About five million should cover it."

I frowned. "Cover what?"

"To buy him back."

I lowered my fork, buying a few seconds to calm myself, or my first reaction might have been to grab Renick by the shirt and stab my fork through his hand. "Let's be clear. You don't own him."

"Don't I? He's a latent ain't he? They're all the same. The girls sell for maybe twenty k. Keeps the Eastern Europeans happy. Russians particularly like 'em young. I can get thirty k for the little ones." Renick swallowed some more wine around a mouthful of lobster. "Latents are the new Class A, man. Easier to smuggle through customs too."

My heart's heavy thudding filled my head.

"John though, you and 'im got history," Renick continued. "And he's, like, some kind of latent soldier or something. M wanted him for a long time, put a contract out on him. Then he sent that little psycho prick, Max, to track John down before I could make my moves. So I know he's valuable. I reckon you're good for five mill."

I swallowed my wine in one, let it slide all the way down, and set the glass gently aside on the silk tablecloth.

"The Russians want him," Renick said. "The Yanks want 'im. Everyone wants a piece of John Domenici, even the boss of Kempthorne & Co... but not for a weapon." He winked. "You're fuckin' him in the arse, right? Or does he fuck you?"

I wrapped my fingers around the glass I'd set aside, needing to grip *something*.

"Yeah, figured so." He picked lobster from his teeth. "He's in demand. If you wan' him back, you gotta pay."

Air filled my lungs, expanding them slowly. The beat in my head slowed. Robin had said to be careful. That meant not acting on the impulse to grab Renick and blast him through the Shard's triple-glazed windows.

"Five million?" I asked in a voice as flat as my smile.

"Seems reasonable."

I slipped my phone from my pocket and opened the banking app. Five million. "Bank account number?"

"Oh fuck... Now?" He laughed too loudly. I raised my eyebrows at him and he reeled off the sort code and account number. "It's a charity," he said. "Can't be traced back to me, if you're wondering. You'll get a tax break for your kind donation."

I filled in the necessary information, called the bank, jumped through voice recognition hoops, and made the transfer, and all the while greed sparkled in Renick's dark eyes.

Once the transfer was made, I showed him the payment confirmation on the phone's screen.

"All right." His smile grew again. "You just bought yourself a five-million-pound fuckboy." Someone at a nearby table glanced over and he snickered, then hunkered down and whispered, "It's not like they're even human, right? You wanna make that five mill back? Film a snuff video. The Arabs pay *insane* amounts for that shit."

"Noted." I dragged a tight smile onto my lips and held his gaze. "I'll settle the bill."

Renick arched an eyebrow. "Ain't gonna say no." He wiped his mouth and hands on the napkin and stood.

"You can have your boy in your hands tomorrow morning, at the club."

"Thank you."

He nodded and glanced around him, then thrust out his hand to shake mine and end our business.

I smiled but pointedly ignored his hand.

"Whatever." He shrugged his jacket into place and smoothed back his hair, then sauntered out, pulling a few curious stares after him. I waited a beat, then another, all the while hearing Robin's voice telling me to be careful, that I didn't have to do this. I was *always* careful.

Anger had burned away much of the booze in my blood by the time I left the table, told the waiter to put the meal on my account, and headed into the elevator.

The floors counted down. I was a few seconds behind Renick. Not too close—close enough.

The elevator dinged, and I spotted Renick with his phone to his ear leaving through the foyer's front doors. He turned right and headed toward the Thames, still on his phone. Tucking myself in behind a few pedestrians, I stayed close. I knew the area well. The riverside walk along London Bridge Pier was quiet this time of night. All the river cruises and passenger ferries had stopped. Perfect.

Renick ended his call and stopped at the edge of the pavement, about to hail a cab or wait for his driver. Spilling a little trick into my fingers, I came up fast behind him and laid my hand on his lower back.

He jolted. "What the fuck—"

"Don't make a sound. That warmth you feel, that's trick, and I'm fairly certain you know exactly what it can do to your internal organs."

More trick flowed, and Renick went very, very still.

I eased his phone from his hand and dropped it into my pocket. "You and I are going to take a riverside walk."

"You're a fucking latent?" he seethed.

"The world's full of surprises. *Now move.*" Guiding him with my hand, I walked him toward London Bridge —not the infamous bridge everyone thinks of but its uglier 1970s cousin farther down the river. A few late-working commuters rushed along the pathway, their heads down, focused on their phones. Renick and I were nothing more than a pair of well-dressed men taking a stroll along the waterfront.

The pier area widened and the amount of people thinned. Nobody was here to admire the view. The Thames was a churning soup of darkness.

I marched him to the railing and cast a few careful glances up and down the river. High-rises sparkled. Traffic hummed and honked, but Renick and I were alone.

The Thames sloshed some thirty feet below the other side of the rail. The smell of earthy wetness filled my nose and laced my throat.

I slipped his phone from my pocket and let it fall. The Thames took it—the splash lost in the sounds of rushing water.

Renick twitched, about to put some weight into trying to shove me off. I pushed more trick through my hand, into his back, under his skin. He spluttered and slumped against the rail. "Fuck—WHAT IS THIS?! You gonna fuck me?"

I pressed my lips to his ear. "In a manner of speaking."

I switched my grip from his back to his neck and shoved him down hard. He gasped, grabbed the rail. The shimmering water boiled below. His face turned white. He tried to lever back—I spilled more trick through my hand, into him. He ticked and twitched, the trick dancing through him, picking at his nerves, threatening to burn him up.

"You'll-pay-for-this, you-spoilt-rich-cunt! I'll fuckin' *ruin* you. Put a bullet in your bitch-boy's head! The-fag-deserves-it-for-what-*hedidtohisdad*—"

His voice, the words, their meaning, faded into background static, just like the rest of London's noises. Below the Thames, *far* below, under the layers of mud and time, a different river flowed, one made of golden threads, overflowing with power. Renick couldn't see it. But I could. London's golden vein. *The source.*

"Some people are worth saving," I snarled in his ear. "Unfortunately for you, you're not one of them."

12

————

D^{om}

I tried to open the Snooker Room's doors but they rattled, staying firmly locked. It was still early, but Renick had called late the previous night to tell me to meet him there at the crack of dawn for *important news*—whatever that meant. I tucked my hands into my pockets and backed up. The building had never been much to look at—old brick, boarded windows painted black for ambience. Someone had spray-painted a dick on one of the boards. But it was unusually quiet; there were always people around.

I sauntered around the back of the club but had the same luck there. Maybe the Business had moved operations and nobody had told me.

Using the burner phone Renick had given me, I dialed his mobile. The line clicked and went straight to Renick's generic answerphone message.

I'd been out of the game so long, I didn't have any other contacts in the Business. A week out of Wordsworth, and Renick had been keeping me on a tight leash to make sure I didn't get any ideas about wandering off. He'd even put me up in a manky flat, so like Max's old digs it might even have been Max's. When I'd looked in the mirror that morning, I figured I was one psychotic episode away from *being* Max. And doubted my decisions all over again.

The prick was always late. Renick would show up, eventually. He always did like to make everyone wait on him. I sat on the ground, leaned against the Snooker Room's front door, and stared at my phone. I knew Gina's number. If I called her, let her know I was fine, she'd lay into me, and deep down I'd have known she was right. Then Robin would have gotten involved, and then Kempthorne would...

A silvery Aston Martin pulled up to the curb a few meters away and idled there, engine purring. The car gleamed, as though it had just rolled from the showroom. Early morning sunlight glinted on its shiny paint. A few seconds passed. *Did I dream him up?* Maybe it was some other rich guy cruising Hackney? The color was off, not quite Kempthorne's car, but spookily close.

The window rolled down. Kempthorne leaned across the passenger seat. His chestnut-colored hair flopped over blue eyes. He swept it back, and his lips found a small, tired smile. "Get in."

I should have argued, told him I'd made my decision to walk away and it was final, that if I went back with him, someone would get hurt, but instead, I got to my feet and climbed into the car.

The interior was warm and familiar, like slipping on an old glove, even though it was a different car to his usual ride. A rental? I glanced down at Kempthorne's hand, resting on the gear lever. Scratches and bruises marked his knuckles. I had similar marks from the shit Renick had me doing. A few specks of dried blood stained Kempthorne's rolled up sleeve. His expensive wristwatch glinted. A bit of blood had dried on the watch face too.

"Busy night?" I asked.

"Something like that."

I breathed in, filling my lungs with the smell of leather and whatever spicey aftershave Kempthorne wore. "What happened to your other Aston?" How many did he have?

"It had an altercation with a security gate. This one's a rental."

Kempthorne had driven through a security gate? It had to be something drastic, for the car to be out of action. Interesting. I could have asked for more info, but seated next to him, everything felt... *normal*.

I hadn't seen him since... My memory was shot by whatever the fuckers at Wordsworth had done, but the last time I'd seen Kempthorne outside of Wordsworth's visitor room, I was pretty sure we'd had a *moment* that Robin had walked in on. I hadn't dreamed that kiss. Although it seemed like I should have. Shit, that felt as though it had happened to someone else a million years ago. Not me.

"Where would you like to go?" he asked.

The thought of going back to Cecil Court filled me with dread, and not just because Gina would bury me in an avalanche of questions. The IRL would be all over me too. I was still technically on the run, even though I'd never been convicted. I puffed out a sigh. I just needed... space. "I dunno... Can we just drive around for a bit?"

He changed gear, flicked the car's indicator on, and drove, just like I'd asked, no judgment, just the quiet hum of the tires on the road and the precision burble of the car's engine, and Kempthorne, just being *there*. No questions. No small talk. Just knowing I wasn't alone. He'd come for me.

People didn't do that. Not for me.

Driving around for a bit turned into a few hours of M25, then M5, then we were in the depths of the rolling hills of Somerset, arriving at a pretty seaside village full of wonky houses and narrow roads.

Kempthorne parked in the village car park, paid for the parking on an app, and looked over. Blue eyes shone with tiredness and something else I couldn't make sense of. It might have been the first time I'd met his gaze since he'd picked me up, hours ago. I wanted to thank him, to tell him I was an idiot for not calling him, but I knew, if I spoke, I'd choke up.

"Fish and chips?" he asked.

Fuck, I think I loved this man. "Hell yes," I croaked, "and curry sauce."

He frowned. "What monster forgets curry sauce?" He

climbed out, closed the door, and I watched him stride across the parking lot in his creased twenty-thousand-pound suit to the pokey little fish and chip shop with the flashing neon *OPEN* sign. He'd probably never ordered fish and chips in his whole life.

He returned with a white paper bag with a blue fish on it, then drove us up to a clifftop carpark, where a few other cars were parked, their passengers having the same idea we had. We unwrapped the meal and poked at the battered fish with small, wooden sporks. The quiet was... nice. Didn't need to be filled, or at least I didn't think so, until Kempthorne cleared his throat and said, "When I created the Kempthorne Agency, it was just me. And it quickly became clear that alone, I'd never get anything done. I needed someone who... well... someone who could organize my chaos."

"Robin," I said with a grin.

He cocked his head as a yes. "I had perhaps... fifteen applicants for the position of personal assistant. Most of them, honestly, could barely string a sentence together. One even asked me to sign their... well... anyway... They didn't get the position."

I found my appetite and dug into my meal. "Sign their what? C'mon, you can't hint and not tell me."

He smirked—actually smirked. "It's not important. Robin was the final applicant," Kempthorne said. "I'd all but given up hope of hiring someone. I was late to the appointment, she was early. And she made of point of telling me so. I mentioned she looked beautiful, which is apparently the wrong thing to say to a woman during a job interview."

I snorted; that sounded like Robin. And Kempthorne.

"She went on to tell me how, if I was interested in any funny business—her words—she'd sue me. Naturally, I assured her that would not be the case. She then insulted my book shop, told me it looked like a condemned charity shop, then told me to fire my cleaner. I told her the cleaner was me. She said that if I couldn't afford to hire a cleaner, what kind of rich toff was I?" He chuckled at the memory and stabbed some more at his fish.

This was priceless. I laughed into my hand, feeling something warm and soft unfurl inside. A warm, human part of me I'd kept locked up for safekeeping while I'd been *away*. "So, wait. Robin was rude?" I marked them off on my fingers. "Told you if you looked at her sideways she'd sue you for sexual harassment, insulted you and your shop, and you hired her anyway?"

Kempthorne nodded, eyebrows raised. "I needed someone who didn't care who I was, who would tell me everything I needed to hear. Kempthorne & Co wouldn't exist without her."

"And Gina?"

"She fell into my lap during a charity dinner, called me a tosser, and flounced off."

I laughed so hard I almost choked. Kempthorne hastily opened a bottle of water and handed it over. "That's not how it ended though?" I asked, once I could breathe again.

"No." He laughed. "She came to the shop the next day and apologized. I was speaking with a client at the time, she overheard and said she'd like to make it up to me by having me hire her. Honestly, I wasn't sure—Robin didn't hesitate. Robin knows people. The both of them do. They're brilliant. I'm lucky to have them."

"And me?" I asked, carefully chasing a piece of fish around the paper tray with my spork.

"You? Well, you know how that came about, but I'd only seen your military photograph..." He hesitated, swallowing as he peered down at what remained of his chips, then lifted his gaze again. "You walked in, dropped your hood and bag, and looked as though you should be a club doorman, not an agent. I had no idea who you were, even having seen your photograph. I was a beat away from telling you to leave, and then you smiled."

"I smiled?" I remembered it. I'd walked into the shop with no idea what to expect and had three strangers staring back at me. Robin had had a pissed off expression on her face, Gina had grinned, as though she'd won the lottery, and Kempthorne... I'd really only noticed the suit and the watch, and thought *fuck, he's out of my league.*

"Yes..." He waved his spork in my general direction. "The smile softens everything else. Then, of course, Gina swooped in, scenting fresh blood. Robin later told me you were a work in progress."

"Wow."

"High praise from her. Trust me. She despises the Queen."

"Christ."

"Exactly."

We both laughed and the ache left over from the past few days faded until it was just me and Kempthorne, sitting in a car, eating fish and chips. I'd thought I'd liked the quiet ride, liked the silence with him beside me, but his stories were so much better. They reminded me of the people and the job I'd loved, the place that waited for me to go back to.

"I er…" I'd been about to say something soft, but choked on it at the last second and switched it with something daft instead. "The Aston's gonna smell of fish and chips for weeks."

He snorted. "It's worth it. To have you back."

Before I could comment on *that*, he'd bundled up our used wrappings and climbed out to stuff the rubbish into a nearby bin. The wind whipped around him, mussing his hair and shirt. A light rain had blown in off the sea, too, dampening him down. He looked wild and undone. And when he climbed back into the car, wet and ruffled and smelling of the sea, it was all I could do not to grin like an idiot.

"It'll take four hours to drive back to London," he said, hitting the ignition. The engine purred.

"Premier Inn it?" I suggested. "If it's not too cheap for you."

The arched eyebrow and sideways smirk tripped my heart. "You presume I can't do cheap?"

"I mean, it's not the Hilton." Christ, that smirk. It was going to get me in trouble.

"Hilton is overrated." He twisted, caught the back of my seat, and peered through the back window to reverse the car. "Just so we're clear, I'd go anywhere with you." A little muscle jumped in his cheek. He swallowed, and with him so close, I tracked the movement down his neck to where his collar gaped.

We'd kissed a million years ago, but somehow it felt like yesterday too. Like I could shift in the seat, move closer, and the tension sizzling between us might explode.

He swung the car around and faced ahead, pointing the Aston toward the road. "I'm glad you're back."

He just meant... like... Nope, I couldn't think of a way to twist the words that didn't mean he'd *go anywhere with me* and that he *was glad I was back.* As though he cared. "Premier Inn's not so bad," I said, for something to say so the tension didn't choke me. "They have little sachets of Nescafé, which kinda tastes like dirt, but the beds are... er... really..." I swallowed. "Comfy."

He cast me a glance that, in the glow of the car's instruments, looked a hundred percent as though he had every intention of putting the beds to the test. Or maybe this was some drug-induced fantasy? I pinched myself to make sure I didn't wake up on my Wordsworth bed.

"Premier Inn, it is," he said.

It doesn't matter where in the UK you go, Premier Inns were all the same. No-frills hotels positioned near major roads, with some kind of chain restaurant attached so you can grab a greasy fry-up at 7 a.m. and be out the door at 7.30 a.m. The one Kempthorne found was no different. We were 'sharing a room,' he told the receptionist, and smiled when he added, "Twin beds." She glared at the both of us through her Perspex screen and Christ knew what she saw. Kempthorne, in his crumpled shirt and black trousers, had probably gotten lost on his way back from a stag night, and I was the thug about to mug him the second he turned his back.

"No bags?" she asked.

"They're in the car," Kempthorne lied smoothly.

Then without further fuss, we were inside our tiny room with its comfy purple-and-white twin beds, and I still wasn't sure how I'd ended up here. With Kempthorne. In a Premier Inn. When I should have been in Hackney getting scuffed knuckles.

He hadn't asked a bloody thing about anything, and he was acting strange, even for him. His phone hadn't rung once, which meant he'd turned it off. Every now and then, he cupped his bruised knuckles, thinking I hadn't noticed. So what was going on here? If he'd taken me back to Cecil Court, that would have made sense—that would have been work. So what was this?

Personal... it was *personal.*

"Look, I—"

"I just—"

I laughed, "You go."

Kempthorne sat on the edge of the bed nearest the window and sighed. "*This...*" He gestured at the room. "It doesn't have to mean anything. We're a long way from home and I thought... Well, I needed some space for a while and I thought you might need the same, so here we are. No strings."

"In a Premier Inn." I tested the bounce at the end of my bed and found it perfect.

He glanced around the room. "It's not nearly as horrific as I thought it would be."

"See... you should get out of your posh bubble more often. It suits you. And it's only eighty quid a night, not five hundred or whatever five-star places are?"

He smiled. His smile warmed me through, and I

found I didn't really care why we were here, or what he was thinking, just that we *were* here and I'd needed this more than I'd known. More than I deserved.

"Dom, I'm sorry I couldn't get you out—"

I lifted a hand and shook my head. "Can we not talk about it?" His face fell. "It's fine, I just don't want it here, now. I just need *this*. Can we talk about everything tomorrow?"

He nodded. "Yes. Of course."

"Thanks." I swallowed. "For picking me up, for everything."

"Always."

My heart tried to fall over itself. I tucked my thumbs into my jeans pockets, then took them out again and stepped backward. "I'm just gonna shower and crash. If that's... okay?"

"Yes. Definitely. That's fine." Was he sad? I couldn't bloody well read that face, with all its charm and softness and his looking-after-me, as though I was worth it.

In the tiny bathroom, I stripped and showered, half wishing Kempthorne would open the door and join me, then hoping he didn't because everything was already complicated without adding sex to it all. When I stepped out of the steamy bathroom, a towel tucked around my waist, he scooted by, avoiding meeting my eye or any part of me, and disappeared into the bathroom to shower. I flopped onto the bed and listened to the sound of water sloshing off him. Maybe I could go in there? Just open the door. He'd either yell, and I'd ruin all this, or he'd give me those come-hither eyes and I'd go down on Kempthorne in the shower.

I chuckled at the fantasy. "Whatever, Dom."

Sleep tugged on my thoughts. I tried to cling on, to stay awake, to make the evening with Kempthorne last forever, but golden wires fell from the ceiling and tied me in knots and plucked on my limbs, as though I were someone's puppet. Somewhere distantly, I knew it wasn't real, but the dream wrapped me up so tightly, I couldn't escape. My trick flowed out of me, veins of light draining everything away—

"Dom—"

Kempthorne. Golden eyes. Lit by trick.

"Fuck!" I recoiled, shoving myself into the pillows and him away.

"Sorry—you were thrashing." He straightened and swept his hair back. "And you er... your trick."

I lifted my fingers to find them glowing in the dark. "Jesus. That's never..." I shook it free and propped myself on an elbow. "My control is s-shot," I explained or tried to. "Whatever they did to me, my trick is all over the place."

"Ah." He moved from his bed and took something from his back pocket. "These will help, I think. The Met had them. I've had them... a while. Meant to give them back, but... with everything..."

A familiar tickle seduced my latent senses. "My deck..." I scooped them from his hand, fighting the urge to go all Smeagle on him. My trick spilled through each card, stirred awake by the deck's dirty resonance. On reflex, I spilled the cards free and fanned them across the quilt. Golden light filled the small room. Yes, this was better. With an artifact to focus on, the trick didn't feel nearly as loose. "Thanks, I..." Kempthorne's blue eyes had glazed over. And I realized my mistake. "Sorry." I quickly scooped them up again. "I wasn't thinking."

"I like it, actually. It's hypnotic." He tucked a hand into his pocket. He was still fully dressed, unlike me, wearing only a towel while sitting on top of the quilt.

The clock on the wall blinked 3:05 a.m. Too early to get up, but the trick, woken by the dream, had me buzzed. Had Kempthorne slept at all?

Kempthorne tore his gaze away. "We'd best get back to sleep."

I took a card from the deck and flooded it with trick, softly illuminating the room. Kempthorne's stride hitched. He glanced over his shoulder.

I danced the lit card through my fingers, spinning it multiple ways. It glowed like a kid's sparkler. Kempthorne returned to my bedside. I kept my gaze on the card, deliberately avoiding looking at him, and flicked the card into the air. He snatched it, lightning fast, and for a second, held it there, then my trick spilled like honey over his fingers and vanished, absorbed *into* him. His moan wasn't far off the sound he'd made when I'd kissed him, and the sizzling affect it had on me went straight to my cock. I had another few seconds of wondering how the fuck I was going to hide a hard-on under a towel, when I found myself pinned to the bed, between his arms, his eyes glowing golden in the near-dark.

"I shouldn't—"

I cut him off with a kiss before he could think up an excuse. Like before, he didn't respond, just froze, and just like before I wondered if I was the twat for forcing this—then the floodgates opened and whatever was holding him back gave way. He came alive inside the kiss, thrusting his tongue in and taking with all the force of a starved man having his desires fulfilled. I had his shirt in one fist, and ran my free hand underneath, stroking his warm chest. He propped himself on an elbow. The kiss slowed, becoming less about desperation and more about enjoyment. I kissed him as though I could make it last, fearful it wouldn't. And right on cue, he pulled back and lowered his gaze, turning his head away.

My trick had spilled out and glowed under his shirt. "Er...sorry?"

He chuckled darkly, unfazed by my trick leaking all over him, and rolled onto his side, with his head propped on a hand and all of his heat and hardness pressed against my hip and thigh. The shift in position broke whatever the fuck my trick was doing and the tingling glow retreated back into my fingers. I rubbed my hands together, watching the light fade, until the room was again in darkness. Only now I had Kempthorne plastered to my side and a raging erection that wasn't going to get any relief while he breathed against my naked shoulder.

"I mean..." I cleared the squeak from my throat. "I feel like we could maybe follow this through and see where it goes?"

"Ah, yes, but no."

Okay. He was probably right. Fucking the boss in a Premier Inn was not one of my better ideas, but it had kind of felt like maybe he'd wanted to. And I definitely wasn't going to say no. We were two consenting adults, so what was the problem?

"This is just... it's not how I do things," he said.

Now that my eyes had adjusted to the darkness, I saw the outline of his jaw, the glisten of his eyes, and the haphazard floppy mess that his hair had become. And I didn't need to see his expression to know he was struggling with *all of this.*

"You mean rescuing a mob boss's son from a life of crime and taking him to a cheap motel for a night of wild sex isn't your bag?" I sighed, dramatically. "It worked for Julia Roberts and Richard Gere."

His soft laugh had my dick pricking up again.

Then he said, "Who are they?"

"*Pretty Woman*?" I prompted, slightly alarmed.

"Perhaps she is, I just—"

"No, she's not a she. Well, she is a she. It's a movie." Wait. Was he screwing with me? His eyes grew bigger in the dark, and his expression was all muddled and sheepish. "You've never seen it? Soppy rich guy buys a streetwise prostitute for a night? They fall in love? It's not ringing any bells?"

"I don't believe so." His eyes glittered. "You don't strike me as the sort who enjoys romances."

I snorted. "Pfft, me? No." *Maybe.* "But everyone has seen *Pretty Woman.*" Everyone except Alexander Kempthorne. "You have a TV, though?" I'd seen it. He definitely had one.

"I watch the news, mostly. And documentaries."

"About?"

"Latents."

Of course. Which meant he'd never understood *any* of my movie refences. "We have to change that." A movie marathon was in order. Netflix, with popcorn.

He snickered a dark, little laugh. "If you think so."

I could lean into him, subtly roll to my side, kiss him until he couldn't stop. He wouldn't be able to resist for long. But that didn't seem fair. Besides, this was... nice. "I know so."

"I missed you," he said, and in the dark, the words carried a whole lot of emotion.

"You did?" *Christ.*

"We all did."

"Ah." So his *I missed you*, was more of a *We missed you like a friend.*

"You've been through an ordeal. I don't want to take advantage of you."

Now I snickered, I couldn't' help it. He was being way too cute and my heart couldn't handle it. "Take advantage of me?" What was I, a seventeen-year-old virgin? "I'm pretty sure I'm a big boy who can handle his hot, complicated, neurotic boss—"

His hand smothered my mouth, and then his lips were at my ear, his breath tickling, and my dick went from bored to hell-yes. "*When* we do this," he whispered, his voice all kinds of low and menacing, "it will not be in a cheap hotel right after you think you owe me, when you don't."

I breathed through my nostrils, so aroused it hurt, but gutted, too, because he was bloody right. I might have done anything for him then. I owed him, and not just for the pickup—for buying me from the military, for getting me out of a downward spiral, for managing my trick in all the subtle ways. We weren't equal, and that wasn't right.

"You don't owe anyone anything," he said, as though he'd read my mind. He eased his hand away, kissed me on the cheek, then hesitated, breathing so damn close I felt the tension strumming through him. "Rest assured, this is killing me as much as it is you." Then the stubborn man made his way off and around my bed and fell onto his.

There wasn't much left to say after that, and after listening to his breathing slow and settle into an easy rhythm, I fell asleep. And this time, for the first time in months, no dreams assaulted me.

Alexander

Dom slept so long I paid for a second night. While he dozed, I visited the breakfast spread at the chain restaurant next door, cautiously optimistic I wasn't about to get food poisoning after having slept in a surprisingly comfortable bed. The food was basic, but functional. I settled for a continental selection with coffee and ruminated over events of the previous day as the other guests filed in, most of them families with kids in tow. Dom sauntered in around ten, grabbed a coffee from the machine, and sat at my table. He pushed his hood down and dumped too many sugars in his coffee. "Sleep well?" he asked.

"Some." I'd slept well *after* our discussion. Not before.

I'd only been able to sleep because he'd been safe, and known it, which meant everything.

He eyed my phone on the table. "You should turn that back on. Robin will be losing her shit. She'll blame me."

"I will." I wasn't ready. Not yet. I wanted Dom to myself a little while longer, before the trials of the real world outside the Premier Inn tried to pull us apart. And there was a lot we had yet to deal with. The IRL. Wordsworth. Montgomery.

Dom leaned back and sighed. "Okay, here it is." He told me about his escape, about calling Charles Renick and not me—skimmed over why, with reasons such as keeping us safe, but when I opened my mouth to tell him we—the team—would always come for him, he rushed into another topic. "I had a dream," he said. "At least I think I did. There were these golden tubes or wires— Anyway, that's not the important bit. I saw Penny, you remember her? The girl we saved from Olivia's rampage?"

"I recall." I recalled the tubes, too, but no more wanted to talk about those than he did.

"Her surname... Do you remember that?"

I remembered the girl because she'd reminded me of my sister but knew little else of her or her family and waited for Dom to enlighten me.

"*Montgomery*," he said. "That can't be coincidence, right?"

"Coincidences are also facts."

"Exactly."

Penny Montgomery. That *was* interesting. "She seemed innocent in those events."

"Yeah, she was. Like I said, maybe I dreamed her up

or something, but... the name niggles. Like it's in my head."

It had merit. Montgomery was a common name. But both being latents and involved in recent events made the coincidence less of a fluke and more by design. "Olivia had no love for M, although I'm unsure whether she knew who he was before she died," I said. "Perhaps she was making a point by singling out Penny? If Penny *is* related to Thomas Montgomery, Robin will know."

Dom eyed my phone again, silently suggesting I might like to turn it back on.

"Not yet." As soon as I turned it on, the bloody thing would demand all my attention, and I was quite content with Dom and nobody else.

"I wanted to call you," he said, shoulders hunched. "The second I got out..."

"I understand why you didn't." I didn't, but the fact remained he hadn't called me, so that was that.

He flicked his eyes up. "I can't go back to Cecil Court."

"If it's the IRL you're concerned about, they have no legal grounds to hold you, especially with Max's surviving victim's testimony. I'll have my lawyers throw multiple injunctions at them. They'll have no choice but to leave you alone."

"And Montgomery? He's a part of this. He's an absorber, and he's right in the heart of Wordsworth."

"Yes, he and I have met." I closed my hands around my mug of now-cold coffee and tapped my fingers. "Montgomery is a problem. Kage and I *visited* his facility." I explained our visit and dramatic escape. As Dom listened, his eyes widened and all his soft warmth turned to ice until he was sitting dead still, alert for threats.

"I thought I dreamed it," he said to himself, and then with a deep breath, plowed into an explanation of the experiments they'd performed in Wordsworth. I kept my expression measured, even as he described procedures I'd undergone years ago. Flooding, and siphoning off excess trick, leaving the latent spent, used, and halfway to madness.

By the time he was done, I'd rubbed my left wrist raw at the memory of being held down. "I'm sorry you had to go through that."

"I'm out... that's all I care about." He could shrug it off, but he'd paled, and his fingers trembled. He sighed and cleared his throat, then nodded toward my hand wrapped around my coffee mug. "What happened?"

I lifted my hand, having forgotten my bruised knuckles. "Oh that?" I flexed my fingers. "I hit a wall."

His expression remained unchanged. I waited for the questions to begin, but instead, he said, "You wanna get out of here?"

I'd become accustomed to the noise from the gaggles of families and the feel of the sticky floor under my shoes. "Not particularly."

"Don't tell me I've converted you to cheap motels and buffet food?"

"Perhaps." No, but I'd let him have the win.

He laughed, sensing I was joking. I'd missed his laugh, the way it rumbled through me and tugged on my heart. I'd missed a great many things about John Domenici, things I'd only realized I'd come to crave after he'd gone. He was back now, and yesterday, after picking him up outside the Snooker Room, had been one of the most real and amazing days of my life. Because he'd been in it. "Alas, we must return to London. It's time Gina and Robin were introduced to the murder wall."

His eyes sparkled. "*Alas*? Seriously? I swear you're havin' me on half the time."

I laughed and had to look away to keep from showing too much of how I'd loved this—loved being around him, loved... *him*.

Gina threw her arms around Dom the moment he stepped from the car, almost knocking him over. All manner of high-pitched squeals erupted, then she punched him on the arm and demanded to know why he hadn't called her. I knew that feeling. He rubbed the back of his neck, sheepish and adorably shy. My heart leaped to defend him. I swallowed instead, stifling the unexpected surge of emotion, and approached Ravenscourt's front door, where Robin waited, face stern.

"You disappear for two days and waltz back in with Dom like nothing happened?" she said.

I stepped around her and unlocked the door. "Yes?"

She leaned in. "How did you get him out?"

"I didn't. He got himself out."

She glanced at Dom and Gina, heads together, plotting something, and smiled. She acted tough—one of us had to—but deep down, she cared about all of us, especially Dom, now she knew him. "I guess he's one of us now." She turned a rare smile on me.

"He really is." I shoved open the door and for Gina's benefit, said, "Welcome to Ravenscourt."

The housekeepers had been in and stocked the fridge,

lit the fires, and made the place welcoming, then made themselves scarce again. We were the only ones in the old house, and as much as having Robin and Gina here had my heart racing, it didn't feel as awkward as I'd anticipated.

"Wow." Gina wandered into the hallway. Dom sauntered in behind her. He caught my eye and we shared brief smiles. He reached out and touched the stair banister, then drifted into the lounge, so familiar and relaxed with the house that I almost envied him. Ravenscourt didn't hold the same ghosts for him that it did me, although as an authenticator, he naturally felt much of the old house's past in its fabric. And, of course, there was the study, which I kept locked, and had a whole other feel to it that was far from welcoming.

"Is it just you in this big old place?" Gina asked, then realized her mistake in mentioning my lack of living family. "I mean, of course it is."

"I'll put the kettle on. Why don't you all take yourself on the tour and meet me back in the kitchen."

Their voices echoed about the house, drifting to me in the kitchen as I made up a tray of tea and biscuits.

Showing Dom the murder wall had been a leap of faith. It could have gone either way—he might have laughed me off as insane or joined me. As it happened, he'd responded with a little of both and had admired the wall through his smiles. But I had no idea how Robin or Gina would react. Kempthorne & Co didn't do personal. *I* didn't do personal. My murder wall was my life's work laid bare. Bringing them here, exposing my past and with it, the real Alexander Kempthorne, filled me with fear.

As I reached for the tap to rinse out a cup, the scrapes

and bruises on my knuckles caught my eye. I flexed my fingers and winced, not at the pain, that was minimal, but at the memory.

"Your house is gorgeous!" Gina bounded into the kitchen, filling the large, high-ceilinged room with her personality. "I can't believe we get to stay here tonight. I bet it's totally haunted."

She was more right than she knew. "There's more to see," I said, perhaps too brightly.

Robin and Dom arrived, and the three of them scooped up their steaming mugs of tea and attacked the biscuits, trading small talk. This was the right time to take them to the murder wall, to tell them everything about me, but instead I kept my eyes down and sipped tea.

"Oh... my God..." Robin gaped at her phone.

"What?" Gina leaned in. "Oh... isn't that..." She glared across the island counter at Dom.

Robin's glare, however, landed on me. Her green eyes narrowed. She set her phone down on the countertop so we could all see the BBC news app headline:

Body Discovered in the Thames Identified as Charles Renick

I backed up to my safe place by the sink and sipped my tea. "How unfortunate."

Robin humphed and faced Dom, adding to Gina's glare.

He blinked. "What?" Then frowned. "Not this again. Why does everyone assume shit like this is my fault? I didn't kill the prick. Although, I would have, given the chance. He's had it coming for years."

Robin picked up her phone and scrolled down the

article. *"Last seen at the Oblix with Alexander Kempthorne. That's why Detective Gomez has been calling…"* She slid her acute glare back to me again.

"Like I said, unfortunate." I sipped more tea. For some reason, none of them appeared to believe me. "Any witnesses will note how my conversation with Charles Renick was light. We left separately."

"When was this?" Dom asked.

"Two nights ago," Robin said. "The body was fished out of the Thames yesterday."

Dom nodded, as though he'd moved some things around in his head and slotted the solution together. "He probably got on the wrong side of the Eastern Europeans."

"Or a faulty handrail," I suggested. But instead of alleviating their suspicions, all three frowned.

Murder Wall suddenly sounded rather on the nose.

Robin scrolled through the article some more. "They're looking for a latent. Renick's body probably has burns."

"He was trafficking latent kids," I said.

"He was?" Dom asked, his face troubled. "That bastard."

"Worse, in many cases," I added, remembering Renick's comments regarding snuff films. Dom didn't need to know about the money I'd paid. It was of no consequence. I'd meant what I'd told Renick. It didn't matter who said what, or how much money changed hands: Nobody owned Dom. "One of his victims likely got the better of him."

A thick silence fell. The bruises on my knuckles chose

that moment to itch. I cleared my throat and headed out the door. "Please follow me. I have something to show you all."

Grateful for the distraction, I took the group upstairs, unlocked the murder wall room, and let the group file inside, following them. Gina and Robin drifted closer to the spread covering the entire wall while Dom hung back, hands in his pockets, admiring all the things he'd seen before.

"Thomas Montgomery," Robin finally said. "He's M? You have proof?"

"He is," I confirmed. "But proof? No. He's too careful for that. I Just have a lot of coincidences, all of it circumstantial."

"Well then," she said, straightening her glasses. "We need to find that proof."

Gina backed up and smiled as I approached her side. "This means a lot to you, doesn't it?"

I swallowed and visually skimmed the wall, with its thousands of clues and people and articles. "Since I lost my parents, it's been my life."

She nodded. "Thank you... for showing us."

"Thank *you* for being here. I couldn't have come this far without you both. And Dom."

They all looked at me—Robin curiously determined, Gina sympathetic, and Dom, oddly proud. Was this what having a real family felt like? A family who cared? I'd been so afraid to show them this, show them the real me, that I'd shut myself away. Alone for so long, I hadn't known there could be any other way.

I scooped up a nearby file from the table, flicked it

open, and handed Gina Google Earth aerial prints of Montgomery's laboratory.

She studied the photos and turned toward the wall. "Let's Kempthorne-and-Co the shit out of this."

Dom Ravenscourt hummed, as though the old house was happy about us being here. It sounded ridiculous—Ravenscourt wasn't alive—but it felt like it sometimes. Within a few hours of being back, Kempthorne had turned into his loose, frazzled self, enigmatic and unhinged. And I couldn't keep my eyes off him. Gina and Robin had fallen into his enthusiasm while he bandied theories around, thoroughly hooking them into his work. He'd been worried about bringing them here. I'd seen it in his eyes, and how quiet he'd been on the drive back to London. He needn't have worried. We were all on board with him.

But there was one team member missing. And his absence had left a gaping hole.

Kage.

I hadn't mentioned him. It didn't seem the place or time. The fact nobody else had mentioned him suggested he wasn't welcome. I figured something had happened while I'd been away—something that had shut him out. I'd ask, when I got a chance, but for now it was all about bringing Robin and Gina up to speed with everything. And there was a lot.

I left them discussing the auctions and M's systematic collection of artifacts and headed for the bathroom, but only made it halfway down the hallway when the whispering pulled me up short. *John...*

I'd been here before, hearing voices, *that* voice. It came from the study, several doors, corridors, and rooms away. Kempthorne's *not*-ghost. A shadow. Or... a dead latent. I couldn't go near it because of the dirty table— that artifact was lethal. In my current twitchy state, the bloody thing would set me off.

John...

I wasn't going to go inside—Kempthorne always kept it locked—but I could listen at the door? The shadow inside wanted something, and Kempthorne said it never left that room, so just listening wouldn't hurt.

With everyone occupied in the murder wall room, I followed the whispers through the house to the heavy curtain slung over the locked study door. A thick, heated beat throbbed from behind. I shoved the curtain aside and pressed my hands to the door.

John... the voice whispered. "Not helpful," I mumbled back. I'd seen the shadow's face up close, felt its icy touch, and was glad for the door between us. But if it was just going to whisper my name, there was little point in hanging around.

A little *clunk* and a shiny piece of metal slid under the door. Thankfully *not* a dirty pen, but it was an artifact, and one I was familiar with.

I knelt and eyed the old pound coin. It had to be *the* coin, didn't it? The one Anya had wanted to get her hands on. The coin Olivia Barnes had needed. The one everyone seemed so interested in and the one I'd thought Kempthorne kept in the wall safe in Cecil Court's basement. Apparently not. Because it was here.

Had the shadow pushed it under the door? Could they do that?

John... the whispers urged.

Bollocks.

I picked up the coin and took a step back from the door, putting distance between me and the study's cloying waves of psychic energy. The coin tingled between my fingers. Cool. Hard. And still very hot—psychically speaking. *The girl with the ponytail, a knife through the chest.* I remembered everything I'd seen before, but did I want to see more? I already had a ton of memories in my head that weren't mine.

Kempthorne hadn't wanted me delving any deeper, or he'd have asked me before now.

I slipped the coin into my pocket. As artifacts went, it was hot, but I could filter out its noise. Reading the coin without speaking with Kempthorne first felt like a violation, and we'd both had enough of those. I'd ask him later.

"Oh hey." Gina bumped into me as I made my way back to the murder wall room. "This place is huge, I got turned around." She lifted four empty mugs hooked into her fingers. "Wanna help me make the tea?"

"Sure."

I rinsed the mugs in the kitchen sink while she dried and set them on the drainer. It was the kind of domestic simplicity that, after the never-ending nightmare of Wordsworth's, felt surreal and had me choking back a sneaky swell of emotion.

"So, you and Kempthorne?" Gina asked, unable to hold the question in any longer. She waggled her eyebrows.

I'd missed her. Missed her smile, the way I could tell her anything and she'd be cool with it. Although, I wasn't sure there was much to tell between me and Kempthorne. "It's kinda complicated." I handed her the last cleaned mug.

She wiped the mug dry and set it down with the others, then filled the kettle. "It's Kempthorne, so *yeah*. But you know, are you... like... a thing?"

Were we a thing? I leaned against the counter and folded my arms. One hot kiss in his bedroom a lifetime ago, and then whatever that had been in Premier Inn? And then there was Kage... "I don't know." I shrugged. "My head's all over the place. I don't know a lot of things right now."

"You know what I know?" She flicked her springy curls back from her face and looked me dead in the eyes. "We care about you," she said, like a threat. "We're glad you're back and we'll fight in your corner, no matter what. You get me?"

I didn't know whether it was the near miss escaping

the lab, or just all of the shit that had been thrown my way for the past few months, but her words levered under my armor like a crowbar. I tried to stifle the surge of gratitude, tried to smile it off, but when I spoke, my voice wobbled. "You have no fucking idea how much that means."

She threw her arms around me a second time, and this time I pulled her in, needing this.

I'd never had a family who cared for each other. My mum had tried, but Dad had cast a shadow that hadn't left much room for caring. Most East End families kicked their latent offspring to the curb. I'd learned early on that latents didn't get loved. But Gina and Kempthorne, and even Robin, had become more than colleagues. They were friends.

Gina pulled back and squeezed my hand. "We got you. Don't leave again, okay? I can't handle Robin and Kempthorne without you. They're off-the-scale intense." She rolled her eyes and turned her back to collect the tea bags and finish making the tea.

"Yeah, right. Next time, I'll try a bit harder not to get wrongly accused of murder."

She snickered. "Sorry about Kage. Turns out the pretty ones are always dicks, huh?"

I frowned. "What happened with Kage?"

Her shoulders stiffened and she glanced back. "Oh shit, you don't know? I just thought..." Her eyes widened. She'd let something slip she shouldn't have. "I thought Kempthorne told you?"

"Told me what?"

She pressed her lips together.

I glowered. "C'mon, you can't clam up now."

After wincing, she picked up the kettle and poured boiling water into the mugs. "Okay, so, don't freak out?"

"Spill."

She faffed about refilling the kettle again for no reason, buying herself time to come up with the right words. Once she set the kettle down on its stand and flicked it on, she had nothing left to stall with she puffed out a sigh. "He's LOA."

"Huh?"

"Latent Observation Agency. Like the FBI, but you know, they make latents go *poof*—disappear."

"I know what the LOA is. Kempthorne told me his suspicions. But there wasn't any proof."

"Yeah, no. Kage admitted it to Kempthorne, apparently. Hence why he's not here and we are."

The cogs in my head turned. "He's definitely LOA?"

"Yeah."

The kettle simmered louder and something inside clicked over, some part of me I'd been keeping in-check. "Okay," I said carefully. Latent Observation Agency. All this time. He killed latents to order. He'd admitted it.

"Okay?" she asked.

I slumped against the counter. "I mean, I dunno. Like... shit." Now it was sinking in, the feelings were coming with it. I'd liked him. Liked him a lot, and then the note in Wordsworth... which sort of seemed like he'd liked me, and he'd made me feel like a dick for suggesting he might have poisoned me. Made me think Kempthorne was paranoid.

The bastard had gaslighted me. What the fuck was all that *I'm waiting for you* shit, if he was an active LOA agent? Waiting for what, for me to get out so he could turn me over to his bosses or put a bullet between my eyes?

Kage Mitchell, with his cocky smiles and light hands and the way he'd made me think he fucking cared was *fucking LOA.*

The water inside the kettle bubbled and boiled, grumbling and spewing steam.

I swallowed.

"Dom?" Gina's voice seemed far away.

"Yeah?"

"Er... Does it normally do that?"

Trick dripped from my fingers. *Shit.* I fumbled my deck from my pocket, needing them to soothe the trick threatening to boil over, but the cards slipped from my fingers and scattered across the floor. "Fuck." The big, glossy kitchen counters tipped around me. The walls moved. I grabbed a counter's edge. Trick seeped over the work surface and into the sink.

I was *leaking.*

Gina knelt and began collecting up the cards. Trick flowed down the counter doors, seeking the cards and their dirty hum. I tried to recall it, to get a hold of myself, but I couldn't focus. Couldn't think. This had happened before, at the London docks... but I'd been drugged then, by Kage. I was *spiraling.*

"Gina... you have to leave—"

I only knew the trick had touched the coin when the memories slapped me across the face and forced themselves through mental gates. I heard my yell, heard Gina cry out. I clutched at my head and went to my knees. I was somewhere else—someone else. *The flash of a knife, the smell of perfume. A punch in my chest. I gasped, knew I'd been stabbed, knew it was bad. Terror flushed hot across my skin. I thrust out a hand, trying to hold myself up, and pressed a wet, blood-slick hand to a table. Coins clattered to the floor. Tried to hold on. Slipped. Knees hit the floor. Blonde hair shielded my face. Couldn't breathe. So cold. So much blood. Help. Help me. I reached up. Someone was there. Blue eyes. My brother. Alex? I reached out a hand, and... he stood there, bloodied knife in his hand.*

The knife. Max's knife. Wait... Alex... Alexander.

Alex? He watched. Eyes so blue, flecked with gold. I reached for him, my brother. I loved him. Why? The knife dripped blood. My blood. He had done this. My chest, it didn't hurt anymore. Alex had done this. Why? So cold. I just... I needed to sleep, just for a little while...

"Dom?"

I blinked and scuttled backward, away from Kempthorne's reaching hand. My back slammed into the counter door. *Alex. He'd killed me.*

Wait. No.

Remember. Remember who I am. Not her. Me. Now.

"Dom, you're in Ravenscourt," Kempthorne said. But he was Alex too, just older. He'd killed her. His sister. Charlotte Kempthorne. I touched my chest and breathed. I wasn't bleeding, I wasn't hurt. But she had been. The coin had shown me everything.

"Dom?"

"I'm here," I croaked, then lifted my gaze. The blood I tasted was hers.

Kempthorne knelt and watched, concern sharpening his handsome features. Gina and Robin stood behind him, their faces in shadow. The memory of who

Kempthorne had been flashed in front of me. A young man. Eyes so cold. But the same eyes fixed on me now.

Knife in his hand. Blood on his knuckles. Blood on his sleeve. Kage had warned me. Kage wasn't the enemy. Kage had been right.

Alexander Kempthorne had murdered his sister.

D^{om}

LOA be damned, I had to call Kage.

Gina fussed, ignoring my attempts to tell her I was fine. Just a glitch from my ordeal, I'd said. I said the same to Kempthorne but had a hard time meeting his gaze. He didn't know I had the coin. He didn't know *I knew*. I had to keep it that way. I couldn't look at him, not yet. He'd see it all on my face.

"I'm just gonna get some air." With my cards back in my pocket, I stumbled outside and swallowed gulps of air. Thankfully, nobody followed. The Aston glinted under the sun, unlocked. I grabbed my burner phone, walked around the back of the posh oak frame garages, and dialed Kage's number. "C'mon, Hollywood, pick up."

It rang out.

"For fuck's sake... why can't you stalk me when it's useful?"

My phone blipped. A text came through. Unknown number: *Who is this?*

Dom, I sent back.

It rang once, and I picked it up before the second ring. "Fuck, Kage..."

"What's going on? Are you all right?" I couldn't ever remember being so relieved to hear an American accent.

"Shit..." I slumped against the garage wall. "I dunno." I could still feel it, the cold, hard punch of steel straight through my ribs, into my heart. She'd bled out in seconds and he'd watched. He'd told me how he'd watched an agent die to keep his secret. But that hadn't been all of it. He'd watched his sister die too. "I need you to tell me the truth."

"All right," Kage replied carefully.

"Are you LOA?"

"Yeah, but I can explain—"

"You fucking twat."

"I know—but it's not what you think."

"Shut up. Listen. Kempthorne." I checked the driveway—still alone. "You told me he's dangerous. What do you know?"

"This isn't a conversation for the phone."

"Dom?" Kempthorne stepped around the side of the garage.

I hung up the call, slipped the phone into my pocket, and ran a hand through my hair with a cracked smile. "I'm fine."

"What's going on?" He started forward. Face worried

—I couldn't look at his face. Couldn't let him see how fucked up I was.

"Nothing. I'm fine... I just... lost it for a second back there, that's all."

"You were talking with someone?" he asked.

I laughed. "No, just myself." It sounded strung out and forced and was an obvious lie. What if I told him? What if I just said, *I looked into the coin and I saw what you did.* He'd probably kill me and I'd be buried in Ravenscourt's back garden. Oh Christ, was that what he'd done. Was Charlotte's body in the yard somewhere?

"Dom." He touched my arm.

I jerked away.

The pain on his face was real, and that made everything so much worse. I trusted him, didn't I? But the coin, its burn, it was in my head; memories that weren't mine had been scorched into my past. I couldn't fucking think straight. "Shit, look... I think I just need a minute, okay? Can I just get a minute on my own?"

"All right." He backed off but his frown darkened, and when he turned, he almost stopped, almost came back and asked, because he was too bloody clever and he'd figure it out, like he figured everything out. The hesitation in his step lasted a second and he walked away. "I'll be indoors."

"Thanks."

I listened to his footfalls crunch on gravel until they stopped altogether.

I had to leave.

I couldn't stay... knowing what he'd done. But Gina and Robin? They'd be fine. They'd been fine this long. Long before I'd come along. They'd *be* fine as long as they didn't know the truth about him—everything was fine just so long as they didn't know the truth.

The Aston glinted on the driveway. Had he left the key inside? If I took his car, he'd know I was on to him.

I gripped my thighs and breathed. Kempthorne was a killer. I'd known he was capable, hadn't I? Was any of this news? I squeezed my eyes closed. The fucking memories bubbled at the front of my thoughts, fresh, like new, as though it had happened in the study moments ago. I knew how to handle this—I'd been trained to read artifacts—I just needed to get my shit together. Needed to get away.

My phone buzzed. One new message.

Unknown number: Where are you?

Kage was LOA. Kempthorne was a killer.

I typed a reply and hit send: *I DON'T KNOW WHAT TO BELIEVE.* Then I turned the phone off, slipped it into my pocket, and jogged toward the Aston.

***

An hour later, I hit Kage's Docklands building's intercom buzzer and waited. "Hey, Dom?" Kage's American tones sounded through the tiny speaker.

"Yeah." My voice echoed around polished steel and glass.

He waited a beat. A hesitation. He hadn't expected me to show up and that was exactly why I was here. I'd had time to think on the drive over, time to get my head in order, and I needed a lot more answers than Kempthorne's crimes.

The door lock buzzed. "Come on up."

The reason for his hesitation became clear once I reached his apartment. Annie was inside, looking comfortable on the sofa, shoes off, legs tucked under her. Half a bottle of wine sat on the coffee table.

The scene was so perfect, so domestic, that I almost turned around. "Sorry. I didn't know you had company—"

Kage leaned against the open door. His dark eyes were glassy, and his gaze crawled lazily over me, the wine making his thoughts clear on his face. He wore loose-fitting black trousers and a pinstripe shirt, untucked and gaping, as though he'd thrown the clothes on without a care. "It's fine," he said. "C'mon in." He left the door open and sauntered toward the kitchen area. "Wanna glass?"

"Yeah, thanks. Hi." I gave Annie a small wave, feeling like a third wheel.

"Hi, Dom." She smiled but it was barbed, as though I'd gate-crashed their party of two.

"Maybe I should come back—"

"Kempthorne's nothing like who he pretends to be," Kage said, half filling a glass and handing it out. If I took the wine, it meant I'd be staying, and I still wasn't sure if I was in the right place. Kage hadn't been honest *at all*. He worked for an agency that was well-known for 'dealing' with latents—worse than even the IRL. But Annie was here, and I knew she was cool, so...

I took the glass, briefly frowning into it. At least it wasn't almond coffee. They'd been drinking from the same bottle, so it couldn't be poisoned. Could it?

"Alexander Kempthorne was sixteen when his parents' light aircraft went down in the English Channel," Kage said in his serious, FBI voice. "All lives were lost. The records show that the flight recorder was never recovered. The records are wrong. The UK government squirrelled away the flight recorder, but two years ago, the LOA was granted access in exchange for cutting edge research on latency." Kage perched on the edge of his swish leather sofa and cradled his wine glass in his fingers. He wasn't wearing socks. An unimportant detail at that moment, but my brain was having a hard time with everything, and the fact he wasn't wearing socks was a nice distraction from what he was about to say, which would probably be a horrible new fact about Kempthorne. "The flight recorder showed the plane went down due to multiple, simultaneous catastrophic failures of its primary systems. In other words, a bomb. The UK government suspected terrorist activity. The LOA believes the Kempthornes were targeted because of their groundbreaking latent research—extracting trick from latents and storing it."

Now *that* was information worth holding on to. The Kempthornes had been working on the exact science I'd been subjected to? I lowered myself to the edge of the sofa next to Annie, feeling fragile all over again. "Wait... This research. What was its goal?"

Kage's mouth turned down. He shrugged. "I don't know for certain, but considering we're dealing with both the US and UK governments, I'm guessing the ultimate goal was to find a way to harness the trick as a weapon. So any soldier could wield it, not just latents."

That tracked with what I knew of the military, and my time in their ranks. I'd known Kempthorne's parents had been at the beginning of all of this, Kempthorne had said the same to me. "All right, so what does any of that have to do with Kempthorne?"

Kage straightened and breathed in, about to deliver bad news. "The bomb on that plane wasn't a terrorist act," he said. "It was a personal one."

"Wait…" I laughed. "You think Kempthorne killed his parents? He was sixteen."

"He knows how. You said he planted a bomb on his Lexus, right? The LOA has a list of persons of interest, persons being watched. Mostly, that list contains latents who are unstable and in some way deemed a security risk, but some names aren't known to be latents—or hadn't been, until recently. One of those names was Thomas Montgomery, the head of research at Wordsworth Latent Correctional, who I now know to be M, and a second name is Alexander Kempthorne of Kempthorne & Co. Both on the LOA's list, both buying up dirty artifacts, and both recently reclassified as latents."

He was still perched on the arm of the sofa, drink resting on his knee, all calm and perfectly in control. He hundred percent believed everything he'd said. He really was LOA.

I sipped my wine and adjusted a few things in my head. "You told your bosses what he is?"

"I had to." Said with all the conviction of a man in the right. Even when he was wrong.

"And me?" I asked, raising my eyebrows.

"What about you?" He shifted his position.

"Where do I fit in all this—you, the LOA, your bosses, everything?"

LOA Agent Kage Mitchell gazed out of the vast apartment windows. A little twitch upset the handsome line of his jaw. "You were a way to get to Kempthorne."

I fell back against the sofa cushions. And there it was, the stark, ugly truth. No wonder he couldn't meet my gaze.

"But," Kage added, looking over, amber eyes somehow warm even after everything he'd just told me. "I didn't expect to like you."

Annie cleared her throat and stood. "I think I'm going to leave you two alone. You have private things to discuss."

"Thanks," Kage told her.

She smiled and slipped her shoes on. "It's fine, really." She turned her soft smile on me. "We've all done things we didn't want to for reasons we thought right at the time," she said, trying to stick up for Kage.

I didn't have the words and tried to smile a goodbye as my thoughts churned.

She collected her things and left. In the quiet that followed, I swirled my wine, wishing my life were different. I hadn't asked to be a latent. It was just a part of who I was, and every damn day I'd had people use me because of it. Didn't matter which way I turned—home, the military, even Kempthorne & Co—I was just another pawn in someone else's game. Like all the rest of the latents. Like Max, the poor kid. Montgomery had gotten his claws into Max, like he had all the other latents in his care.

We were all fucked.

I downed my wine, grabbed the bottle, and refilled my glass.

"I'm sorry."

"Sorry?" I laughed. "Fuck off."

"I couldn't tell you."

I didn't want to hear his excuses. I didn't have enough headspace for them. "Do you kill latents?" The first time we'd met, I'd seen him execute a latent. The latent had been a mule for an illegal artifact auctioneer; just another latent, trying to survive in a world that hated us. Kage had shot him between the eyes.

"No, I mean... yes. Not unless I have to."

Narrowing my eyes on the prick, I tapped my fingers on the arm of the chair and tightened my hold on the wine glass in my free hand. "Do you get off on it?"

"Dom, you're angry, I get it—" He got to his feet, was probably thinking he could comfort me or something, but my next words stopped him dead.

"You got your gun on you now?"

He held my gaze, weighing his options, then turned and lifted his shirt. His gun was tucked against the small of his back.

"They order it and you shoot us down like we're nothing, right?" I had it right the first time I'd seen him. I should have trusted my gut, not my dick.

He winced—so he did feel something—then placed his glass down on the coffee table. "Most of the time. Until I met you."

I leaned forward and tilted my head up. The angle put me low, the same height as I'd be on my knees. "And what happens when they do order you to shoot me? Not like a graze, like you did on the docks, but in the head. Execution style. You gonna do it, Hollywood?"

He sighed out through his nose. "I'm hoping it doesn't come to that."

"But you're gonna shoot Kempthorne?"

That jaw twitch happened again, only this time it tugged on his lip, hinting at a snarl. "It's not my call."

"Fuck. You."

"He's dangerous. He's been absorbing trick from artifacts and you for years! He's a walking, talking latent bomb. That kind of power can't be left to roam free. He's stayed in the shadows for a long time, Dom, but as an unregistered latent with an insane amount of power, he was always going to get caught. It's just a matter of time."

His spiel sounded a lot like the years of propaganda latents had been forced to swallow. We were dangerous, we couldn't control our tricks, we should all be locked up for our own safety. The more he talked, the more he made my decision for me. "What will your bosses do to him?" I asked.

"Take him away. If the IRL don't get him first, but the Brits aren't acting, so..."

"Your people will lock him up?"

"Probably."

"Shit." Kempthorne had already been subjected to horrible things. His parents had routinely tortured him. Maybe he had killed them; would it have been wrong? I couldn't exactly take the moral high ground when I had my dad's blood on my hands. Was Kempthorne the monster-in-waiting the LOA had made him out to be?

What I'd seen in the coin made everything more complicated. The hollowed-out look in young-Kempthorne's eyes. He hadn't felt a bloody thing as he'd watched his sister die. She'd cried for help and he'd just... *watched.* Then there was the blood on Kempthorne's knuckles after he'd picked me up outside the Snooker Club, and Renick's body in the Thames. Another coincidence. *'I wonder if I am touched by death itself,'* he'd told me. He'd even tossed the coin at me, daring me to look deeper. Did he *want* to be caught? To be stopped?

But that didn't feel right either.

Kempthorne was a killer. All the suave charm and sophistication was a mask. But that wasn't all he was. He ran an agency that tried to *help* latents. He'd helped me, saved (bought) me from the military. My thoughts flip-flopped between good and bad.

"What happened?" Kage asked. He'd lowered himself to the edge of the sofa cushions, no longer towering over me, delivering his speech about all-bad-latents.

If I told him what I'd seen in the coin, he'd tell his people. And maybe that was right. But whatever Kempthorne had done, Montgomery had to be worse. Kempthorne didn't experiment on latents. He didn't have facilities built to drain them of trick. And if the LOA scooped up Kempthorne, who was left to stop Montgomery? The useless IRL were clueless. The Metropolitan Police weren't interested. So that left... me, Gina, and Robin.

"What do your people know about Montgomery?" I asked.

"He's the same as Kempthorne but with government backing. The LOA is very interested in that man's activities. Especially since they now know he's a latent."

Thanks to Kage. Maybe he'd get Agent of the Month and a pay raise? "Do they want the man or his research."

"Both, probably." He picked up his glass of wine from the table. "It's not perfect. I'm not pretending anything is—"

"Did you drug me with that fancy coffee?"

He hovered his glass near his lips, took a sip, and swallowed. "Yeah, I did."

The glass I'd been holding shattered. Wine and jagged fragments rained over my leg. I turned my hand over, watching blood mingle with trick. It didn't hurt. It probably should have.

"Shit, Dom. Come over here." Kage dashed to the kitchen and ran the faucet. I went, weirdly detached, as though I was here but not. I let him take my hand and wash blood and glass from my fingers. The cuts weren't deep. He grabbed a first aid kit and sprayed something cold onto the cuts.

"You've been through worse," he said, half smiling while wrapping my hand with a temporary bandage.

I looked at him, at his pretty amber eyes and too-long, wavy dark hair. Everywhere I turned, everyone wanted a piece of me. I'd thought that once I got out of the East End, I'd stop being someone else's tool, but it had gotten worse, not better. The world didn't beat me down with a whiskey bottle, it didn't have to. I was a latent, and because of that, I was always someone else's fucking tool.

"I get it if you hate me," Kage said, tying off the bandage. His hand folded around mine and he looked me in the eyes.

"Yeah, I kinda do."

His smile faded. "For what it's worth, I thought you were just some clueless piece of ass who would get me close to Kempthorne, but you turned out to be all kinds of awesome and before I knew it, I was looking for ways to get you away from him, to keep you safe... when the time comes."

When the time comes to take Kempthorne in and kill any

latent who gets in my way. He didn't say it, but I heard the words anyway. "Wow. You sure know how to make a guy feel special."

"You wanted the truth. There it is. All of it." He peered through his dark fringe, smile twitching.

He executed latents to order.

I killed people in war.

Kempthorne killed because... the jury was still out on that one.

I lifted my wounded hand and touched Kage's cheek, then slipped my fingers higher, teasing them into his hair. He tilted his head, lips parting and eyes widening. If I was the bad guy here, I'd run my trick through him and end him because he was LOA, and my enemy. Kempthorne could have sent me to his door to do exactly that. But Kage trusted me, I saw that in his eyes. So maybe I wasn't the bad guy. Maybe I never had been. Maybe everyone else just wanted me to be.

"*Just a piece of ass,*" I said, adding a terrible American accent. "Was any of that gay stuff real, like the story you told about Annie sticking up for you, you worried about coming out—all that?" I tightened my hold on his hair, just a little, enough to make him still. His free hand dropped to his side, within reach of his gun.

"It was all real," he said, voice rough. "There's more you don't know, about my past, about... my life. But a little truth goes a long way in a lie."

I smirked. And Kage thought he wasn't like Kempthorne. I pulled him close and hovered my lips over his mouth. His eyes blew wide, filling my vision with all that pretty. "I just got out of prison," I said, struggling to keep my voice above a growl. "Just learned my boss is a bad guy. And my sometimes-fuck-buddy works for an agency that will issue orders to kill me without batting an eye."

He breathed hard, his chest pressing against mine. I slid my hand around his waist and danced my fingers over the gun, then plucked it free and dumped it onto the counter without taking my eyes from his.

Now he was unarmed, unless that rod sticking in my thigh was a second gun down his trousers, but I figured not when I adjusted my stance, leaning hard against him, and he sucked in a sharp breath.

"I'm walking the fucking line, Kage. One step away from losing my shit."

"I'm... getting... that," he panted.

"Let's get something straight." I brought my hand around his hip and molded my fingers to the bulge in his trousers. "This piece of ass has had enough of everyone else's shit." I rubbed. He shuddered, eyes rolling. His lips brushed mine, seeking the hint of a kiss sizzling between us. "I don't fuck guys who'll throw me away once they're done. So find some other dick to fuck you, Kage Mitchell." I freed him from my grip and stepped back. He slumped against the counter, breath racing, and glowered, looking all kinds of sexy with it.

"It's different with you," he snapped. "I really... I mean, I want us—this to be something." He started toward me.

I flashed him a cold smile. "It could have been, if you hadn't lied."

"Yeah, but I've told you everything!?"

I laughed. "So I should be so grateful that I'll get on my knees and suck you off? Then what? You put a bullet in my head tomorrow morning once the order comes in?" I gave him the finger of my newly bandaged hand. "I. Can't. Trust. You. Ever." I turned on my heel and headed for the door.

"I had a brother!"

I stopped dead.

"A latent. He... died."

If he'd told me before, maybe it could have changed things, but how could I trust anything he said was real when he'd lied, manipulated, and drugged me?

I shook my head and continued toward the door. "I'm not doing this."

"Go back to Kempthorne and I can't save you!"

"Whatever. I'm just some latent piece of arse anyway." I slammed the door on my way out and jogged down the stairwell, feeling halfway to normal for the first time since I'd been carted off to Wordsworth.

I was done being used. It was time I walked my own path. Fuck everyone else.

From now on, I was doing things my way. And I had a plan for that.

16

D^{om}

Registered Latents are Safe Latents! Posters around the pastel-colored office declared. *Report Suspicious Latent Activity to the IRL. IRL—We CARE.*

"Miss Worthington will see you now, Mr Domenici."

I followed the receptionist down the hall and into a plush little office with potted plants and a great view of a park. The trees outside had lost their leaves for winter, but the crisp February view still enticed, unlike the view inside. Miss Worthington was perched behind her desk like one of those angry parrots at garden centers that peer at each customer as though choosing which eye to peck out first.

"Hi, Doris," I beamed.

"Mister Domenici." Doris blinked as if she blinked enough, I might vanish and she could carry on with her day without further unwanted interruptions from troublesome latents. "I see you're out of Wordsworth and lawyered up. How unexpected."

I smiled a *fuck you*, tossed a photograph onto her desk, and flopped into the chair. "The posters outside say you protect all kinds of people, including latents, so maybe you should start doing that?" She opened her mouth to squawk something, but I spoke over her. "The Kempthornes and the rest of the people in that photo experimented on latent kids back in the seventies, eighties, and into the nineties. They flooded latents until they were about to go boom, and then drained them of trick. You don't know what that feels like, but I assure you, Doris, it ain't fun. Now, I know we all wish latents would go away, but it doesn't matter how many institutional holes you stuff us in, we keep coming back, like weeds. Maybe—" I spread my hands. "—we could try something groundbreaking, like... I dunno... treating latents like people instead of something you scrape off your shoe?"

Doris had turned a bright shade of pink. "Mister Domenici, I'm finding your tone rather alarming—"

"You know what's fucking alarming, Doris? It's that latent kids go missing every day and nobody gives a shit. Some are sold abroad, did you know that? I just found out. This shit is happening all over London and I'm apparently the only person who knows! Little ol' me? A nobody. Seems sus, right? You'd think the IRL would be all over that and doing something to stop it." I thumbed over my shoulder at a poster without looking. "Because: *You Care.*"

Doris cleared her throat. "Mister Domenici, I advise you change your tone or I'll be forced to call security."

"Thomas Montgomery." I leaned over the desk and tapped the man's image in the photograph. Doris's eye twitched. "I see you know him. Nice guy, until he rips out your trick. He's an absorber, by the way, in case you weren't aware, because the IRL doesn't seem to know its arse from its elbow. The LOA—maybe you've heard of them, they're like you, but ten times scarier with guns and American accents—they're really interested in his activities, so maybe you should be too? If you were actually interested in doing your job?"

She picked up her desk phone. "Security to my office at once please."

I was surprised it had taken her that long. I got to my feet, anticipating the heavies would charge in and be on me any second now. "You see, those latent kids who go missing? Some turn up in Montgomery's super-secret labs, hooked up to machines and sucked dry of trick. Some don't come out. Some go mad and go on killing sprees with a dirty artifact given to them by *Montgomery*." I slammed my hands onto her desk and sneered. *"Ask me how I fucking know."*

Security lurched in and grabbed my arms. I didn't fight. I wasn't here for that. "Do your job, Doris. Then maybe you'll be able to sleep at night." I winked, got dragged from the office, and had the door slammed in my face.

Security threw me out of the processing center, to the curb, literally. Ignoring their sneers, I shrugged my hoodie back into place and thrust my hands into my pockets. They could have arrested me, so all things considered, it had gone pretty well. Next stop: Rebecca Stevens, *London Today*. I climbed back into Kempthorne's Aston and launched away from the IRL, leaving a cloud of tire smoke behind.

17

Alexander

"I just had a call from Doris Worthington at the IRL." Robin entered the room, frowning at her phone. "Dom was there a few hours ago—"

"Dom was at the IRL?" Gina looked up from her position at the table.

"Apparently he was acting *agitated and irrational*. She threatened arrest." Robin came toward me. She'd be asking questions next. Questions I wasn't ready to answer.

A younger Dom stared out from his picture on my murder wall. He'd been stable back then, but now he was in a bad place. Anyone who had been through everything he had would be suffering. But something had happened in the kitchen, something triggering.

I wanted to go to him, to call him, collect him, hide him away from the world. If that was all I wanted, he might even agree. But Dom's trick was too tempting. I feared, if I got too close, I'd drain him, just like I had all the dead artifacts on Cecil Court's basement shelves. I'd resisted so far... but when he'd spiraled, when his trick surged, half of me checked out, taking my control with it.

I didn't want to hurt him. But could.

"The IRL can't touch him," I told Robin, making sure to keep all the uncertainties out of my voice and off my face. "Not without going through the courts. My lawyers made sure of it."

"He steals the Aston and then shows up there? What's going on with him?" Robin asked, because she knew I had theories. Probably thought I had the answers too. And perhaps I did.

It wasn't something I could discuss with Gina or Robin. Whatever had happened in the kitchen, Dom hadn't been able to look at me afterward. He'd seen something, knew something.

"Kempthorne?" Gina prompted. "*Do* you know what's going on?"

And now the pair of them were closing in. "He'll come back when he's ready." If he came back, I suspected we'd either be friends or enemies. How he'd found out, I had no idea, but the fear and disgust I'd seen on his face in the kitchen and outside, by the garage—meant one thing: He knew who I really was.

Gina folded her arms and narrowed her eyes, suggesting she knew I was keeping secrets and that nonsense wasn't going to wash with her for much longer.

But if they knew the truth, they'd leave. Everyone left, eventually.

It was inevitable.

And out of my control.

The only thing I could control was my murder wall and how to stop Montgomery from torturing more latents and harvesting trick.

"What does Montgomery want?" I asked, turning toward the wall to find the black-and-white photograph of my parents and the rest of the benefactors of their work at the academy, with Thomas Montgomery among them. The photo had been buried in a box in my mother's things. I'd dug it out and pinned it to the wall. I hadn't recognised Thomas Montgomery before recent events, but there he was, alongside the Kempthornes. "All this time, he's been perfecting what my parents began, turning their discoveries into an industrial operation. But why?"

"Money, most likely," Gina suggested.

A man like him, money wasn't enough. He wanted something, was searching for something. He was a latent. An absorber. One of the first generation. Shunned for who and what he was, just like the rest of us. Draining latents... harvesting trick... There was more to all of this.

I turned to the table and pushed various papers aside to reveal a map of central London. With Gina's borrowed pen, I marked an *X* over Wordsworth on the map, right on the bend of the Thames. I marked a second *X* where the lab was, again close to the Thames. "Of all the places in all of London, or the entire UK, why put a lab there?" I tapped the lab's *X*.

Gina moved closer and pushed the last of the documents aside, clearing all the map.

"Wait..." Robin grabbed a green pen and her phone, scrolled a while, then began to mark more little *x*'s all over London. "These are the places where Olivia's latents spiraled, you remember? All over London. We had a hard time keeping up."

"I remember."

Her glasses slipped and she shoved them back up her nose, then began making new *x*'s over the first in her green pen. "These marks represent where the more recent surge killed multiple latents."

"They match," Gina said.

"These locations aren't random," Robin confirmed.

"There's a pattern." Like my murder wall, I drew a line through each *x*, joining them up, and at their center? Montgomery's lab, close to the Thames. Close to the *source*. "But we're missing something." All the little *x*'s, scattered all over London. It was just the surface. "We're only seeing the top layer." Dread chilled my veins and skittered down my back. "London is where latents first began emerging. Every latent knows London has a heartbeat, we feel it every time we pull on the trick." I tapped every *x* with my pen. "And right here, these crosses mark her pulse points. Underground caverns, sewers, reservoirs, old parts of forgotten London. If we take a look under these *x*'s, under the streets, I suspect we'll find voids beneath, spaces closer to the source."

Weak points where the source could bleed through.

"If Montgomery pierces those points," I went on, "it'll be as though he's sliced open an artery." The source would come rushing through. It could bleed out, become unstable. The resulting surge might kill all latents unless there was a way to harness it, control it. Montgomery's lab.

The latents weren't Montgomery's targets. They were a trial run. Montgomery wanted to tap *into* the source and harvest its power.

The fine hairs on my arms and the back of my neck lifted.

He had the years of knowledge and government resources behind him.

He didn't want money. This wasn't about governments or weapons. It wasn't like with Olivia and raising a god beneath London. Montgomery—one of the first generation of latents and a man who had hidden his true self for decades—wanted to *make* himself a god.

"We need to destroy that lab," I said.

If he couldn't store the trick, he wouldn't risk tapping into the source. The surge would kill him. The lab was exactly what he needed—a storage facility—a way to flood himself slowly. He was building up a resistance, absorbing more and more. That was why his trick undulated like it did—it wasn't natural.

Gina and Robin stared, faces touched by fear. "Aren't there latents in that lab?"

"If there are, we'll get them out."

"How?" Robin asked.

There had to be a way. But we needed more than the four of us, assuming Dom would return. We needed an outside force, someone who wanted Montgomery stopped as much as we did, someone with access to resources outside the influence of the IRL and the military—we needed the enemy of my enemy. "We need Kage Mitchell."

Gina frowned and shook her head. "We can't trust him."

I removed my phone from my pocket and dialed Kage's number. "I never have."

"I did," she mumbled. "Dom did."

Robin said, "He'll turn you over to the LOA."

"Inevitably."

"Kempthorne?" Kage answered, sounding strained. We hadn't spoken since our escape from Montgomery's lab. I'd assumed he'd be reporting all the new information he'd discovered to his superiors. I hadn't expected to ever be calling him again. But here we were.

"I need your help."

His dry laugh carried a note of derision. "Am I still part of Kempthorne & Co?"

"I need you as LOA. No more lies. I'm serious. This isn't about me, it's about Montgomery."

"...I'm listening."

I told him my theories, and the more I spoke, the more Montgomery's plan solidified in my mind. Montgomery and I were similar. We both knew the trick was a never-ending tease, and as absorbers, we were never satisfied. The more we took, the more we wanted. Normally, harvesting trick would kill a latent. But not if Montgomery had taken my parents' work and perfected it.

Kage and I talked, reasonably. I hadn't noticed Robin and Gina had left the room until Robin returned, mouthing, *"Dom's back,"* from the doorway.

My heart squeezed. A thousand feelings rushed in at

once. *He came back*. I hadn't realized how afraid I'd been that he might not.

"Will you help?" I asked Kage.

"I'll see what I can do."

"We can't do this without you."

"I'm not a bad guy. Maybe you could tell Dom that, huh? Does he even know you've called me?"

Robin left, and a few seconds later, Dom sauntered in. He jerked his chin and planted his backside against the edge of the long table. His mouth was pressed into a thin, defiant line. He had a hand tucked into his hooded jacket's pocket. One of his boot laces was undone. I swallowed the urge to yell at him for leaving and fought back a different need to wrap my arms around him.

"He will," I told Kage, hung up, and turned off my phone.

"You and me need to talk." Dom took something from his pocket and tossed it onto the table. The coin rolled halfway across the map of London, looped around the Tower, and came to rest on its side near the London Eye.

Such a small thing, but it had my past forever burned into it. I didn't move. I wanted to. Wanted to go to it, scoop it up, and drain it of all its power over me. I'd hidden it away in the study, where all the nightmares lived. "I was very clear in asking you not to go into that room."

He chuckled without humor. "I didn't. Your skeletons want out."

It didn't matter how he'd gotten the coin. Just that he had, and he'd seen its secrets. *My* secrets.

"What I don't understand is why you didn't just absorb it?" he asked, looking at me now. "Then nobody would ever know."

I approached the table. The coin's tarnished metal didn't appear dangerous, but I could feel its soft background throb, like a living heartbeat. I knew what he'd seen. It was a wonder he could stand to be in the same room as me. "I've tried," I admitted. "But I can't bring myself to do it."

"Why?"

"Because..." The words clogged my throat. But this was Dom, and he deserved to know. "While it's an artifact, some part of her is still alive inside it." I reached for the coin but only managed to make it halfway before pulling my hand back. I didn't need to be an authenticator to know what lay hidden inside it. I'd been there.

He closed his eyes and shook his head gently. "I wasn't gonna come back, yah know?"

I wanted to ask him why he had but feared the answer wouldn't be the one I desperately wanted to hear. "Where did you go?"

"I had to get a few things straight in my head. I told Kage what I thought of his almond coffee and then, a few hours ago, I dropped in to see Rebecca Stevens at *London Today*."

The journalist. My throat dried. "What did you talk about?" I croaked. What had he told her? He knew everything about me. He could ruin me in multiple ways. I'd laid myself bare, shown him everything I dared.

"You."

He didn't seem the sort for blackmail. But he could. My lies were crumbling around me. Years of pretending and lying and being someone I was not... I was ready to let it go. The truth was always going to come out. It was almost a relief. I didn't have to live the life of Alexander Kempthorne anymore, the man who didn't exist.

Dom cocked his head. "You told her you're gay in exchange for her help getting me out of Wordsworth?"

"Oh, that." I laughed a little, despite none of this being amusing. "As it happens, you were already working on your escape, so my efforts came to nothing anyway."

"That wasn't nothing. Nobody has ever done anything like that for me." He fell quiet, and when he next spoke, his voice was almost a whisper. "You keep saving me. Why?"

"I keep *trying* to save you, but you invariably get there first." I tried to smile. It felt lighter on my lips when he smiled back.

"I told Becky about Wordsworth," he said. "And who Thomas Montgomery really is. She was quite eager I don't sue her for the crap she printed about me—not that I can afford to. She's also convinced you're my sugar daddy." I blinked and Dom laughed his dark chuckle. "She's going to do her own investigating, but if her poking around doesn't shake something loose, nothing will."

"Oh... that's good." And almost a disappointment. I leaned against the table's edge, feeling the weight of all my secrets pushing down. What did it say about me that I wanted the truth to be out there—all of it. I touched my forehead, rubbing away a new ache. "I'm so tired of pretending." I stared at the murder wall, where I controlled everything. Every picture, every note, every article, it all had its place. It soothed me to admire it.

"The memories, when they come..." he began softy. "They can be too hot to handle for a while. I wasn't expecting it. The coin was in my pocket, my trick leaked. I was going to ask you about it, and then... well... it ambushed me and I didn't have a choice. It hit hard and I was already fucked from Wordsworth." His voice cracked. "But I know, sometimes... the things I see are skewed. So maybe it wasn't what it looked like?"

He was giving me an out. I closed my eyes and tilted my head back. The memories came, memories I'd tried to hold back. I'd stabbed my sister—I recalled how cleanly the knife had sunk in, hard to begin with, then soft, as though her skin was no more resistant than butter. "It was exactly as you saw."

"You know I feel it, right? Like it's happening to me? I'm right there... at the end, when she dies."

I swallowed and when I opened my eyes, I forced myself to meet his gaze. The same fear I'd seen on his face in the kitchen was echoed in his expression now, but he'd had time to process what he'd seen, and anger had seeped in too. Perhaps he'd strike me. God knows I deserved it.

"Why?" he whispered.

He wanted me to tell him it was temporary insanity, or that I'd had a good reason, something to excuse me and make me better somehow, but there were no excuses.

The memories were older for me, not as sharp or as raw as they would be for him now. I knew I'd done it. I remembered plunging the knife in, remembered the look of betrayal and fear in her eyes. "Knowing why doesn't change the outcome."

He turned his head. "You killed her? That's what I saw. That's what I felt. You did that?"

"I can't deny it."

"Fuckin' hell, Kempthorne. At least tell me you're sorry."

I wanted to, but would it be another lie? When I didn't reply, Dom pushed away from the table, away from me, and paced across the room. He ran a hand through his hair and swore. I was losing him, but that was likely for the best. Everyone I got close to, everyone I cared for, they always died. It was safer for him if he stayed away.

Bowing my head, I breathed out. "This is all irrelevant and has no bearing on what must be done today. While you were gone we—"

"Irrelevant?! Like fuck it's irrelevant." He laughed, the sound wrung tight with stress. The glare he threw at me accused and hit like a physical blow. "What happened to Renick?"

My left hand reflexively twitched into a fist. I touched my forehead with my right, saw my fingers tremble and folded them into my palm. "He was trafficking latent children—"

"What about the agent you said you watched die?" Dom plowed on, leaving me no room to breathe or think. "Did you help her along a bit, huh? Maybe she saw who you really are and you couldn't let the truth get out, so she had an *accident*, like your parents?"

I reeled. Every word hammered home the guilt I'd felt, every accusation driving nails through the carefully placed barriers in my mind, keeping all the bad things at bay. "No, I didn't... That's not—I let her die, yes, I could have saved her—"

Dom's face had hardened, turned cruel. "What's the real reason you've been absorbing artifacts for years?"

"T-to get them off the streets. To save latents—"

"So you murder people on Tuesdays and save them on Wednesdays, and that balances the scales?"

"Dom, please. That's not who I—"

"I fuckin' trusted you. *They* trust you." He flung a hand toward the door, where surely Robin and Gina were somewhere in the house and could probably hear us. "Is Kempthorne & Co a front for you to power up? As an absorber, it takes more and more for you to get your kicks, right? Absorbing trinkets just doesn't do it for you anymore. Is that why you bought me? I'm *irresistible*. You know, I'm starting to wonder if you got to Olivia in Wordsworth. She knew a whole lot of things about you and *poof*, she's gone too."

The words, the lies, the past, the memories, all of it spiraled. "No, no—" I didn't—I hadn't done all those things—some, perhaps. "Olivia used to be a friend—"

"So you bought me out of the kindness of your heart? I believed it, but now I can't believe a fucking word that comes out of your mouth, Kempthorne. Maybe I'm on the wrong side, huh? Montgomery is starting to look like a saint next to you."

"Enough!" I was on my feet and in front of him with no memory of having moved. Trick tingled through my veins and when Dom lifted his chin, daring me to lash out, trick shimmered in his eyes. "Whatever you think of me," I said through my teeth, "Montgomery is *far* worse."

"Says the man who murdered his own sister."

My fingers twitched, the trick simmered, I imagined myself wrapping my fingers around his neck and pinning him to the murder wall. His trick would flare, he'd go for his cards, and I'd drink him down like the elixir he was. He didn't stand a chance against me.

"You gonna murder me too, *Alex*?"

I reached for him—almost did exactly as I'd seen unfold in my mind—but instead of wrapping my fingers around his throat, I brushed them against his cheek. Tension made him twitch, almost tugging him away, but he stood firm, kept his chin up and his eyes ablaze. His trick made him glow, and where my hand touched his cheek, the golden shimmer flowed over and into my skin, tingling up my arm and feeding into the heart of me.

"It's almost as though you want me to."

"Maybe I do? Maybe I'm pushing to see how far I can go before you snap because I need to know who you really are."

His hand pushed against my chest, warm and tingling. More of his trick passed through my shirt and into my skin. Did he know every beat of his heart fed more of his power into me, and every beat of his heart thumped through me, teasing my control, wanting me to take more and more of him?

"I've never wanted to hurt you." I hadn't meant to sound so breathless, but at some point his anger had ignited another kind of heat, one I was hopeless to resist.

"But you could?" He had to be standing on his toes because now his mouth was close to mine. An electric tension simmered between us and sparked through my veins.

"Oh yes."

"Why can't I hate you?" His sultry, Italian eyes searched mine, seeking answers I didn't have.

I tilted my head, brushed my lips over his. His mouth opened, surrendering under me, even knowing who and what I truly was. His lips met mine, setting my soul ablaze. His hand twisted in my shirt, making it clear there would be no escape. I could never say no to him. Now I had my hand at his throat and shoved him back against my murder wall, just like I'd imagined, but for a very different reason.

He gasped from the kiss. His glare burned mine, part anger, part lust. "What if we stop fighting who we're supposed to be and just go with it?"

A strange kind of mad hope danced in his eyes. I almost wished such a thing could happen. "If I stop fighting, I fear you and everyone else might be right about me."

He sank his hand into my hair, bared his teeth, and pushed trick through his touch—all at once power scorched, lighting him up, blinding me. I almost pulled away, but his grip held and then the soft touch of his lips at my neck undid my mental restraints further, loosening my control. I breathed him in, soaked in every tingling touch, absorbed everything he gave and wanted more, so much more. More of his trick tingling on my tongue, more of the taste of him on my lips, more of the hard feel of his hands, the solid press of his cock—

"Oh! Oh shit—" Gina turned on her heel by the door and covered her eyes. "I'm never gonna unsee that."

I nearly snarled at her to leave, but Dom's twitching smile and the laughter in his eyes smoothed the crackling, shifting surge of power, calming the part of me that wouldn't have cared had she watched whatever happened next.

"I'll just erm... go," she stuttered, then left.

Dom had withdrawn his trick and now my thoughts were washing back in, bringing some clarity with them. I lowered my hand from his neck, stroked down his chest, wishing there were no barriers between us, and found the firm evidence of his need at his crotch. Lifting my gaze, I discovered his trick-flecked gaze locked on me.

"You're so fucking hot when you let yourself go," he said.

Is that what I'd done? Let myself go? The idea was terrifying. I couldn't *ever* do that. I stepped back, turned away, tried to breathe through the sudden, age-old panic.

That's good, Alex. Let yourself go.

"Shit, sorry..." Dom's warm fingers caught my wrist.

I shook him off and focused on the table, its map, and everything we'd researched so far. "While you were gone, we discovered some pertinent information regarding Montgomery's plans." Spreading my hands over the map grounded me again, bringing me back to myself and what needed to be done.

What we'd done, what had just happened, that had taken me somewhere I had no control, and to lose control was dangerous. I hurried into an explanation of the source's potential weak points where the surge had broken through. Then told him what I suspected to be Montgomery's masterplan. I relayed everything as facts and avoided looking into his eyes. The task at hand, the murder wall, stopping Montgomery—these were things I knew how to control. Whatever was happening between Dom and me? That was uncontrollable.

"Wait, you did what?" he asked.

"Kage Mitchell is bringing in the LOA to lead the raid on the lab," I said again, then finally looked over. He stared at the ceiling and licked his lips. "Why, is there a problem?"

"Nope."

Clearly a lie.

"It's fine," he added, seeing my expression. "I just feel like maybe any goodwill we had with him might be gone since I told him to go fuck himself."

He had? It was difficult not to feel some swell of satisfaction in that. "Ah."

A knock at the door drew both our gazes.

"Are you both decent?" Gina called.

"Come in."

Her smile was a little wooden and she couldn't meet my eye. Good lord, this was going to be awkward. "I apologize for what you saw—"

She waved a hand. "Let's just pretend it didn't happen. Robin said to tell you both that Annie is here."

"Annie?" Dom asked, then glanced at me.

"No idea," I said.

"She was with Kage this morning," Dom said, then added, "Before him and me er... got into it."

Gina's eyes widened. "You went to see Kage?"

"Not in the way you're thinking," Dom told her.

"I'll see what Annie wants." I left Dom and Gina to their discussion about Kage and headed down the hallway, thoughts bumbling over pieces of my conversation with Dom. Despite his harsh words, or perhaps because of them, something had changed between us. He knew me now, all my secrets, all my lies, and all the nightmares. He knew what I was capable of, and he'd *come back*. Nobody ever came back. The people I cared for always left.

He knew me. And he'd come back. That was good, wasn't it? I didn't do relationships. I didn't do personal.

Because, invariably, it always went wrong. But with Dom, it didn't feel wrong, or as though the card castle might fall at any moment. It felt as though we were building something stronger than the both of us. Or perhaps I was delusional? Dom would be the first to tell me, if I was.

I smiled, and my steps lightened. I opened the lounge door. "Robin, I—"

Annie stood with her arms around Robin—with Robin clutched against her chest, both facing me. A knife... *the* knife trembled in Annie's hand, and where the blade pressed against Robin's neck, blood swelled. The knife's throb was familiar, warm and inviting, like a home I hadn't known I'd been missing.

Tears glistened on Robin's cheek. "Please," she sobbed. She clutched Annie's arm so tightly her fingers had turned white.

Annie's eyes fixed on me. "Thomas will no longer play games with you, Alex. There are consequences for all our actions. Join him or your friends die."

"No, wait!" I moved, summoned the trick, but knew, with terrible clarity, it was all too late.

The knife flashed, blood splashed the floor, Robin crumpled.

And everything changed.

18

D^{om}

"I mean, Imma just gonna say it. You and Kempthorne are hot A.F. together," Gina said. "His sophistication, your..." She waved a hand. "East End charm."

"Thanks."

We'd rapidly moved on from the topic of Kage after she'd learned I'd told him how it was and were now on the topic of how she'd seen Kempthorne and me tied up in knots.

If she hadn't walked in when she had, I'd have been all over Kempthorne, and that hadn't been the plan. I'd come back to Ravenscourt to deliberately push his buttons, needing to know if he'd lash out, if he meant to harm me, but the opposite had happened. For both of us.

He was dangerous all right, but he was also in control.

I knew what I'd seen in the coin and I knew what he'd told me matched with the past, but something about it all didn't feel right. As an authenticator, I sensed when the resonance was off, and the coin, his supposed past? Something was missing from that picture.

"Oh god, I'm so conflicted." Gina laughed and fanned her face. "Is it wrong that I kinda wanna watch?"

Heat touched my face and I laughed with her. "Yeah, G. It's wrong."

"So are you a thing? You are, right?" She bounced on her feet. "Is it serious? Please tell me it's serious. I ship it so hard. My heart can't handle it if you break up."

"Stop. You're making me nerv—"

A shout barreled through the house. Gina froze and glanced at the open door.

Kempthorne.

A shiver ran through the floor, under my feet, and up the walls. I knew what it was, having felt the same in Syria as soon as the bullets had begun flying. A traumatic psychic blast.

Oh no.

I dashed down the hallway, flew down the stairs. The lounge—the house's trembling came from there. My trick sparked alive, rushed through my veins, kicking my heart and head into fight or flight. I skidded into the lounge and tried to make sense of the scene. Kempthorne on his knees. Robin under him. Annie standing over them both. Knife in her hand. A memory flashed—Max's knife, Kempthorne's past, it was here in the room with me.

The knife. The same bloody knife Max had used. The same wretched knife I'd seen in the coin. The knife Kempthorne had killed his sister with... It had been the same knife all along. The same artifact. But its past didn't matter, not when Robin was down—unmoving.

Blood covered Kempthorne's hands. The deep scarlet of it mixed with his flowing trick. He was trying to fix her, but her eyes were open, her mouth too. She wasn't breathing.

I moved closer to Kempthorne, to try to help, to do something. But Annie brought the knife up. The charged card left my fingers on reflex. It spun, burst against her hand. She yelped and dropped the knife. It clattered out of sight, but its menacing allure still permeated the air and my thoughts—it was close by, waiting to be picked up, crooning for attention.

A memory flashed. The same knife in a boy's hand— driven through his sister's heart.

"Dom, the knife—get back!" Kempthorne yelled, rooting me in this room, this time.

That fucking knife.

Annie caught my eye. She cradled her hand to her chest. Her darting eyes were red. She lunged toward the floor, and the knife. I flung a second card, missing her head by inches, and bolted around the furniture. She scooped up the knife, raised it like a prize, then slashed wildly at me. I skipped back, arms out, charged card between my fingers.

"Don't make me hurt you, Dom!" Her mouth twisted. Panic and fear drove her to the edge. I'd seen the same in so many latents. Watched them spiral in front of me, knowing it was the end.

"Annie, put down the knife. It's poisoning you. Don't listen to it."

"Robin," Kempthorne whispered—begged.

No—*no*—not Robin. I couldn't look. Didn't want to know. She would be okay, she had to be. Kempthorne would fix her like he'd fixed Kage.

I raised my spitting card. "Annie, put the knife down or I'm going to have to make you."

"He knows *everything*," she said, buckling as though the words pained her. "I told him everything!" she screamed. Tears fell freely down her cheeks.

"Annie, please?"

"I took photos... in the attic at Cecil Court, I was there at the charity party, I saw all of Alex's plans. And here too. When you were hurt, Dom. Do you remember? I helped care for you. I saw the wall! I've listened and watched, and I told Thomas *everything*. He has all the evidence he needs to ruin you both. This is his warning." She stabbed the air toward Robin's prone figure. "I had to do it," she sobbed. But then her crying eyes sharpened on Kempthorne's back. And whether it was the knife whispering to her or Montgomery's orders, I couldn't tell, but she meant to bring that knife down on Kempthorne.

She lifted the knife in both hands, pulling her lips back in a sneer. Her trick sparked, spilling out of her in a terrible aura, out of her control and about to blast us all into the afterlife.

Kempthorne wasn't looking at her, or anyone else. He hunched over Robin, pouring more and more trick into her.

Annie plunged the blade down. Her trick retracted, about to blow.

I let the card fly, setting it ablaze. It spun, straight and true, struck Annie's chest, and blasted her backward against a sideboard. She collapsed, limp and doll-like.

Her trick fizzled and hissed to nothing. And in her chest, where her heart used to be, was a gaping, smoking hole.

Oh Christ.

What have I done?

I had to.

The knife... it lay in Annie's limp fingers, throbbing hot and hungry, demanding to be picked up, for the cycle to go on and on.

Gina whimpered close behind me. "*Robin?*"

"The knife—take the bloody knife away!" I yelled.

"Robin...?" Gina stumbled against me, ignoring my order. She dropped to her knees beside Kempthorne.

Robin still wasn't moving. And Kempthorne was still bent over her, pouring his trick into her body. It spilled over her edges and leaked into the floor, mingling with a growing pool of blood, making it shine.

"You can fix her?" I heard myself say, still standing back, as though glued to that one spot on the floor. "Right?"

Kempthorne's shoulders folded in. He hunched over her, his hands on her face, then he scooped her up and pulled her into his arms. He pressed his forehead to hers. I'd never seen him cry before. His spilled trick withdrew, leaving Robin cold and blue in Kempthorne's arms.

Gina's sob squeezed my heart. I couldn't breathe.

"Kempthorne, just fix her! Like you did Kage—"

"*I tried!*" He laid Robin down and braced himself over her, head bowed, tears falling.

No... He *had* to fix her. Just put his hands on her and make her all right again. Jesus Christ, this was Robin. Out of all of us, she didn't deserve to die.

Kempthorne suddenly grabbed the knife from Annie's hand and bolted from the room.

I couldn't think about what came next. This wasn't right. How had this happened? Annie's dead eyes leaked cold tears. Annie... and Robin. Gone.

Why?

The knife... That fucking knife. The worst kind of artifact. Poisonous, dangerous, a serial killer's weapon. The knife turned good people bad.

Shit, Kempthorne had the knife.

"Call the police," I said, leaving Gina sobbing on her knees. I had to find Kempthorne. Outside, on the driveway, Annie's car was parked next to the Aston, but there was no sign of Kempthorne.

Drizzle cooled my face. Mist had rolled in, obscuring everything more than a few meters in front of me. "Kempthorne?" He was out there somewhere. Close by. He wouldn't have gone far.

The garden.

I staggered across the gravel, spotted a disturbed trail through the lawn's wet grass, and followed it out into the field that swept away from Ravenscourt. Thick fog hugged the ground. I could only see a little way ahead, but I *felt* him close, felt the beat of his trick, and the knife. "Kempthorne?"

The fog swirled, wafting away, and there he was, standing with his back to me, facing into the mist. The knife was in his hand, out at his side.

"Kempthorne?"

Slowly, I waded through the long, wet grass.

His shoulders heaved. The knife glinted. He had good control. Better than me. But that bloody knife was seductive, and after what he'd just witnessed, the knife's whispers could slip through any cracks in his barriers. "Alex?"

He staggered, tilted his head back, spread his arms, and *shone*. Golden light rolled out of him and washed over me in a blast of heat and crackle of restless power. Shit... what if he blew? I squinted behind my arm. He was a figure of black encased in sunlight—a black hole spewing light. He bellowed into the rain and flung the knife into the fog, then collapsed to his knees and sobbed. His explosive trick collapsed, vanishing back into him as quickly as it had come.

I drifted closer, and when he didn't move to stop me, I sank down beside him, wrapped an arm around his shoulders, and pulled him against me.

"What good am I if I can't save the people I love?"

Even if I'd thought of anything to say, it would have gotten stuck in my throat behind the tight knot holding back my own swell of emotion. I held him, until we both shivered in the cold and wet and the sounds of sirens drew closer.

19

D^{om}

Montgomery had made his move, and I couldn't help but feel responsible. If I hadn't forced his hand by rattling a few cages, maybe he wouldn't have had to send a message. Maybe Robin would still be alive.

I sat at Cecil Court's kitchen table alone. The clock ticked. The faucet dripped into a sink full of dishes.

The IRL had come to Ravenscourt and taken Kempthorne away while the cops were still working the crime scene. They'd had an anonymous tip: Alexander Kempthorne might be an unregistered latent. The anonymous snitch had provided CCTV footage of Kempthorne using his trick, or so I'd overheard.

They'd shoved Kempthorne into the back of an IRL van as though he were some stray dog they planned on beating, and slammed the doors on him. He hadn't fought. I almost wished he had.

I'd given my statement to the Met. Told them how Annie had burst in, brandishing a dirty artifact, and how she'd killed Robin. I'd acted in both self-defense and to protect Kempthorne and Gina. I'd used *reasonable and proportionable force* in killing her. I was still an agent, so I had that in my favor, although my escape from Wordsworth had raised a few eyebrows. As far as the cops were concerned, I'd been cleared of being a serial killer, but I was also a latent who happened to keep getting mixed up in bad shit. They had kept me in as long as they legally could but eventually released me without pressing charges.

Gina had given a statement, too, as far as I knew, but she wasn't at Cecil Court and she wasn't answering her phone. I didn't even know if Kempthorne was coming back.

Was Kempthorne & Co a thing anymore?

The used mugs stacked on the kitchen drainer, the jar of custard cream biscuits on the side, and Robin's chair beside mine. It all felt so... empty. Death wasn't supposed to take her. Me, sure. I'd come close often enough. But not her.

It had broken Kempthorne.

He hadn't spoken when we'd sat in the misty field. He'd only nodded when the IRL cuffed him. He'd never looked so beaten. It had taken every ounce of control I had not to break him out.

So now I waited, in the cold and the quiet and the dark of Cecil Court. Waited to see what happened next because I had no fucking idea where to go or what to do.

Robin was gone. Gina probably wasn't coming back. If the IRL had any solid evidence on Kempthorne, they'd shove him into Wordsworth so bloody fast his lawyers wouldn't be able to stop it. Where did that leave me? This place, these people, they'd become my whole life. I loved them.

The front bell buzzed.

I dragged a hand down my face, brushing off cold tears.

The bell buzzed again.

Robin usually had the front door video feed on her laptop. I didn't even know where her laptop was.

The bell buzzed again.

"For fuck's sake." I trudged down the stairs and yanked open the door.

Kage blinked through wet bangs. Rain glistened on his long swish overcoat. His eyes were a little red. "Can I come in?"

"No." I folded my arms and leaned against the doorframe.

He nodded, expecting nothing less, then kicked at the step. "I had to call Annie's family. Tell them… she's gone. I couldn't even tell them why." His face was hard, but his voice quivered.

I swallowed, not knowing what to say. He'd probably heard the early news reports, knew how it went down, knew an unnamed artifact retrieval agent from Kempthorne & Co agency had acted in a professional capacity to stop a dangerous latent.

He had to know I'd killed his childhood friend.

Would he blame me? Would he shoot me? The seconds ticked over. London traffic hummed far away.

"This was Montgomery?" he asked.

I nodded. "He had her working for him this whole time. Probably from the first time Kempthorne and me met her at that fancy Chelsea dinner. Did you know?"

"Shit. No. I had no idea." He shifted on his feet, restless, as though he might hit something. Like me.

Maybe I was too tired to argue, or maybe it was his bloodshot eyes and the way he swayed, but I believed him. He hadn't known. Montgomery had used him too.

"He's a bastard who needs to be stopped before he does something worse," Kage said with a fire in his eyes. "You wanna go somewhere and talk about how we do that?"

Rattling around an empty Cecil Court was killing me. I knew Kage now, knew who he was and who he worked for. I couldn't trust him, but if he was offering help in bringing down Montgomery, then I was all for it. "I'll grab my coat."

20

Alexander

"On a scale of one to ten, how competent do you believe yourself to be, Mr Kempthorne?"

"Ten, obviously."

Doris Worthington was enjoying herself. I'd been questioned, re-questioned from different angles, had my blood extracted, my mouth swabbed, my fingerprints mapped—all in the name of registration, *for my own protection*. I wasn't an idiot. This wasn't about keeping me safe, it was about fear. Theirs. My name was now in their database as a registered latent. From this day henceforth, I'd be tracked, judged, and monitored wherever I went and in whatever I did.

The competency test was another hoop to leap through and after dealing with the police for hours, I'd had enough of the IRL and Doris Worthington's thin smile.

"Well, that's a surprise." She harrumphed, sitting back in her fake-leather chair. "You passed."

That made two of us surprised. Perhaps I *was* stable. Interesting. "Now, unless you want my shoe size or if I'm under arrest, I shall be leaving." I plucked off the thumb sensor and stood, and when she didn't stop me, I made for the door.

"Things will be very different for you now, Mr Kempthorne." She wasn't smug, or sly. If she wore any expression, it was one of firm belief.

"I don't doubt that, Doris."

Jordan collected me outside the processing center, in the subtle Mercedes. "Kensington, sir? The police are still at Ravenscourt, I'm afraid."

"Cecil Court." As Jordan drove, I plugged my dead phone in and waited for the screen to blink back to life. Dom or Gina may have called. Theirs were the only numbers I wanted to hear from.

"Alex, are you all right?" Jordan asked, eyes flicking to the rearview mirror.

Jordan had been the one constant in my life through everything. He knew more than most but said very little about anything personal. "Regarding having my latency status revealed? Yes. Relieved, actually." I tugged on my shirt cuffs and straightened my collar. "It's been a long time coming. As for... everything else? Not in the least." I couldn't linger on events that had happened at Ravenscourt. It would be *dangerous* to do so. I bounced my foot and stared out of the window. Montgomery would pay for this. I'd been of a mind to stop him, now my mind was set on *destroying* him.

We drove through London, the world outside muffled by the car's snug interior. Word would soon break regarding what I was. Once that happened, the media frenzy would be difficult. My whole life would be dragged through the papers and splashed online for all to see. Streetlights blinked as we approached Trafalgar Square. The grand stone lions presided over a swathe of intrepid tourists wrapped up in their winter coats. London might not be the friendliest of places once my status as a latent was public knowledge. Jordan pulled the car against the curb at the end of Cecil Court's pedestrianized street.

"Here we are, Alex. I'll return to Ravenscourt and oversee matters there, but should you need me, please do call." His soft eyes were almost too much to take.

"Of course. And thank you. For everything." I tugged the handle to open the rear door and paused as I caught sight of Dom leaving Cecil Court with Kage at his side. They were talking, heading in the opposite direction, away from the car. Neither saw me. Dom had his hands shoved into his pockets and Kage's dark coat flowed, accentuating his slim build. They looked... good together.

"Was there anything else, Alex?" Jordan asked when I didn't leave the car.

"No. Thank you."

The pair vanished around the corner and I climbed from the car. I loitered, tugging on my gloves to walk just a few feet. The car slipped back into traffic. Tourists bumbled about. Panic tried to claw up my throat. Everything appeared to be the same, but everything had changed.

I opened Cecil Court's door and a horrible silence yawned ahead of me. I almost closed the door again. I could have walked to Soho but banished that idea. What if Dom and Kage were there?

My phone vibrated, messages and notifications finally coming in. Mostly from Gina. They ranged from asking if I was all right, to a few that had been written while she'd been either distressed or drunk, perhaps both. I used the texts to distract me from thinking about the silence I'd walked in to. Gina wasn't coming back tonight. I couldn't blame her. Although, from the tone of her messages, she blamed me for everything.

I climbed the stairs, grabbed a bottle of whiskey from the collection in my attic apartment, and carried it all the way to the basement. The grotty old lamp behind my desk lit the racks of dead artifacts, but I liked the gloom. It softened all the sharp edges. I slumped into the chair and took the coin from my pocket. Perhaps it was time to absorb the bloody thing and put Charlotte to rest?

Alone, I drank the whiskey and stared at the coin, as though it could somehow fix all the things I wasn't able to.

I'd tried to heal Robin.

It hadn't worked.

Why hadn't it worked? I'd been able to save bloody Kage Mitchell without much effort, and his wounds had been far more devastating. I'd have traded his life for Robin's in a heartbeat. The knife... the bloody thing had tugged on my thoughts, whispering the whole time. I hadn't been able to focus.

I refilled my glass a third or fourth time. I'd lost count. Some whiskey sloshed over the sides.

The coin hummed, wanting me to take it and swallow its power. But if I did that, she'd be gone. Like Robin was gone. Like my parents were gone. Like everyone I'd ever cared for was gone.

Not thinking about that.

More whiskey went down.

I wasn't thinking about how my parents had died, or how I'd watched a good agent die in front of me and done nothing because I'd been a selfish coward, or how I'd shoved a disgusting prick of a man into the Thames while he was unconscious, knowing he'd never survive the river.

"Kempthorne, you down here?"

Dom's call dragged me back from the fog. "Y'here."

He approached through the aisles of dead artifacts, eyeing them warily now he knew I'd absorbed them, and stopped by my desk. His gaze skimmed the whiskey bottle, then me. "You wanna be alone?"

"—No." I'd replied too quickly. "Definitely, no." He looked good. A bit haggard, like he'd had a rough few hours, or like someone had had their hands on him, perhaps to hold him against a wall and kiss him as though he was the only thing that truly mattered in this godforsaken world. "Did you have a nice chat with Kage?" That had sounded a lot more spiteful than I'd intended. Dom could screw whomever he wanted. Even an American. It wasn't any of my business. His cheeks were a little pink, from the cold probably, or from screwing Kage—it was all too easy to imagine the two of them pressed together, breathless and desperate.

He narrowed his eyes. "Are you drunk?"

"Possibly." The bottle was half empty. It had been full

to begin with. And it was bloody good whiskey. "It's five thousand pounds a bottle."

"Then pour me some."

After a brief search of the desk, and with no luck finding anything for him to drink from, I shoved my drink toward him and raised the bottle to my lips.

His eyebrows lifted. "We're getting *that* pissed, huh." He pulled up a chair and sank into it. "You saw me leave with Kage?"

"You make a handsome pair." I attempted to sound normal, but in trying to reveal nothing, I may have revealed all of it. I really wasn't very good at being intoxicated.

Dom's eyes narrowed. His lips twitched around a smile. "Wait... are you jealous?"

"I'm not." Was I? "He is attractive, in an American way." I dismissed the whole idea with a wave. Or tried to, but the imagery of the two of them together clung on, summoning a snarl. "Good lord, I'm so very drunk."

Dom laughed, short and sharp. "He poisoned me and works for American dickbags, so yeah. Him and me, we aren't a thing. But I *can* tell you, he'll do just about anything to end Montgomery. He wants him gone just as much as we do."

"Good. He'll bring the LOA. God knows, the IRL are toothless." I drank some more whiskey and down it went, burning in my belly. The soft basement lighting blurred. Dom smiled. I liked his smiles. He smiled more than any man I'd ever met, even though he had little reason to.

"How'd it go with them?" he asked. "I bet Doris thought Christmas had come early?"

"I am officially registered." I tipped the bottle and

Dom chinked his glass against it. "And surprisingly stable. A quirk I suspect of my low resting heartrate, not my actual stability, which we both know is highly suspect."

"Welcome to the latent club. You're one of us."

He's one of us now, Robin said in my ear, my memory. Just yesterday. And now she was gone.

I wasn't supposed to think about her. But how could I not?

"Will you give the scoop to Rebecca Stevens before it leaks?" Dom asked.

"If I want to get ahead and control the narrative, yes." I'd have to organize that. Robin wasn't here to book a meeting in my diary. She'd never scold me again for my tardiness. How could I run Kempthorne & Co without her? I gripped the bottle and pressed my hot forehead against it. "I couldn't save her." No... I couldn't—wouldn't think about it. "Have you eaten?" I forced a smile. I could focus on Dom, make sure he was all right. That was a lot easier than dealing with the yawning hole inside, one that alcohol didn't appear to be filling.

"No. The cops kept me in all day."

"Well then, we need to fix that." I stood too fast but ignored the moving walls and made it halfway around my desk before catching sight of Dom grinning into his drink. My exceedingly unbalanced state was clearly amusing him.

"Have *you* eaten?" he asked.

"No, but that's not the point. I'm sure I can rustle up something in the kitchen—"

His hand brushed mine where I'd propped it on the desk to steady myself. I looked down and watched his trick spark from his fingers into my skin. A tingle travelled up my arm—and like a fleeting kiss, it stole my breath and teased the promise of more.

"It's going to be all right," he said. He seemed so innocent in that moment, although I knew him to be far from it. There was too much to say and no words adequate enough to convey it all. So I did the one thing I'd been wanting to do since he'd walked in—perhaps since we'd met. I braced an arm on the arm of his chair, gave him a few seconds to escape, and when his tongue swept across his bottom lip the shreds of my restraint fell away and I kissed him. Slowly, at first. Carefully. Because it always felt too good, as though he might turn to dust and slip through my fingers. The first time he'd kissed me, I'd expected him to be hard and rough. His gentleness had been a surprise. It was no surprise now; he opened, deepening the kiss. His hand came up to slip behind my neck and pull me down, and now I was the one caught.

The gentleness between us roughened and the whiskey-tainted kiss lost all its edges. I had a hand at his shirt, half hauling him out of the chair as he dragged me toward him by the neck. I didn't want this, couldn't have him, but none of that mattered when he tasted so sweet, and his hands scorched my skin, my neck, my lower back, his mouth on mine. Then he stood, pushing into me, driving me against the desk. His hands untucked my shirt free of my trousers and sank confidently down my back, then we were as close as two people could be, and it was all I could do not to draw on his trick and drink him in.

He pulled back to breathe, his hand on my face. "Are we doing this?"

Yes. Everything in me wanted this, even as the voices

told me no, that I could hurt him, wanted to hurt him, because it was who I was.

"Screw overthinking." He pulled me into a kiss that banished all doubts. I wasn't even sure what "this" was, just knew I needed more. His trick-warmed hands swept down my back, nails digging in at the same time as all of him pressed close. It was too much—all of him, every-where, all at once. His mouth branding mine, then skim-ming to my neck, where his teeth nipped—his hands spilling their trick, lighting me up wherever he touched. My own trick simmered inside, tugging and twitching, trying to reach him through me. The sensory overload threatened to tip me over into somewhere terrifying.

I gasped free, caught his hand—the one that had begun to work at my trouser fly—yanked, sidestepped, and before either of us knew what had happened next, I'd bent his arm behind his back and pinned him face-down over the desk.

"*Fuck*," he grunted.

Was it too much? Was *I* too much? Holding him with one hand locked around his pinched wrist, I ran my hand up his back, scrunching up his hooded top, revealing his muscular back and how he quivered beneath my hand. His trick shimmered beneath his skin, invisible to most, but not me. Where I ran my hand, his trick swirled, sweeping away and then rippling back in, as though it played with me. *Teased* me. I'd called his cards hypnotic, but really, all of Dom was hypnotic. His trick sang, lured me deeper, promised pleasures I knew I shouldn't take.

He pushed, trying to work his wrist free, but he could have tried harder. Leaning over his back pressed my hardness against the back of his thigh and startled a small gasp from his lips. There was no sweeter sound, and my own groan sounded.

"Wait... let me up."

I *was* too much.

I freed his wrist and retreated, almost falling over my own feet in my haste. "I... This was... Sorry—I shouldn't have—"

"No." He twisted, grabbed my wrist, and reeled me back in. "Just some practicality?" he whispered, head tilted back, lips mine for sampling.

Practicality? What?

He produced a condom packet in his right hand. I hadn't even considered getting that far, let alone the practicalities of *everything*. Wait... was he suggesting... penetration?

Dom huffed a gentle laugh. "You've seen me almost blow half of London to bits and a condom frightens you?" He hopped onto the edge of my desk and spread his knees and guided me between them. "You can't tell me you don't know what you're doing? You went to a private boys school, right?" He smirked then threw both arms over my shoulders, locking me inside his embrace. "If you really don't know, I'll show you." His dark eyes dropped to my lips, then flicked back up, full of questions and laughter and the careless joy he carried with him that had brightened Cecil Court from the moment he'd arrived.

I captured his lower back under both hands and yanked him tight, trapping the bulge in his trousers against mine.

"Fuck, yes," he breathed. "C'mon, Kempthorne. I

know you want this. You just gotta get past all those years of being told you can't have it."

I'd known him to be a temptation, but now *he knew* he was a temptation, and was pandering to my weaknesses, the need to take him was a thousand times sharper. There was nowhere to hide, not with him. He knew everything, and he still looked at me as though I was worth loving.

He wasn't ready for what I wanted. I'd hurt him. I'd ruin it, ruin us, ruin him.

I caught his jaw, held him still, felt the throb of his trick beat between us alongside the occasional twitch of his cock in his trousers. "You know I care for you, John?"

"Yeah?" He swallowed. Hope widened his eyes. "*Alex*," he drawled, teasing my name, teasing me.

"Good." I tightened my hold and pushed the next words against his lips. "Because I'm going to fuck you like I don't."

21

D^{om}

His words went straight to my cock, and instead of unleashing the strangled noise of pure lust making its way up my throat, I kissed him as though he was expensive whiskey, not meant for the likes of me, like I'd devour him all at once before he could change his mind about fucking me as though he didn't care. He twisted his grip in my hair and kissed me back with the same ferocious panic I'd thrown at him.

I'd known when the dam that was Kempthorne finally spilled over, he'd be unstoppable, but knowing it and feeling it were two very different things.

He hauled me into his arms, then dumped my arse back down onto his desktop, rattling the whiskey bottle and glass. He pressed close, suddenly everywhere, his hand still knotted in my hair, his tongue teasing mine, his lips hot and wet. *Fuck.* I drove a hand under his shirt, feeling my way across hard muscle and warm, smooth skin. He moaned into my mouth and a surge of lust filled my cock to beyond hard. I needed to feel him there, and clutched at his arse, grinding him so close that his heat and hardness burned against mine. God, I didn't know what this was but it was crazy, and wonderful, and I needed all of him, at once. To kiss, to fuck, to touch, to lick. He tasted of whiskey and rage. His hand in my hair might have hurt if I hadn't been so bloody fired up. And maybe I liked that, him holding me too hard, this happening too fast. Slow and gentle wasn't happening. Not tonight.

He pulled away, freeing me. "Fuck," he said, that sharp Queen's English, and licked his lips. His gaze burned when it met mine. I panted, raging hard, mindlessly hot.

"I can't..." He took a step back and ran a trembling hand through his hair. "You're too bright."

I was having him, and the only word I would listen to was *no.* I made the distance between us vanish again, dug my fingers behind his belt and eased its end from its loop. Kempthorne watched my face, his eyes glazed, either drunk on whiskey or lust. Probably both. I tugged his belt open, let its ends hang loose, and started on the fly, teasing my knuckles against his cock, pushed hard against the inside his trousers. "I'm going to have you like I should have months ago. If you're gonna run away, do it fucking now, because I'm not letting you go after this." To drive my point home, I squeezed his heated cock through his snug boxers—delivering a hint of what I planned to do with him.

He heaved out a breath, nostrils flaring as though I'd pissed him off. If he said no, I'd back off. But he wasn't saying a bloody thing so that was my cue to get on with it. Surrender glittered in his eyes. He didn't like to resist temptation. I had him now. I parted his fly all the way, shoved his trousers down an inch over his hips, just enough to loosen them, and freed his heated, veined cock. Alexander Kempthorne, with his floppy hair, his flashy watch, and his quick, clever smiles, was finally fucking mine.

A hand on his chest was all it took for him to step back.

The second I went down on him, he arched his back, leaning his hips toward me. I sealed my lips around him, easing him in deep. His fingers speared into my hair, more gentle this time, but that would soon change. From my angle, on my knees, his cock in my mouth, I looked up the length of his chest and over his crumpled shirt and found him peering down. Fuck, was there anything hotter than meeting a man's gaze while getting him off? He filled my mouth, then my throat, so smooth, warm, but so very hard. My own dick throbbed, heavy and neglected. We'd get to me, but this was all about him— the insanely complicated bastard.

I'd wanted this for so long. Wanted *him*. And I needed it now more than ever. I wanted to feel something, have something fill me up and chase away the god-awful trauma, turn me back into who I was before, not the empty thing I was afraid Wordsworth had made me. I needed this, needed him. And I was pretty sure he needed us too.

His grip on my hair tightened with every thrust between my lips. Whatever fear had held him back was long gone. I took him tip to balls, fighting not to gag. He wanted to fuck me any way he could; the need was raw in his eyes. He needed control, too, and I'd give it to him. Did he see that in my eyes? I hoped so, because words were off the table.

I pulled free, licked him from base to crown, and tongued the salty slit.

He made a gulping, moaning sound that I'd bet nobody had ever heard from Kempthorne, and then I swallowed him so fucking deep he twitched at the back of my throat.

"Oh God."

Yes, I wanted him to beg me to finish him, to hold me tight, to fuck me into his desk. None of it would be enough. I'd dreamed this, hadn't I? Him taking me. And here we were. It was happening, it was real, and I wasn't sure what I'd done to deserve him.

He suddenly hauled me off my knees, pulled me into his arms, and thrust a kiss on my lips that left my head spinning. I was back against the desk, driven there with his hand on my cock and his mouth on mine.

He cupped my face, made me look into his dark eyes. "Do you want me to?"

"If you're asking if you can fuck me, I'd have thought that was bloody obvious."

His gaze dropped to my lips, then back to my eyes. "I haven't... I mean... not like this, for a long time."

I kissed him loosely and mumbled, "It's like riding a bike."

His little laugh undid me. "I'm fairly certain it's not."

What was this? Kempthorne getting cold feet after he'd told me what he was going to do? "Shit, stop being cute." I twisted in his arms, bent over the desk, and grabbed his bottle of posh whiskey, then waggled it, hoping he got the idea.

He arched an eyebrow. "It's a five-thousand-pound bottle of whiskey."

"It's *wet*." I flung a look over my shoulder that left him no doubt that if he didn't do this right now, I'd pin him to the fucking floor and do it myself. His eyes sparkled with need and want and that mixture of gentlemanly coyness and wicked slyness that he did so well.

"It also burns. Top drawer," he growled and jerked his head, telling me to hurry up.

Leaning over the desk, I managed to work the drawer open and found some fancy sensitive hand-cream—*Christ, he moisturizes*—and handed it back.

He yanked my trousers down, revealing my arse to the cold air, spread my cheeks, and lightly skipped a finger over my hole. When a finger explored deeper, I breathed out, focused on relaxing. Alexander Kempthorne knew exactly what he was doing.

When a dribble of warm whiskey hit my lower back, a surge of doubt hit, too, and then his wet tongue slid across my skin, lapping up the liquid, while his finger teased, and fuck if my knees didn't almost give out.

"Say the word and I'll stop."

"*Ughdontstop*," I garbled.

He clamped a hand around the nape of my neck, bent

my shoulders back toward him, and with his free hand, angled his sheathed cock against my hole. He was already wet, thank fuck. He slid in, opening me wide, almost to the point of too much, and then his cock rode over my prostate and delicate tremors spilled down my spine, making me forget how to breathe. I choked, he thrust, my aching cock got clamped between me and the desktop, and then he was fucking me, filling me, riding me. The whiskey bottle rattled. His glass toppled, rolled, and thumped onto the carpet. I thrust a hand out, gripping the edge of the desk, and lost my mind to the fullness and spiking waves of toe-curling ecstasy.

He fucked hard, like I'd known he would. I bit my lip but failed to stop my grunts and moans. When he hauled me upright, my shoulders close to his chest, shallowing his angle, his cock found a new way to pour pleasure through me.

His soft mouth kissed my neck—so damned lightly it almost slapped me out of my daze. Firm fingers wrapped around my slick, straining cock, and as he mouthed my neck, he pumped, and with all of him still firmly embedded, I rode the cresting pleasure higher, didn't want to come, not yet, but I would, and soon. My trick was out, lighting me up where he touched, sinking into him in some kind of weird, erotic exchange that I was too far gone to question. With his mouth at my neck, his hand on my dick, his cock filling me, the storm that was Kempthorne swallowed me whole.

I came hard, shuddering and swearing mindlessly, spilling over his fingers as his teeth bit down.

With my head still spinning, he drove me facedown on the desk, and as the climax wrung the last drops from me, Kempthorne thrust once, twice, and on the third, his desperate shout was every bloody thing. He shuddered, jerked, cock unloading, and bloody hell if he wasn't off-the-scale hot with his hands on my hips, and his eyes half-lidded, lips swollen, and face flushed. He caught me looking, and the corner of his mouth twitched into a wicked smile.

Something dangerous and wonderful sparked alive inside my chest. My withered heart beat faster. We fit so well together, him and me. Like this moment was the only one that had ever made any sense. As though everything had been building to this.

He withdrew, dealt with the condom, and my body shivered, parts burning pleasantly. I winced and laughed at my own desperate idiocy. "I'm gonna be feeling this for a while."

"Are you all right?" His brow creased, and he stood there, shirt all askew, belt undone and his half-hard cock hanging free, and he was so fucking unhinged and beautiful.

"Yeah. I really am."

He kissed me on the lips, tilting my head up, and the gentleness in his touch shocked after his savage roughness. "That was... everything," he said, bumping his forehead against mine. Wintery, glistening, trick-touched eyes filled my vision.

It was everything, but it also wasn't enough. I wanted more and wove my fingers with his. This didn't have to be an end, it could be a beginning, but how could I say that without sounding like a tit?

"I have a perfectly good apartment upstairs—" he suggested, all growl.

"Yes." Whatever he was asking? Yes! I smiled, hoping I wasn't coming off as needy, and he smiled back, then led me upstairs by the hand. Inside his loft apartment, he kept the lights low. I glimpsed the spread of papers on the large glass-top table and drifted toward them.

"Don't," Kempthorne warned. He stripped off his shirt and casually dropped it to the floor, then climbed the two steps to his bedroom area. With his trousers slung loose, clinging to his hips, he beckoned me with a sultry glance. There wasn't a man or woman alive who could have resisted that look.

He stopped at the end of the bed, undid his glinting watch and set it down on the bedside cabinet, and all the while the soft light played over his body. How many times had I imagined touching what he kept hidden beneath his expensive shirts? All those times he'd rolled up his sleeves and I'd wanted to see just an inch more of skin... I was getting it all now.

He shucked his trousers into a pile at his feet, so all that was left were his socks, and damn... where was I supposed to start? Everything about him teased. I knew one thing. I was going to devour every inch of him and savor it. Fighting a smirk, I climbed the steps, tore off my hooded top, and watched his gaze drink me in. I wasn't shy, but his widening eyes had my heart thumping.

He lifted his hand. I didn't hesitate to link his fingers with mine. The trick flowed, spilling golden light over us both. It didn't hurt; maybe it was never meant to. He raised our linked hands between us. Trick reflected in his eyes and flowed between us, tingling and warm and so right.

His fingers skimmed my jaw, drawing my gaze back to

his face. "I find I am at a loss for words to describe what your being here means to me."

My heart beat harder, as my head clutched at the idea that I might have worth. "That's a lot of words for *fuck me, Dom*."

I leaned into his touch and his warm palm cradled my cheek. So close to a kiss, he whispered, "I've wanted this since we met."

"That's a hell of a coincidence..." I folded an arm around his neck, leaving him with no escape. "So did I."

"Coincidences are also facts." He smirked.

I flicked my tongue over his bottom lip, twisted and fell backward onto his bed, dragging him down over me. He laughed and nudged my jaw, then nuzzled my neck. I locked a leg around him. Maybe I'd flip him onto his back, maybe I'd take him in my hand and pump him until he cried out—

He caught my wandering right hand and pinned it above my head. "You're mine now, John Domenici." His eyes glowed with devilish desire.

I squirmed so he could feel my hardening cock against his hip. "Oh really?"

He caught my other wrist and pinned that over my head with the first. "Do you doubt it?"

"Hm... maybe."

He chuckled, let my wrists go, but only so he could slide down and suck a nipple between his teeth. Darts of lust danced down my spine. I bucked. "Fuck."

"Hm... yes," he purred, "I think we will."

22

D^{om}

Waking up next to Kempthorne in his swanky apartment had not been on my bucket list, but it should have been because it was one of those pristine moments of my life. Sun leaked through the blinds and Cecil Court's background noise bubbled up outside the window. I should have woken him, but he'd told me once how he rarely slept, and right now, he was out for the count, breathing heavily, lips slightly parted, dark hair a chaotic mess, and his face so relaxed he almost looked like a different person.

I extracted myself from under his arm, tugged on my jeans, and padded to the kitchen area. His loft apartment was all open plan, which meant I had to try to make the coffee quietly, so as not to wake him.

He groaned awake once the smell of freshly brewed coffee filled the air.

"Oh dear." He flung a hand over his eyes.

This could go one of two ways: He'd either regret last night and blame it on the alcohol or he'd shut down and go into distant Kempthorne mode. Whatever happened, my pristine morning was about to get really awkward.

"Coffee?" I asked.

He stared at the ceiling and touched his fingers to his temple.

My insides tried to tie themselves in knots. Okay, so this was bad. He was thinking of all the ways to tell me to get the hell out of his place. I'd known I should have done the right thing and stopped *everything* before we'd— before I'd indulged in the kind of bone-melting sex that should come with a warning label. He'd been off-his-head drunk, and I'd still gone along with it, which made me a dick.

"I'm sorry," he said, *not* looking over.

"It's fine." I swallowed. I should have been the one saying sorry. "Let me get dressed and I'll—"

"What? No, God no. That's not—" He straightened and the sheet slipped, pooling in his lap, leaving the glorious-bastard's-glorious-chest bare. He didn't regularly work out, didn't need to. The morning light dappled his chest and ran like liquid down muscle and golden skin. Memories of last night tried to warm me though and rekindle the heat we'd shared. I'd swept my tongue where the light touched now, sucked his nipples between my teeth, making him hiss.

He slumped and groaned some more. "Last night, I

hadn't meant..." He waved a hand and lifted his gaze, looking utterly wrecked.

Well, this was right up there on the awkward scale. I set my coffee down. There was no point dragging it out and watching him try to politely tell me to fuck off. I grabbed my shirt from the floor and headed for the door. At least I didn't have to go far, my room was only downstairs.

"Dom, stop." He stumbled from the bed, clutching the sheet around his waist as though I hadn't seen all of him gloriously naked in that bed behind him.

He tripped down his steps, swore, and growled at the sheet when it got stuck on the corner of the kitchen unit. Finally, he stopped in front of me, his face a muddle, part frown, part plea. "I just meant that I hadn't planned on us being together quite... like that." He winced again. "You may have noticed I'm not terribly good at this."

Apparently, when flustered, he became even more upper class. Half of me wanted to tell him it was fine and I'd leave, and we'd never speak of any of this again. But the other half liked this, and last night, and him, standing there, wrapped in a sheet, looking lost and vulnerable, with his blue eyes hiding all the horrors of his past. But he wasn't the only vulnerable one here. My CO, Sawyer, had been the last person to thoroughly fuck me like Kempthorne had, and he'd later fucked me over, so wasn't it better to cut to the chase and be done with all the emotional angst, when we both knew how this ended? "Look, if you want an out, just blame it on me or the whiskey, okay?"

"I don't. No. That's not..." He ran a hand through his

hair. "Oh hell." And kissed me. Softly. As though I was the most precious thing he'd ever held. His thumb skimmed my cheek and when I opened my eyes, he was there, that intense mix of everything Kempthorne. "What I'm trying to say is that I had hoped we might have gone to dinner first, during which I would have behaved in a far more gentlemanly manner than I did last night."

"You mean you don't start all your relationships by getting blind drunk and hammering your dates into your desk?" It came into my head and went straight out my mouth and now there was nothing I could do to take it back.

He blinked, like a deer in headlights, swallowed and hesitated, doubts widening his eyes, as though he was trying to think of all the ways he could backpedal, then he said, "I could blame it on the whiskey but honestly, I've wanted to fuck you over my desk since the first time you walked into Cecil Court."

I couldn't stop my smile. "Okay then." This was better. Much better. Terrifyingly better. Because I wasn't sure I deserved him—setting aside the homicidal aspects the both of us were still working through. "We're good?" I asked, hoping he didn't hear the quiver in my voice. I could put on the smiles and the swagger, but inside, I was all glass. I'd been here before, fallen for someone so deeply that their betrayal had blindsided me, and I didn't want this to be that.

"Yes, we're er... good. This is good. At least, I hope it is. Is it?"

I almost laughed, but he was trying and struggling with the morning after. He smiled back and turned with a swish of sheet, then swore again as it tangled around his feet. "Bloody, wretched thing."

"You know, you could just—"

He dropped the sheet—all of it—spoiling me with a show of his fine thighs, pert, peachy arse, and the rippling musculature of his back as he climbed the steps toward the bedroom area and disappeared into the bathroom.

I shut my mouth and stood in the middle of the apartment for a while, going over the conversation in my head. So, if he wanted to take me to dinner, but hadn't, were we a thing? Was there a Kempthorne and Dom? It had felt like there might have been an us, but there had also been some very expensive whiskey involved in last night's decisions and if I'd been a better person I wouldn't have taken advantage of the situation, but I had—his warm hands on my chest, the hard pumping motion of his hips against my arse—and didn't regret it.

Christ.

I made him a coffee to the sounds of the shower and was equal parts relieved and disappointed when he reappeared, wrapped in pressed trousers, fingers working at his shirt buttons, and his hair all wet and smoothed back. He spotted his coffee, said thank you in his gravelly morning voice, and leaned against the kitchen counter.

"So." He cleared his throat. "Would you like to go to dinner this evening?"

I tried unsuccessfully to stop smiling like an idiot. "Yeah, I'd like that. But don't feel you have to ask because of last night."

He frowned, turning serious. I'd have said he looked more like the Kempthorne I knew as my boss, but he'd also had that serious expression on his face when he'd grabbed me by the hips and made it clear I was going to get fucked. "I'm asking you to dinner for no other reason than because I want to and because I'm mortified to recall I fell asleep while we were... during a... well, you were there so you know exactly when I fell asleep."

My heart was going to explode. "You did. But it's fine."

He winced. "God."

"But really, don't worry. It was cute." I sipped my coffee and he sipped his, and this strange, soft warmth made it feel as though everything was going to be all right.

If I'd thought him intense before, last night he'd been off the scale. I'd mistaken his aloofness for inexperience. And I'd been very wrong. I shouldn't have been surprised. He attacked everything else with ruthless obsession. It made sense he'd be ruthless in bed too. But with the trick sparking alive between us, adding a dimension I hadn't even known was possible, it seemed we'd crossed over from screwing around to a whole lot of something more. He'd had an insatiable fire in him, and at one point, I hadn't been sure where his trick had begun and mine had ended, as though if I'd taken an ounce more, he'd have burned me up. And I'd have liked it.

Then I'd got to work on seducing every inch of him, and he'd fallen asleep and started snoring before I'd reached any of the exciting parts. Which was honestly, insanely adorable.

A distant hammering on the shop's front door soured the morning after glow.

"Robin will get it—"

And just like that, reality slapped us both in the face.

He set his coffee down and pulled in a deep breath. "I'll just—I'll get it."

I listened to his footfalls on the stairs and sipped coffee. Maybe we could stay in his apartment all day and pretend the world outside didn't exist, then go to dinner, on an actual date, which was a thing normal people did but I never seemed to.

The sound of barked voices shot up the stairs, followed by boots on the risers. I straightened at the sight of the all-too familiar black-clad IRL troops spilling into the apartment. My trick tried to spur me into reacting. I reined it back under control.

A short guy came through the door and made a beeline toward me, flashing an agency badge. He raked his gaze from head to toe, took in my naked chest, then the rumpled bed, made his assumptions, and curled his lip. "Under the Latents Act of Nineteen-Seventy-Eight, we are hereby legally obliged to confiscate any and all artifacts and/or items suspected of being artifacts from known-latents."

"The fuck you do—" I came out from behind the kitchen counter and might have gotten into it if Kempthorne hadn't appeared.

He shook his head, face severe. "Let them work. There's nothing we can do." He stopped at my side, trick simmering quietly, unseen by these IRL idiots.

"*We got Aladdin's cave down here!*" a voice announced through the short guy's radio.

Agent Shorty smirked into his radio. "Take it all."

"Everything in the basement has been neutralized," I said, the threat in my voice thinly veiled.

"That remains to be seen," Shorty said.

"I'm an authenticator and a qualified agent and I'm telling you the artifacts here are all dead."

The little prick squared up to me, angling for a punch to the face if he didn't back off. The guy hardly reached my chin. If I hit him, I could knock a few more inches off. "You're a *latent*," he snarled. "You'd tell me anything to stop me taking artifacts." He backed off and cast a disgusted frown at Kempthorne. "How the fuck two latents ended up with this much power is beyond me."

He said two latents, but meant two *homosexuals*, and if it hadn't been for Kempthorne's hand coming down on my shoulder I'd have pummeled the twat into Kempthorne's posh floorboards.

"What about all this?" one of the black-clad men asked, eyeing the paperwork strewn across the table.

"Just research," Kempthorne said. His hand fell from my shoulder as he stepped forward. "It doesn't come under the remit of the Latency Act—"

"Take it all," Shorty barked.

Kempthorne stilled; then, without making a fuss, he moved behind the kitchen counter. "Tea?" he offered, as though they weren't gleefully tossing his research into bin bags.

By the time they'd filled their bags and filed out, slamming the doors behind them, I was seconds away from losing my shit. "The fucking pricks. This is that bitch Doris's doing—"

Kempthorne opened his mouth, but his trilling phone interrupted him. "Kempthorne." He listened and sighed. Whoever was on the other end of the call didn't have good news. "I see..." His cheek flickered. "No, that's fine, thank you, Jordan." He hung up and slumped against the kitchen units.

I reached for him without thinking, but he thrust out a hand, warning me off. "Just..." He rubbed the bridge of his nose, squeezed his eyes closed, and winced. "Just... give me a moment."

Feeling useless and awkward, I shoved my hand into my back pocket and touched my cards—still there. The IRL agent hadn't thought to search me, probably too afraid he'd catch the gay.

"The IRL raided Ravenscourt," Kempthorne growled. When he opened his eyes, trick made the blue shimmer a shade cooler. "They took everything." He swept an arm out and knocked his coffee flying, then was in motion, pacing the apartment, the static charge of his trick rising, prickling my skin. "Everything in the study—*all of it!*"

"The murder wall?" I asked.

He made a strangled noise and thrust his hands into his hair. "*Everything.* I am a latent. Therefore, I cannot be trusted with *sensitive information.* Never mind it's *my* property, in *my* fucking house." He paced some more, stopped at the window, and sighed, deflating.

I'd known they'd come for him, in all the ways. He must have known it too. Didn't make it right, though. "I'm so sorry."

He heaved a breath. "This is Montgomery's doing. He'll turn the screws until he believes I have nothing left. That man has grossly underestimated me—*us.* He must be stopped. Now." He scooped his car keys off the table, then hesitated. "I fear our dinner will have to wait."

Of course it did. And that made sense. Even if I tried

not to wince and reveal just how much I'd wanted that tiny slice of normality.

"We're going to see Kage," he added.

"Right." *Fuck.* "Great."

It hit me as Kempthorne cruised the Aston into Kage's building's underground garage, that I was about to try to have a reasonable conversation with a man I had a complicated past relationship with, alongside a man who I had just spent the entire night engaged in mind-blowing, trick-infused sex with. And while there were more important things happening that did not revolve around my sex life, I couldn't help but worry that having Kempthorne and Hollywood in the same room together was asking for trouble.

Hopefully our mutual hate of Montgomery would be enough to eclipse their mutual hate of each other.

Kage buzzed us through the building's front door with a gruff, "sure" via the intercom. Kempthorne had at least called ahead, so our arrival wasn't a surprise.

Kage opened his apartment door and invited us in. Kempthorne wore his typical smile and voiced a few pleasantries about the apartment, not having seen it before. But Kage wasn't smiling, and when he caught me looking at the kitchen—where I'd snubbed him and, before that, thoroughly fucked him—his frown became a permanent fixture on his pretty face.

"Montgomery is making moves," Kage said, cutting to the chase. He approached the sofa, suggesting he might relax, but thought better of it and stopped in the dead centre of the room instead. "I have orders to close the net."

Kempthorne tugged off his leather gloves and tossed them onto the kitchen countertop. "Then our timing is perfect."

"Look..." Kage ran a hand through his too-long hair and sighed, exasperated. "It's better for you both if you stay out of the way. You're latents, you're on the wrong side of this fight."

I crossed my arms. He just had to get that dig in, didn't he? "So the LOA can squirrel Montgomery overseas and have him work for the US Government? I don't think so."

Kage spread his hands in a what-am-I-supposed-to-do-about-it gesture. "Dom, you're questionably a prisoner at large—"

"Wrongly accused—"

"I know that but the LOA doesn't. Kempthorne is, honestly, considered only slightly less of a threat than Montgomery. The LOA are unlikely to authorize your involvement. And even if they did, I'd be putting you in cuffs at the end of it and despite what you think of me, I don't want to be *that* guy."

At least he was being honest, for the first time in forever. "We all do things we don't want to do," I said, echoing Annie's exact words. Kage's eyes widened. Perhaps she'd tried to tell us in that moment, and maybe she'd said things before, hinted at her own trouble, and none of us had been listening, too wrapped up in our own shit. "Montgomery is dangerous," I said. "The LOA won't change that. We can. You just have to let us in on the operation."

Kage studied my face, then glanced at the quiet Kempthorne standing behind me. He obviously really, *really* didn't want us in on this. He thought the worst of Kempthorne, and here he was, standing behind me. Could Kage sense something had changed? Did he know Kempthorne and me were a thing? Tension simmered. Was the bloody heating on? Christ, it was hot in here.

"Need I remind you, Agent Mitchell," Kempthorne began in his holier-than-thou voice, "had you been doing your job, you might have realized Annie was being manipulated before events came to a head as they did. Robin and Annie might still be alive."

Kage laughed bitterly. "Fuck you."

Kempthorne moved up, putting himself a few steps in front of me. "Perhaps if you weren't so focused on Dom and me, you'd have seen how your friend needed your help? I lost a good agent, a good friend due to your incompetence. If you're a good man, as you say you are, then you'd be looking for ways to make this right. You should want to help us."

The glare Kage threw Kempthorne had me glad he wasn't a latent, or he'd have likely tried to spontaneously combust Kempthorne where he stood. His attention then skipped past Kempthorne, found me again, and burrowed deep. "I didn't stand a chance, did I?"

"This isn't about us," I said.

He chewed on his reply then scowled into the middle distance. "We could have been good."

"If you hadn't fucking poisoned me and then grassed me up to your bosses." I could probably have kept that to myself. "This isn't helping. We've talked—"

"That wasn't—I had orders," he snapped, then came

forward, stopping only when Kempthorne straightened. "*You* talked. Now you can listen." He pinned his glare on me. "You're a good guy, Dom. Kempthorne will twist that goodness, like he does everything else he touches. I wish you'd see who he really is."

Kempthorne's chin dipped. His presence simmered in the corner of my eye. He could put Kage on his arse with a click of his fingers. But he wouldn't because he believed Kage was right.

Kage clenched his hands into fists. "He doesn't know how to care." He swallowed, coming closer, moving past Kempthorne, who just stood like a bloody immovable monolith, staring out the windows.

I snorted, glaze flicking between Kempthorne's back, the hard cut of his shoulders, and Kage, closer now, looking soft and vulnerable. "And you do?"

"I'll quit the LOA."

Shit. "Kage, stop. It's over."

"Please, just listen..." He lifted his hands. "He's a sociopath. And believe me, I'm trained to know. The only thing he cares about is power. Everything else is collateral damage. Even the people he claims to care for."

Kempthorne's shoulders twitched, Kage's words finding a weak spot in his armour.

"You need to stop talking," I growled. Why wasn't Kempthorne standing up for himself?

"I get it, I do. Sociopaths are attractive. Power always is."

Kempthorne turned his head, and I saw his face in profile. The smooth jaw, always set in a firm line. Dark eyes, filled with secrets. On the surface, all the things Kage had said appeared to be true. Fuck, Kempthorne believed it too. Which was why the prick wasn't defending himself. All that fucked up past, his mother torturing him, a life spent hiding who and what he was. Kage was reinforcing all of it.

And now Kage was all up in my face, hands up, as though he were talking down a dangerous latent, talking down to me. Because I was so gullible I'd spread my cheeks for any guy with a fast car and a flashy watch.

"The day will come when Kempthorne reveals who he really is and you will get hurt."

I pinched up my lips, keeping all the vicious insults behind them. I wanted to tell him how Kempthorne and I had something, something that Kage and I never would have had. Whatever Kempthorne was, whatever he'd done, I trusted him. He wouldn't drug me, and he wouldn't use me. He wouldn't ever turn me over to an agency for the greater good. Because he was Kempthorne, and he tried to do good, despite believing all that shit Kage had just spouted. "Are you done?"

He reached for me, and he was damned lucky I didn't put him on his arse. I stepped back, hands up, and then Kempthorne moved—in a single step he grabbed Kage's wrist and spilled a little trick into his touch. Kage's eyes went wide and his mouth flew open.

Kempthorne gave him a slight shove, a hint of what he could do. "John doesn't want you."

Kage stumbled, rubbing his wrist. His glare bounced between us, then sizzled on Kempthorne. "If you hurt him, I'll come down on you with the weight of the LOA, and don't think your pathetic British government will help you."

Kempthorne sighed. "And if you so much as think

about using Dom again, I will prove to you exactly how much of a sociopath I can be."

My lips twitched. Sparks of pride and lust sizzled low, warming my veins. There was my Kempthorne, the dangerous son of a bitch who I, right then, wanted to drag outside, slam against a wall, and kiss until he came undone in my hands.

"When is the LOA making moves on Montgomery?" I asked, voice gruff.

Shaking his head, Kage turned and headed back toward the sofa, putting some much-needed distance between us. "You know I can't tell you that."

Kempthorne and I finally shared a glance, an understanding. The storm had passed. We'd all said what needed to be said. We survived. Nobody got hurt, except maybe Kage's wrist. And we still had a job to do.

"C'mon, Kage." I started forward. "If it wasn't for us, you wouldn't even have found Montgomery. We got you this far. You owe us."

"I can't, Dom. If I tell you anything, I'll get fired. And I'd like to keep my career, seein' as I've got nothing to give it up for." He tucked a hand into his trouser pocket, more of the fight draining out of him. "I shouldn't even be talking with you. You should go."

With his shoulders slouched, he looked beaten. Did he really not know anything about Montgomery getting his hands on Annie? He hadn't seen a damn thing until it was too late? But we hadn't seen it either. I wanted to trust him, and that was the problem with Kage, I couldn't. "We're trying to save latents," I said, getting down to the bones of it all. "People like Annie. You said you had a latent brother? Right?"

His head lifted. And whatever history was there, all the things he hadn't told me, mentioning his brother hurt him. He *did* care about all this. He just had the worst way of showing it.

"We're trying to save people like him."

"Fuck, Dom. I wish... I wish Annie had told me. But she didn't, and for the rest of my life I'll carry that with me."

"A life you owe Kempthorne."

"What?"

"He won't tell you, probably because he regrets it. You died in Cecil Court's kitchen, Kage. I saw you die. Kempthorne saved you."

His gazed flicked behind me, landing on Kempthorne for the truth. "Why?"

"I often wonder that myself." I heard the shrug in Kempthorne's voice. "But there's no mystery. Dom likes you, and I am... That is to say, I couldn't watch another person die knowing I could prevent it."

Kage rubbed his chest and the scars behind his shirt. "You can heal?"

"Sometimes... when I'm focused. Not, unfortunately, with Robin. There was an artifact. It was distracting, and... I couldn't save her."

"Could you have saved Annie?" he asked quietly.

I'd been the one to kill Annie. I wished it hadn't come to that. But I'd do it again in a heartbeat to save Kempthorne.

"No," Kempthorne said. "The presence of the dirty artifact prevented me from focusing enough to manipulate the friction resonance in such a way as to stimulate healing. In fact, it would have been impossible to save either of them, although my guilt tells me otherwise."

Pain paled Kage's face. I didn't hate him, not really. I understood why he'd done the things he had. After this, I'd probably never see him again. He wasn't a bad guy, just one being torn in multiple directions. I knew how that felt. "C'mon, Kage. Montgomery has all our backs against a wall. We need you in this. And shit, we've had our issues, but you told me all that stuff from your past was real. The LOA might be arseholes, but you're not. You said you're trying to do good. I believe that."

Kage tilted his head back and sighed. "They'll ask me to pull the trigger on you. Don't put me in that position."

I shrugged. "You won't do it."

He frowned. "You can't know that."

"Yeah, I do. And you won't."

He sighed. We'd won, I could feel it. Then his smirk proved it. "The best I can do is warn you when the LOA issues the order to bring you in or..."

"That'll do, mate. Just let us in and give us a head start when you get the order to take us out. That's all we're asking."

He flicked his gaze to Kempthorne. "Do not make me regret this, Kempthorne. I'm doing this because I owe you, and Annie would want..." His voice caught. "She liked you both before that son-of-a-bitch got to her. She'd want me to help."

"You're doing the right thing," Kempthorne said.

Kage snorted and checked the clock on the wall. "The raid on the lab is four hours away. I'll tell the lead agent we need your intel on the ground. The LOA will swallow it because they want you both close, but they'll try and take you in as well. Just... watch your backs." He plucked the phone from his pocket, rang a number, and spoke all official-sounding into it, asking to speak with his contact.

I wandered back to a rigid Kempthorne standing by the counter in the kitchen area. "We're in," I said, under my breath.

"You are," he whispered back, reapplying his gloves. "Whereas I suspect there's a bullet in his gun with my name on it."

23

A lexander

The shadows had been uncharacteristically quiet since Dom had been thrown into Wordsworth. The two events were unlikely to be connected, and their lack of movement was probably related to the surge, but it was a coincidence, nonetheless. I'd always seen shadows—the remnants of dead latents—as flickers in the corner of my eye, sometimes voices, but in recent years they'd been getting bolder, more tangible, more... hungry, culminating in their attack while Dom and I had been under Renick's dubious care in a Hackney flat.

Now Dom and I were a few warehouses away from Montgomery's lab, waiting in the Aston on the arrival of the elusive LOA. Kage and his cohorts wouldn't be the only danger tonight. The shadows were close—flickers here and there, shadows light didn't penetrate, movement in the dark. Strange how the shadows should be stirring now. It meant something, but I had no idea what.

"You all right?" Dom asked, his face illuminated by the cool blue of the Aston's instrument panel. He'd just ended a call from Gina. She'd asked for a few weeks' leave. She was within her rights to take time off, but I couldn't help wondering if she'd ever come back to Cecil Court. There was very little of the "Co" left in Kempthorne & Co.

Outside, a parade of armed agents spilled from a conspicuous line of black Range Rovers.

"Yes, fine." His gaze lingered on me. "I *am* fine," I reassured him. "Just not fond of waiting."

"I always used to get angsty before an op." He plucked his deck of cards from his pocket and began to shuffle them, not needing to look to know where each one of the fifty-one playing cards was. "Shuffling these helped."

The cards' soft slide through his fingers and their accompanying artifact hum were undeniably soothing. "Did you use the cards during military operations?" His skill with the cards fascinated me. The way they slid between his fingers, the way he made them dance. I'd meant it when I'd told them they were hypnotic.

"They were—are my main weapon," he said.

I watched him tease the cards for a while, losing myself in their flow, then cast my gaze back to the gathering LOA and took the coin from my pocket. The IRL agent who had raided my loft apartment hadn't got his sticky fingers on the coin before I'd been able to slip it up my sleeve.

Dom stopped shuffling his cards and eyed the coin.

"You have your cards, I have the coin," I said.

His relationship with the coin was a complicated one. Mine, however, was simple. It was all I had left of my sister.

"That knife was a nasty piece of work," he muttered, after a few minutes of contemplative thought.

I stared out the car window. That knife—clearly given to Annie by Montgomery as a means to make her both pliable and unstable—was a thousand times worse than the coin between my fingers. And the bloody thing kept finding its way back to me. I should have absorbed it, instead of tossing it into the field outside Ravenscourt. Not my finest moment. Although, had I tried absorbing it, it would have burned through me. That knife was as dangerous as it was powerful. At least it was out of play for now.

"That knife was the same Max used, right?" Dom asked. "The same knife you used... to... "

"To kill my sister," I finished for him, still staring ahead. I couldn't meet his gaze knowing what he'd seen me do. What he'd *felt*. Why, after all that, he'd let me touch him, let me be intimate with him, I couldn't fathom. He should have despised me. Part of me wondered if all of this was a dream I'd soon wake from, tied to an examination table, judged and dissected, teased and taunted. Part of me wondered if Dom and his magic cards and his brilliant smile were even real.

I swallowed the urge to tell him we weren't discussing the past. That knee-jerk reaction had served me well for years. Protected me. But with Dom, things were different. He'd already seen the worst, and for the first time I could talk about what had happened that day without fear. He already knew how it ended. "She came back from a trip to Scotland early, walked into the study, where I was..." The memories were a muddle. Just the knife in my hand and my sister bleeding, her blood running through my fingers.

"What were you doing in there?"

"I... don't recall. Reading?" I rubbed my head and willed the memories to organize, but they never did, and recalling it all now was no different.

"How did Montgomery get the knife?" Dom asked after too long of a silence.

"The same way he gets all his artifacts—auctions, black market trading?"

"You don't think it's a coincidence it keeps coming back to you? Like maybe it's deliberate?" Dom asked, and I didn't answer. "The knife corrupted Max. It could have corrupted you back then as well."

"Max was a troubled young man."

"Alex, so were you."

I'd forgotten he'd seen my past, stood inside it as though it was his own. To think he'd seen... those things, heard my screams, heard my sobs too. I looked away and clenched my jaw. Those had been my secrets to keep. "The knife was in the study. I think perhaps my mother had it. I picked it up..." And the rest he'd seen.

"You mother had it, huh? What about the pen?" he pushed, because he was good at that. Asking questions, getting answers. "The pen that almost flipped me to the dark side. Do you know how Montgomery got that pen?"

"I really don't know and would prefer not to think about it."

"I *know* how he got it. Your mother gave him the pen, as a gift."

I faced Dom. "She what?" She had? I'd known Montgomery had been close to my parents, always lurking in old photographs, but gift giving? My relationship with my mother was... complicated. Mostly distant. Although I'd tried to change things, to make her... love me. It was never enough. "I wasn't aware of that. And I'd rather not discuss this anymore."

He shrugged. "Okay."

But in the silence, he clearly had more to say, and after a few minutes, added, "Montgomery knows how to use artifacts against latents. He used the pen to fuck with me. He used the knife on Max, and Annie, a knife you have a past with. He was probably hoping you'd use it on me—"

"No. You're too strong a latent to cast aside so frivolously." I had to get Dom off the topic of me and back on Montgomery. "Which is part of the reason we're here. To stop him getting his hands on you and those like you. He'll keep on corrupting latents unless he's stopped."

The car's instrument panel lit Dom's face, highlighting the curiosity there. "But what if he had the knife from *before*? What if Montgomery had something to do with your sister's death? What if he was there—?"

"Dom, please... don't try and excuse it. That's not what happened. I was alone."

"I know you don't want to discuss it, but when I saw into the pen and that time when I stumbled into the study, there was something else there, some other presence. Maybe you can't remember? Our minds block devastating trauma. There's a chance you weren't alone when it happened. If I could just get the knife back, under controlled conditions, I could read it—"

I breathed in through my nose. "Do not *ever* authenticate that knife." I glared, and he glared right back. "Do you understand?"

His eyes narrowed. "As the murder weapon, it will show me everything. I saw into some of it when I touched the knife fighting Max, but it was loud and confusing. Now I know what to look for, I can search through its trauma and find yours. I'll know exactly what happened—"

"Dom—don't ever look into it again. An artifact as potent as that one will drive you insane, if it doesn't burn through you. It's not worth the risk." If I lost him... I couldn't... *That* couldn't ever happen.

"I can handle it—"

"No, you can't!" I grabbed the steering wheel. "And you won't. Not in this." The knife caused death and destruction for whomever touched it. Worse than any artifact I'd known. "It is not to be trifled with."

Dom held my gaze but eventually conceded. "Yeah, okay. You're right." He peered through the windscreen and I plucked my hands free from the wheel, rubbing off the tingling trick before he saw. The LOA agents milled about outside, keeping behind the bushes and out of sight from the lab.

"Sorry."

I looked over.

"It's your past, your sister," he said. "I shouldn't have pushed."

"It's fine... I just... I couldn't bear it if something

happened to you." I mumbled that last part, not because it didn't matter. Because it *did*. In a way that made me want to gather the words up and unspeak them so they didn't leave me vulnerable.

"Really?" His face brightened.

"Yes." He stared and his smile grew, making mine tic cross my lips. "Why are you surprised?" I asked.

"I dunno..." He fought off some of his smile, but it soon came back. "Because you're Alexander Kempthorne and I'm just some East End grunt—*incoming*."

Kage Mitchell's distinct figure broke from the squads of men and women crowded around the Range Rovers, all geared up in boots and helmets, complete with night vision goggles. I assumed they had a plan for raiding the lab, perhaps by cutting the power and taking advantage of the resulting confusion. It's what I'd have done. They surely knew what they were doing, but I couldn't help feeling exposed, as though this were part of a larger plan, beyond the scope of my sights.

"You're not and never were just a grunt."

"Don't you want to know the knife's secrets?" he asked with a sly lift of his eyebrows, apparently not giving up on the knife.

"I was there." I opened the car door and climbed out. "There's nothing the knife can tell you that I don't already know."

Kage glowered, only smiling when Dom emerged from the passenger side and leaned on the Aston's roof. "We're a go in fifteen," Kage said. "But I can't get you in the initial push, they won't okay it. You're both too hot. You have to stay here."

"Oh well, it will have to do," I said.

Mr Mitchell eyed me closely. "I can get you some time with Montgomery after the raid and before he's removed from the scene, assuming he'll talk. But that's all. And I have to be present."

"All right," I said.

"How do you plan on avoiding his trick?" Dom asked Kage.

"Let us worry about that," Kage replied, sounding smug. His eyes narrowed, fixing me under his glare. "What exactly are you planning, Kempthorne?"

"I would like to speak with him so he knows who is responsible for his downfall."

"That's it?"

"What else would I be here for?"

That seemed to partially satisfy him, and with a nod toward Dom, he returned to his people.

Dom waited until Kage was out of earshot and whispered, "Why are we really here?"

"To ensure Thomas Montgomery never harms another latent."

"Deliberately vague much?"

I slammed the car door closed, tucked my hands into my coat, smiled, and nodded toward the horde of LOA agents. "They will underestimate him. People like them always underestimate latents. Montgomery is extremely powerful. If cornered, their guns and Tasers will do little more than slow him down."

Dom gave me a raised eyebrow. "Like someone else I know."

I cleared my throat. "Precisely."

"So are we just gonna hang back and wait for the fireworks?"

I peered through the trees, beyond the gathered agents, at the distant shimmer of the lab under flickering streetlamps. On the surface, the early evening was calm, but a tension crackled at its edges. The presence of multiple shadows lingered in hidden pockets of darkness. "Hope for the best, plan for the worst."

Dom came around the front of the car and frowned at my view, then up at me. "What do you see?"

Of course he'd noticed something wasn't quite right. "We are not alone in our observing. There are shadows here."

"Oh shit." He unfolded his arms and reflexively reached for his cards but stopped short of drawing, remembering how the trick attracted their attention. "How many?"

"Not many, or you'd see them too. They're on the periphery, a hint more than a threat. Let's hope they stay that way."

Sighing, he leaned back against the car and folded his arms. Strong arms I'd had wrapped around my thighs as he'd... "You never did tell me why they seem to want you so badly."

"Hm?"

"*Hm*?" His eyes sparkled with humor.

"That is a discussion for another time."

"Over dinner?" His eyebrows rose in query and some part of me I hadn't known existed warmed my chest. My heart, I supposed. It had been a long time since I'd allowed myself to have one.

"If you like."

"I do like."

He leaned against the car, arms crossed and stance nonchalant, and he was a gift, one I wanted to unwrap again and again. Despite knowing what awaited inside, he somehow always surprised me. This was not the time to be thinking about him on his back in my bed, and it certainly wasn't the time to remember how all of that coiled strength had quivered under me. The more I knew of John Domenici, the more helpless I became to resist him. "Once all this is over, we should spend a few weeks at Ravenscourt." It sounded more like a business proposal than an invitation for him to stay with me, alone in the big house, but I didn't know how to be effortlessly comfortable with such things and was fully aware I was out of practice when it came to intimate relationships.

I fiddled with my cuffs and struggled with an unfamiliar wave of self-doubt and internal conflict. Was it too soon to ask him to stay with me? After the disaster that had been my behavior last night and my terrible attempt to explain myself this morning, it was a wonder he hadn't run for the hills. Sex was uncomplicated. I was confident enough with that, but relationships? I had no idea where to start.

"I'd like that too." He pushed from the car and slipped an arm around my waist. Touching had been one of the more difficult aspects of any intimacy, especially with our tricks having minds of their own, but as he pressed himself close, all the fraught concerns flitted away, leaving the very solid feel and soapy smell of him that I'd come to enjoy—even crave. Heat and weight, the press of strength and muscle, so close. Like last night, when I'd skimmed my fingers down firm shoulders and followed the trail of goose bumps with my tongue.

I almost moaned.

"What you did with Kage earlier today... Putting him down with a few words?" His fingers touched my jaw, pulling my gaze down to meet his. Beautiful eyes, surrounded by dark lashes, they flashed now, full of lust and life and all the things I couldn't resist. From the first time I'd seen him, his easy smile and cavalier attitude—my heart had beat faster, and my murky world had funneled to a sharp point, to him.

I'd have preferred not to talk about Kage. I'd have preferred to push Dom against the car and kiss him like I had last night, only without the muddle of whiskey between us. "I'll not apologize—"

His mouth skimmed mine and his words slipped between my lips. "It was so hot."

Several van doors slammed and someone coughed gently. "We're going in," Kage said, armed with a military rifle and clad in a black Kevlar vest. Dom and I untangled, and Dom's playful demeanor tuned icy under Kage's withering glare.

Not for the first time, I wondered why I'd saved the American's life. He'd been the bane of mine ever since.

Kage threw me a look that confirmed he'd like nothing more than to put a bullet between my eyes and then stalked off to join his team.

Dom took his cards from his pocket and shuffled them. "Time to dance, I guess."

Having Kage see us intimately close had ruffled Dom. He still cared for Mr Mitchell, because Dom cared about people in ways that were lost on me. It was a large part of who he was.

As I fell into step beside him, his feelings for Kage shouldn't have factored in my thoughts. But they did. And as the LOA agents fanned out, the operation getting underway, I couldn't help but hope Kage Mitchell showed Dom his true colors before the night was over.

24

D^{om}

The CO—a muscular guy in his late forties—observed his LOA teams through multiple screens from inside the back of the van, watching each unit close in on the lab. Slick, silent, and efficient. I was almost grateful the UK's IRL were crap because if they'd had this kind of training, there wouldn't be a single latent left on UK streets.

Watching it all unfold brought back memories of Syria, and the urge to charge my cards almost slipped free, but if I did that, I'd make the LOA's command glow like a lighthouse. I had to sit this one out.

A few minutes into the op and I noticed Kempthorne wasn't watching the screens. He stepped back from the van and frowned at the gloomy scenery. "What is it?" I whispered.

"The shadows are moving."

The CO gave us a disgusted look, assuming Kempthorne was full of latent voodoo.

"Oh dear." Kempthorne stepped onto the grass and strode toward the lab, breaking cover.

"What's he doing?!" the CO growled. "Get his ass back here. Now!"

Shit.

I hurried through the wet grass. "Kempthorne?" He strode on, either oblivious or choosing to ignore me. "Hey!" I grabbed his arm but his trick tried to leap all over me. He jerked, I reeled, and it took a second for us both to focus.

"Sorry," he said. "I'm afraid my trick has become rather familiar with yours."

I shook the fizzing sensation from my hand. "You can't waltz down there like you're Alexander Kempthorne."

He bristled. "Of course I can."

"You're a *latent*. If you go in there, doing whatever it is you've got in your head needs to be done, they'll shoot you."

"There are latents in there," he whispered back. "The shadows are converging. Between the LOA, Montgomery, and the shadows, they're all helpless."

"I get it. I do—I was in a lab just like it. But what are you going to do? Huh?"

"What I did before, absorb the excess. Without it, the shadows will dissipate. It's the energy that attracts them."

"—to you. It attracts them *to you*."

Annoyed, he dismissed me with a huff and took off again. Not quite running, but close.

Why did he have to be so bloody stubborn? "For

fuck's sake! Hey—" When I caught his arm this time, I wasn't letting go. He whirled on me, eyes as dark as I'd ever seen them. "You're *not* going in there. I've had the shadows tell me all they bloody want is you and your fancy trick. I'm not watching them devour you." I cared about him. Was that enough to stop him? Would he listen if I told him? "Look..." I more than cared, and if he went in there, I couldn't protect him, but thinking it and saying it were two very different things. What if he didn't feel the same? What if I was about to hand him my heart only for him to laugh—why should he care what I thought?

His glower softened. "I can handle myself, Dom. But the latents in there cannot."

A shockwave hit me like a truck. I didn't remember falling or the explosion, just coughing into the wet grass and a high-pitched ringing in my ears, like a thousand alarms all going off at once. Fire, when it rages, sounds like a vicious storm, like something snarling and alive. I heard the same noise then and couldn't figure out why. The roar and the whistling faded, and I rolled onto my back, trying to understand what had knocked me down.

The lab, the parking lot, the fences. It was all gone. Like an enormous hand had torn out a chunk of London. A latent... or a bomb. Someone or something had detonated.

Kempthorne propped himself on an elbow beside me and blinked at the inferno. Dancing firelight highlighted a line of blood running down his face, from the cut above his left eye.

If we'd been any closer...

He glanced over, face white from shock, probably

thinking the same, then clambered to his feet and staggered toward the burning rubble.

Distant sirens joined the cacophony of car and building alarms ringing in my head.

"Wait..." I dragged myself upright and started after Kempthorne heading down the grassy bank toward the wreckage. There had been people inside that lab, latents, agents...

Kage.

Fuck... he went in.

I loped closer and scanned the twisted fragments of brick and metal and glass strewn all over. This close, nobody would have survived that blast.

He went in... Kage went in with the rest.

A wall of heat pushed me back. We wouldn't find anyone alive. But I still searched for him, telling myself I was looking for *any* survivors. I stumbled over debris and around the twisted wreckage of a black van that had been blasted into the fence. Where were the bodies? There had to be some. There had to be *something*.

Fire raged but was contained in pockets of rubble here and there—most of the building had been blown apart, with just one large corner still intact, somehow avoiding the explosion.

Fire trucks screeched in. The place would be crawling with officials soon and I'd get shut out... I had to know. I picked my way around the wreckage, fighting off old combat memories. Explosions, IEDs had been common, and there were always bodies. Montgomery's lab had been staffed; the rooms were occupied by latents. I should have found some evidence of people. The fact there weren't any, meant something...

Realization hit. It meant the lab had been cleared beforehand.

Montgomery had known we were coming.

Something flickered near the flames, figures shifting in the light. I plucked a charged card free. *Shadows.* Kempthorne had said they were here.

Where the fuck *was* Kempthorne? I glanced back along the path I'd taken through the rubble. I could make out the corner of a fire truck and flashing lights, but little else, and no Kempthorne. Had he gone back?

Smoke wafted between me and those trucks, cutting me off.

John...

"Oh no, no, no," I muttered, still holding up a card, spitting with trick. "Not now." The last thing I needed was more voices in my fragile head. I turned, smoke drifted.

"Drop the card," Kage said.

He was alive! I turned toward the source of his voice, and the smoke cleared. "Kage—"

He held the gun cupped in his palm and peered down its sight, aimed right between my eyes. "Drop the card, Dom."

"What the—"

"Drop the fucking card!"

I ran my tongue across my lips, dropped the sizzling card, and lifted both hands. My thumping heart joined all the other noises in my head. "What are you doing?" My discarded card spluttered and died.

"Now drop the deck. *Slowly.*"

"Kage—"

"Just fucking do it, Dom."

I eased my hand into my pocket and pulled my deck

free. This didn't feel like agency business. Kage breathed too hard and too fast for this to be all part of the job—it was personal. "You goin' to tell me my rights under the latency act?"

He snorted a short, dry laugh. "Drop. The. Deck."

If I did that, I'd lose my main weapon. Without my cards, I could still throw trick at him, but it would be messy and harder to control without my cards to focus on. Slower too. His bullet would hit me before my trick hit him. "I didn't think you'd do this."

He flexed his fingers on the gun. "I wouldn't have... until you killed Annie."

"That was Mon—"

"Drop the deck!"

I dropped it and raised my hands. "Montgomery—"

"Montgomery? Kempthorne? You're all the same. Same as you, Dom. I wanted you to be different. But you're one of them."

And the scary bloody thing was, he sounded as though he believed that. All latents were the same in his LOA book. "I thought *you* were different," I said.

"I am! I was. You and me? We could have—" He choked. "Damn..."

Kage's shadow shifted on the ground behind him, but something else was moving behind him too. More shadows gathered, unconnected to the debris, or even this world. Kage wouldn't even see them. Could they hurt him... a non-latent?

He retrieved a pair of cuffs from their sneaky hiding place at his lower back. "Hands down."

"If you wanted to get kinky, we could have—"

He tossed me the cuffs, no hint of a smile. "No bull-shit. Put them on."

Cuffs were better than a bullet in the head. But they also meant I was probably about to be an unwitting guest of the LOA. I ratcheted the cuffs into place, taking my time about it. Smoke swirled around us. Someone might see, Kempthorne might happen to walk this way... If all else failed, cuffs would slow me down, but I could escape them with some trick and time.

"What went wrong here?" I asked, jerking my chin toward the rubble. If we talked, I could buy a few minutes.

"Bad intel. Montgomery knew we were coming. Two of the guys didn't make it. Three badly wounded." He dabbed at his own split lip. "But it's not a total loss. We'll get you."

If it was a trap, and Montgomery had planned it, then he'd be nearby, watching. I flicked my gaze behind Kage, into the dimly lit streets leading off to neighboring warehouses.

What if the trap hadn't been meant for the LOA?

What if the trap had been meant for the most powerful latent, outside Montgomery himself?

Montgomery needed power. He'd been siphoning it off latents in his lab. He needed Kempthorne. "Where's Kempthorne, Kage?"

Kage huffed. "I didn't stand a chance, did I?"

"If you didn't lie about everything, you might have."

"And Alex didn't lie?!" Kage's aim wobbled, but he caught it and straightened, more determined than ever.

"That's different. Where is he, Kage?"

"Worried, are you? You should be." Something cold

and dangerous lurked behind Kage's pretty eyes. "We might not have gotten Montgomery tonight, but we will get the both of you. I fucking have to... I need this. I need you and him off the streets. I need to do my job. Despite whatever... whatever I might feel. I'm sorry. I am. I warned you this would happen. It has to be this way."

I cast a look back, trying to make out the figures moving in the rippling heat. If Kempthorne had been caught, he was being bloody quiet about it. "You know, even when Kempthorne said you were a dick, I didn't believe him. I wanted to trust you—wanted to *like* you." I could easily have loved him.

Shadows bubbled up behind him, building like storm clouds. Probably, not a good thing. They were dead latents, attracted to trick. Much of the lab's stored trick had fueled the explosion, which left me and Kempthorne their only beacons in the dark. Great.

"Ah, there you are." Kempthorne stepped around a pile of steaming rubble and focused on straightening his cuffs, oblivious to Kage swinging the gun on him.

"Kempthorne!"

He blinked, and sighed. "How terribly predictable." The cut above his eye had dried, but he'd smudged the blood on his face. If it weren't for those small wounds, he might've looked no more ruffled than had he dropped by for a chat.

"H-How are you here?" Kage stammered. "They should have detained you. You can't— Did you kill them?!"

"Calm down." He rolled his eyes and lifted his hands, wristwatch glinting. "I haven't killed anyone... lately." He made a show of glancing over his shoulder and then back at Kage. "What is it you want, Kage? To take us in, to kill us? And where does that get you? A pat on the back and a pay raise? While Dom and I will be incarcerated like animals."

"You're dangerous."

Kempthorne's eyebrows lifted. "So is a man with a gun."

"Annie didn't deserve... that." Kage looked at me, the accusation clear. He might have cared for me, but he blamed me for Annie too. Somebody had to pay, and in his head, that was us. He could deliver us to his bosses and wipe his hands of everything, feeling as though he'd done a good thing.

"Neither did Robin." Kempthorne narrowed his eyes, fixing Kage in his sights. Behind Kage, the shadows swelled and pulsed. Kage was no longer the most dangerous thing here. "We're here to stop the man who killed them. Arresting me or Dom doesn't change the fact Montgomery is still out there, arguably even more dangerous now he knows he's being hunted."

"How do I know you're not working with Montgomery?" Kage said. "You bought artifacts from the same auctions, you met with him, had lunch with him. Do you treat all your enemies to lunch?"

He'd had lunch with Montgomery?! When?!

"Ask Charles Renick," Kempthorne said.

"Renick's dead." Kage's eyes widened, the realization hitting home. He was smart, but sometimes slow. Of course, he didn't know Renick had been trafficking latents, and even if he did, he wouldn't care. Renick was dead and Kempthorne had just hinted at killing him.

Kage had his gun and all his attention glued to

Kempthorne. With him distracted, I snuck a step closer to my deck on the ground.

"Consider this," Kempthorne began. "I will stop at nothing to bring down Montgomery. Things will not end well for anyone who puts themselves in my way."

Kage snorted. His aim wavered, just a fraction. But it was enough. I dropped and snatched my cards into my cuffed hands. Kempthorne's trick flashed. Kage's gun fired with a startling bang, then clattered to the ground. Charging the deck, I straightened to find Kage and Kempthorne standing still, staring at the rippling black cloud towering over us all.

"What the—" Kage began.

"*Run,*" Kempthorne barked.

Running in cuffs wasn't as easy as it looked. I darted behind Kempthorne with Kage ahead of us, but stumbled over loose rubble and almost went down, losing precious seconds. Kempthorne doubled back and with a flash of light and heat from his hand at my wrist, the cuffs fell away. He caught my gaze. The shadows were coming. I could feel their heavy weight at my back, like a thousand eyes all watching at once. The fear on Kempthorne's face said he knew it too. We'd had the Aston before, managed to outrun them. How were we going to outrun them this time?

They wanted Kempthorne—the *boy who was made*—because of his trick. If we could distract them somehow with a larger target, that might buy us enough time to shake them off.

The fire had died down, leaving mounds of rubble and twisted metal. A low-level psychic burn throbbed deep within the building's foundations—the collective trauma from countless trapped latents tortured over time. That could be enough to throw the shadows off our scent, if we went deeper, closer to the heart of the building's trauma.

"We need to get inside," I said.

Kempthorne recoiled, sharing a knowing look with Kage. They'd been here before, together. Something had happened then, something that spooked Kempthorne more than it did Kage. It was too bloody late to worry about it now.

"We get inside and lose the shadows in the building's god-awful resonance," I said.

"What are they?" Kage asked.

A surge of icy air and brittle tension blasted over us. "Go!" I shoved at Kempthorne, jolting him into motion, and followed them through a doorway into the section of lab that remained standing. Darkness swallowed us. Something was alight farther ahead—its warm light drew all three of us forward. What if I was wrong? What if we'd just walked into a dead end? No, it would work. Our tricks would disappear in the background psychic throb. It had to work.

And then the lab's gut-clenching bottomless pit of despair grabbed hold, trying to yank out my consciousness. I gasped and stumbled into the corridor wall. A psychic shock snapped through me like a jolt of electricity. A hundred voices screamed in my ears. The lab boiled with hidden trauma. Yanking my hand back, I breathed.

I could keep it together—I had to keep it together.

But below the ground... not far below... power tremored.

This was a weak spot, just like Kempthorne had said. A place where the source was close to the surface.

Kage ranted, demanding someone tell him what was going on. His bitching helped ground me in the now and drag me back from the past.

He looked half pissed off that he hadn't yet arrested either of us, and part terrified of the things moving in the dark. "Dom—what are those things?"

Yeah, I'd get right on that when my brain didn't feel as though it was melting out of my ears.

"I'm not going another step until someone tells me what's happening!"

Kempthorne threw him a withering glare and pushed off the opposite wall. "Dom, how are you holding up?" he asked, turning to me and ignoring the twitchy American. "The resonance is excruciating here."

"I got a handle on it." And I'd have one hell of a headache, once we got out of this.

He reached for me, like he always had, and when his hand rested gently on my arm, some of the exhaustion of holding myself together dissipated—seeping into him. Deep lines cut into his features, betraying the strain of taking the psychic weight from me.

"What is happening?" Kage snarled.

"They're shadows— Dead latents stirred up by..." I waved my hands. "*Everything.*"

"By the source," Kempthorne added. "The source is imbalanced, probably because of Montgomery's meddling with it."

"What?" He was clearly having a hard time with all of this. I might have sympathized if he hadn't threatened to shoot me.

"Ghosts," I said with a shrug. "With a real hunger for trick."

"Ghosts, shadows, dead latents?" He backed away from us, glancing about him as though only now realizing he was stuck in the basement of a secret lab with two latents who didn't like him and some angry ghosts. "This is insane."

"No more insane than my fingers glowing with psychic energy."

"I can't be here with you. You both need to come with me. Now. Come quietly and it will be easier on you."

I screwed up my face. "Think I'll pass, mate."

"Whether it's now or later, you will be caught. At least if it's me I can try and protect you—"

"You can probably leave," Kempthorne suggested. "I doubt the shadows will—"

The door crashed in. Darkness washed over the walls. Kage whirled, and then he was gone, swallowed inside the surging wave. I'd seen him fall to his knees, his mouth open in a silent scream, but all the screams had started up in my head again and I couldn't hear his.

Kempthorne hauled me into a run and shoved me through a doorway. Down was probably bad, but the stairs ahead were the only option. We took them fast, and with a single card charged, I lit the way.

Had they killed Kage?

Could shadows do that if he wasn't a latent?

We burst into an eerily untouched room full of examination tables and white plastic curtains. Kempthorne slammed the thick metal door behind us, and a hiss of air suggested we were now hermetically sealed inside.

"Don't touch the tables." Kempthorne ran a trembling

hand through his hair. "Or anything." His fraught gaze skipped from table to table. "Just... don't touch a bloody thing."

I didn't plan to. It was enough to be close to them, to hear their writhing madness trying to claw toward us. Kempthorne staggered, his trick sparking. This was bad. If he couldn't remain stable, what chance did I have?

"What is this place?"

"This place"—Montgomery emerged from behind a curtain, wearing matching brown trousers and a sweater, like everyone's favorite uncle—"my dear boys, is where gods are made." His eyes turned molten, mixed with threads of black and gold, and Thomas Montgomery's dark trick *pulsed*.

25

D^{om}

Kempthorne sizzled beside me, reacting to Montgomery or the maddening psychic trauma we'd been locked inside with.

"I really wouldn't get too excited, Alexander," Montgomery said, maneuvering around the examination tables. "As you've seen, the shadows are irritable and any surge in power will lure them right to us. To say little of the unstable source beneath our feet."

Then he knew what he was doing was damaging the source, putting everything out of balance. Of course he did, and he didn't care.

"Where are the latents?" Kempthorne snarled. "Your experiments. What have you done with them?"

"Moved on. Safe. Dear boy, you surely don't believe

I'm hurting them? Wherever did you get that idea?" He somehow looked both amused and evil.

"Aren't you?" I asked, recalling how I'd woken on a table like the ones surrounding us, drained. The memories were muddled, but not the sensation of having my trick syphoned off.

"Goodness no! It seems we've had something of a misunderstanding." He chuckled. "I'm not hurting anyone. I'm *freeing* them."

"You tied me to a table and drained my trick." I started forward, without having a plan beyond punching the sickly-nice smile off the prick's face.

Kempthorne's arm flew out, blocking me.

Montgomery frowned as though I was the stupid one who couldn't understand his genius. I expected crap from him, but not from Kempthorne. "Give me one good reason why I can't deck the tit right now," I told him.

"This is not the place to draw the trick," Kempthorne said, sounding reasonable and restrained. "Isn't that right, Thomas?"

"It's not advisable," Montgomery agreed. "Since the source is unstable beneath our feet, and considering how powerful the three of us are, if we were to further disrupt it, we might cause a surge, killing any weaker latents who happened to be caught in its impact radius. And then of course, there are the shadows."

"If you're helping latents, why are the shadows here at all?"

"Ah yes, the shadows. An unfortunate side effect. The source's defense mechanism."

"An unfortunate side effect that just killed an LOA agent."

"Regrettably, Mr Mitchell isn't dead," Montgomery explained. "Just overwhelmed. The shadows can't harm non-latents. He'll be right as rain in an hour or so."

Ugh, this dick was getting on my nerves. He'd drained latents for his own boost in power, he'd killed people, tried to render me unstable with a dirty artifact, and when that hadn't worked, he'd trapped me in Wordsworth and bled my trick dry over and over. "What is this? Why are we even talking to him?" I asked Kempthorne. "We should be taking him out."

The tell-tale muscle in Kempthorne's cheek fluttered. He stared at Montgomery, eyes narrowed, unblinking. But something wasn't right. We'd come here to stop the man who stood just across the room from us. So why weren't we doing that? "Kempthorne?"

"I'm afraid, John, we've been quite wrong," he said.

"What?"

Montgomery's winning smile grew. Any time he smiled, bad things happened, so what was going on here?

"Indeed," Montgomery said. "Isn't it better for us all to stop fighting and embrace the gifts we've been given? Don't you agree, John?"

"Fuck off."

"Ah, but you're being stubborn, and not listening. It's hardly your fault when all your life you've been told you're something lesser. Alexander understands. He always was a good boy. For the most part. He did take some persuading, but we got there in the end, didn't we, Alex?"

"I'm not sure I understand," Kempthorne admitted.

"Your parents were visionaries, but *you* were the

breakthrough. Without you"—Montgomery spread his hands—"none of this would be possible."

"Kempthorne?" I said. He didn't move. But he had that obsessive look in his eyes. "Don't listen to him. He's trying to get in your head."

"Oh, John, I don't need to try to do anything." He smiled fondly at Kempthorne. "Alex and I have always been close. So close, in fact, we could be family."

"You're not my family." Kempthorne seethed and his trick sparked so violently, I stepped back. What if he spiralled? Could I talk him down? When he lit up, he burned like a star. I couldn't handle all that.

"Kempthorne?" I swallowed. "Easy. All right?"

"A demonstration, perhaps?"

"You!" I pointed at Montgomery. "You need to shut the fuck up. Kempthorne... don't listen to him. Look at me."

But he *was* listening to the old twat. He hadn't looked at me. Trick dripped from his fingers. His cheek pulsed.

"Penny, dear? It's time you made your debut."

A girl emerged from behind a curtain. Her blonde hair had been cropped short since seeing her in my Wordsworth dreams. Penny Montgomery. But what was she doing here now? I'd known her as the mid-teen, sweet girl who wore strappy sandals and had gotten caught up in all this by accident. Penny was the same now, but also different. Taller, thinner, older. She wore cropped trousers and a patched hoodie. When she turned her gaze to me, the spark had vanished from her sunken eyes.

"I'm sorry, Dom."

Kempthorne's trick sizzled tighter. He'd seen something in her. Something only he could see. Something that tripped him into high alert. Power. It was every-where. Simmering off him, but off Penny too. I didn't need his gifts to be able to see it—I felt it thinning the air, making it crackle. Shit, something had to give, and when it did, anyone nearby was going to get hurt.

"Montgomery isn't a friend." I waved Penny over. "We'll get you out of here."

She tipped her face to Montgomery. "I don't want to hurt him."

"It will be the way of things now. Everyone is either with us or against us, my dear. Enemy or ally."

"Dom," Kempthorne said under his breath. "This is a dire situation that we need to extract ourselves from with minimal psychic disturbance." His gaze flicked to me. Trick gleamed in his eyes.

"What the fuck is going on?"

The worry I saw on his face chilled my blood, not because of any fear, but the resignation in it. "Mont-gomery wasn't draining trick for himself. He's been pouring it *into* latents. He's not only making himself a god. He's making them all gods."

"What?"

He breathed in. Then laid his hands on my shoulders and *pulled*. "Forgive me."

26

Dom

I touched my head, hoping to ease its thumping, then frowned at my sumptuous living room surroundings. I'd woken on the sofa, and my body felt as though I'd downed a bottle of Kempthorne's posh whiskey, but there was no evidence of getting wasted, no empty bottles or toppled glasses. Just one hell of a hangover.

This wasn't right. How was I in Ravenscourt?

I sat up, the room spun, and I groaned. If I could think around the pain... I'd been on the LOA mission with Kage and Kempthorne, then it had all gone tits up. The bomb. Shadows had attacked. Montgomery had been there. Kempthorne had—

"That fucking arsehole!" I shot to my feet and

fumbled my phone from my back pocket, then gagged and tried not to throw up as the room spun some more.

"Ah, you're awake." Jordan offered a warm smile and loitered in the doorway. "Would you like some tea?"

"Tea? No. Wait... Where's Kempthorne?" Even as I asked, I'd dialed his phone. It didn't ring and went straight to answerphone.

"He opted not to return in the car with you," Jordan said matter-of-factly.

"He what?"

"You were somewhat intoxicated—"

"I *wasn't* intoxicated," I growled. "I was assaulted. Where is he?"

"I'm afraid I don't know."

I shoved by him and into the hallway. "What did he say, Jordan? Exactly?"

"That I was to get you home and ensure you were comfortable."

"Kempthorne!" I called, in case he was hiding somewhere, like his murder wall room. Ravenscourt's corridors and rooms swallowed my voice. "Kempthorne! You dick!" I caught Jordan's thin expression as he followed me dutifully. "Sorry. About the language."

"Oh, it's quite all right. I've called him a few choice words in my time. Alex can be difficult."

I snorted a laugh, despite the circumstances. Difficult was putting it mildly. He'd *absorbed* some of my trick and dumped my arse into a car like a date who couldn't handle his drink. *Christ.* I tried calling him again and left a colorful message, making it clear he had better call me back and explain himself, or better yet, explain to my face why he'd rendered me fucking helpless in front of Montgomery and Penny and then kicked me to the curb.

Satisfied he wasn't hiding in his murder wall room—now horribly sparse since the IRL had taken the research—or anywhere else in the house, I returned to the kitchen to find Jordan making a pot of tea on a tray as though we were stuck in the nineteenth century. He'd laid out a spread of biscuits on a plate that matched the teacups, and of course, there were the custard creams.

I slumped on a stool at the breakfast bar, feeling the weight of *everything*. If Robin were here, she'd tell me how logically everything was going to be all right.

My anger had boiled dry, leaving me empty and cold. "Was Kempthorne with anyone else last night when he dumped my arse?" I asked Jordan.

"Oh yes, the Montgomerys."

"The Montgomerys? You say that like it's a thing."

"Well, Mr Montgomery was a regular visitor of the Ravenscourt estate for a long time. Not so much since the tragedy took Alex's parents. But I am aware of the man and the girl I assume was his niece?"

"Granddaughter, maybe. What's the deal with him?"

Jordan decided that moment was the perfect time to begin tidying. "Well, I'm not sure it's my place to say."

"Alex could be in danger."

That stopped him fussing. He set down the cups he'd been stacking. "Thomas Montgomery was instrumental in the Kempthornes' early work, as far as I understand it. He was here, in fact, the day Charlotte Kempthorne went missing. Terrible affair."

I picked up a custard cream and attempted to act as

though none of this information was new. "He was here *that same day*?"

"She was due back from Scotland, but never returned." He turned and levelled his steel-eyed gaze on me. "I remember because Alexander was sick that night and Thomas kindly stayed with him."

How *kind* of him. Jordan's tone made it clear he had his suspicions about how *kind* Montgomery was.

"Hm." I dipped the custard cream into my tiny china cup of tea, probably performing some kind of social no-no, but I hardly cared, then turned over the new information in my head as I devoured the biscuit. The knife and Montgomery being at Ravenscourt on that same day? That wasn't a coincidence. Maybe I was clutching at straws, but put Montgomery together with that wretched knife, and bad shit happened, like Robin, and like Charlotte Kempthorne dying in the study. "What's Alex's relationship been like with Thomas Montgomery over the years?"

"I don't recall them crossing paths much. Mr Montgomery mostly met with the Kempthornes at their academy. He rarely had dealings with Alexander, personally. Who was, of course, just a boy then. They wouldn't have had much reason to converse beyond pleasantries."

The academy again. The same academy Oliva Barnes had trained at. The same academy Kempthorne had attended. I wasn't buying the whole—just coincidence— not anymore. That academy had been bad news.

"Were you surprised to see Thomas Montgomery last night?"

"I was actually, yes. And I daresay, surprised Alexander remained with him while I brought you home.

Alex seemed rather distracted, if I'm honest, John. I do hope he's all right."

What was Kempthorne doing? He obviously had some crazy-stupid plan and in his infinite upper-class wisdom thought he could remove me from harm without giving me a bloody say in it. He and I were going to have words about that, once I got him back.

He'd said, before draining me, that we'd been wrong, that Montgomery was feeding trick *into* latents, not taking it. But Montgomery had taken mine when I'd been strapped to one of those tables. So it wasn't all about giving.

This place, my dear boys, is where gods are made.

He wasn't making himself a god; he was making an army of them. Draining some latents, like me, draining the source, and pouring it back into those he'd selected as candidates. Pliable. Gullible. Vulnerable. Kids like Max, like Penny. Latents who wouldn't be missed. Christ, had Renick been selling them to him too?

Kempthorne had put all of the pieces together. He must have. And faced with all that, and the powered-up Montgomery and Penny, he'd knee-jerked and taken me out of the game.

"Thanks," I told Jordan as I dialed Gina's number on my phone. "For the tea, and for bringing me here."

"You're welcome, John. I hope you don't mind me saying, but I'm rather pleased you're still here. I know Alexander can be difficult. But I've rarely seen him as happy as he's been these last few months, and with Robin's death, he needs a steadying force in his life. Someone he can't push away, someone he can rely on."

He smiled fondly, and just like with Kempthorne, I saw the same intelligent sparkle in Jordan's eyes.

"Er... Thanks."

"I'll be seeing to the fireplaces. Call if you need me."

He left the kitchen. Jordan was not to be underestimated. He knew a lot more than he let on.

"Hey, Dom, you good?" Gina answered.

Hearing her voice did something to my heart—made it ache. I sighed and slumped against the counter. "No," I admitted. "Listen, I know you're supposed to be away and stuff, and I get it, but I really need your help, G." The more I spoke, the more I needed to get the words out. "I'm out of my depth here and without Robin— Shit, Gina, I can't do this alone."

"Do what? Slow down. Where's Kempthorne?"

"Montgomery has him."

"What? How?"

"Kempthorne has some mystery plan he hasn't told anyone about. His usual dick move, but G—" I dragged a hand down my face. "We've been good. Him and me, I mean. Really good. And he just... Last night, he absorbed my trick, knocked me out." He'd fucked me over. I'd thought he was different to Sawyer. I'd thought... He'd made me feel like I wasn't a fuck up or a failure, or something to be used over and over again. And then, he literally fucked me and fucked off. "Gina—" The rest of it all got stuck in my throat.

"Oh-my-god-Imma-gonna kick his perfectly tailored arse—"

"This sucks. I'm sorry." It came out as a croaked whisper.

"Dom, this isn't your fault. He's an epic dick. I'm coming back. I'll be on the next train to London."

Relief lifted some of the lead locked around my heart. "I'm at Ravenscourt... and thanks."

"Hey, we've got this."

"Yeah." I hung up and stared at my phone, waiting for Kempthorne to call, but the screen stayed blank.

He'd absorbed my trick in an attempt to protect me. I tried to believe that. I had to because the alternative, that he'd switched sides, was unthinkable. But if there was a tiny chance he *had* switched sides, then Kage had been right all along and we were all in trouble. Montgomery was powerful and so was Kempthorne. And if the pair of them decided they were turning latents into gods, this went further than London. It could change everything, forever. It could start a war.

Jordan left to collect Gina from Paddington Station, so I had all of Ravenscourt to myself. The house had a good soul. I could feel the warmth in its walls as I took myself on a tour. Most of the artwork was of landscapes, but in one of the rooms I spotted a portrait of the late Mrs Kempthorne. Alex definitely had her crystal-blue eyes. Despite her small smile, her eyes were all ice.

With a mug of coffee warming my hands, I wandered from room to room, soaking up the feel of the place. Kempthorne absorbing my trick had left me rattly and anxious and my trick about as powerful as a candle flame. Breathing in Ravenscourt helped soothe some of the dissonance.

Until I got to the study.

The curtain had been pulled away from the door and the key was in the lock—a big old skeleton key that was probably as old as the house. Wasn't the door meant to be locked at all times?

I stared at the door's thick oak panels. The room behind throbbed like a heartbeat. Kempthorne had said the IRL had taken everything, which meant everything behind this door had gone too. But it didn't feel like it had gone.

Behind that door, Alexander had killed his sister.

Behind that door, Alex had been used like a rat in a maze. Poked and prodded, flooded, tested, experimented on, *made*.

Montgomery had been here that day, with the knife. That was no fucking coincidence. Alex had been holding the knife, but Montgomery had been the one to kill Charlotte, I was damn-near certain.

There was one way to know, and that was to go out in the field and pick up the knife. The artifact was beyond dirty—on another level of hideous—but inside all of that madness, it cradled the truth about that night. I wasn't ready for that, not in the jittery state I was in. But I did have another way to get to the truth.

I sipped my coffee and stared at the door some more, as though it had all the answers.

Maybe it did...

I set my coffee down on a nearby windowsill, grasped the door key in my left hand, and turned. The mechanism clunked over. Now it was definitely unlocked. There was nothing left to stop me from going inside.

I opened the door.

Light from the hallway fanned across the sparse floor. The IRL *had* taken everything, including the books from the shelves and the awful examination table. Much of the horrible gut-sickening throb of power had vanished with those artifacts. But not all. Some of it had leached into the walls.

I flicked the light on. The bulb buzzed.

Had the chatty shadow vanished or was it still here, tied to the room, not the artifacts?

I didn't *feel* any presence, just the background throb from psychic stains that would probably never fade.

What had I expected? A ghost hiding in the corner? A shadow to talk to? Maybe I was losing my mind, just like most latents. I huffed a laugh at myself, turned and —*"John"*—froze. Light still streamed in from the hallway, the walls throbbed like before, but I was no longer alone.

An icy breath touched my neck.

The door was just a few steps away. If I needed to, I could run. Kempthorne had said it never left this room.

Was the bulb's buzzing getting louder?

"John." Definitely beside my ear. I breathed. Didn't move. Waited and listened. It hadn't attacked, not yet. Maybe it would; maybe this was a stupid idea.

Montgomery had said we should stop fighting, and I wouldn't normally listen to psychos, but I'd said the same to Kempthorne. The shadows made it bloody hard to reason with them, but this one... This one seemed different. And if they were the ghosts of dead latents, maybe the ghost in Kempthorne's study remembered things. Maybe it was here because it had something it wanted to say.

"I'm here," I told it, sounding like an idiot talking to an empty room.

The lightbulb buzzed louder and popped. Shadows rushed in—just normal ones. The door was open, the light from the hall just a few steps away. Everything was fine. Nothing I couldn't handle.

"Are you..." I licked my lips. *Might as well go all in.* "Are you Charlotte?"

"John," the voice said.

"I'm going to need a bit more than that." I should have asked Jordan for a Ouija board. There was bound to be one somewhere in the house.

"Alex."

A new name, so the shadow could switch things up. "He's not here. He doesn't like people coming in here. Why is that?"

"Knife."

"Not here either." Which was definitely a good thing. I turned my head an inch and got a look at *something*—a hazy blur, like heat haze on a summer's day, but this haze was smoky, made of darkness. It had form, separating it from the rest of the everyday shadows, but no distinguishing features. Maybe, if there wasn't any light...

The door slammed shut.

The lightbulb burst.

Thick darkness rushed it.

I lunged for the door handle, rattled it, but the door stayed stuck. Shit, shit, shit... Okay. This was fine. I was out of trick; it wouldn't hurt me.

"Murder." The word spilled into my ear and ran icy fingertips down my spine. The door still wouldn't budge.

I plastered myself close to it, sensing the shadow breathing down the back of my neck.

"Montgomery?" I whispered. "Was he here? Was it him?"

Each of its ragged breaths hissed against my neck, and each breath spilled more ice into my veins. I couldn't have moved even if the door was unlocked. My trick, spent as it was, did little more than give me pins and needles in my fingers. "Alex blames himself..." I said. "All this time, he blamed himself, but he wasn't alone that day, was he? You came home early. You found Montgomery and Alex in here, and whatever you saw, Montgomery killed you for it, with that knife."

I had to be right. I'd seen half of it in the coin. I knew Kempthorne—knew he was capable of some vicious shit —but he had no reason to kill his sister, despite what he believed.

"Yes."

I'd known it, but to hear it meant *everything*. Alex hadn't killed his sister. He'd carried the weight of her death all these years, but it wasn't his fault. He hated himself, I saw it in his eyes, every time he spoke of his past. He hated what he'd done. He had to know he was innocent. I had to tell him.

"You have to help me." I didn't even know what I was asking, but nobody had talked with a shadow before, and I needed something to come from it. I needed a break, a win. "Montgomery is making gods out of latents, the balance is fucked, the source is out of whack. That's what the shadows are here for, isn't it?"

"Takes too much."

Montgomery. She had to mean Montgomery. "And you—the shadows want it back?"

"*Restore.*"

"Restore the balance." Okay, that made sense. Sort of. The trick was all about resonance and friction and power being out of balance. It just needed to be restored. Easier said than done. "How? How do we do that?"

"*Alex.*"

"Alex what? Alex can restore the balance? Alex knows how?" I tried to see her, to turn my head and get a glimpse of the young woman she'd been before Montgomery had cut her life short, but shadows weren't people anymore, and as soon as I focused on her shimmering outline, a surge of bitter cold blasted through me, ripping out all the heat in my body. I clutched the door handle, yanked, and the door jolted open.

I couldn't run out of that room fast enough and didn't stop running until I'd found a bedroom on the other side of the house. I slammed the door shut behind me and dashed away from that, waiting for the ghost to follow. It didn't.

Gina found me an hour later, wrapped chin-deep in a quilt in the kitchen, shivering as though I'd been buried in ice.

"Oh, bloody hell." She dumped her bag to the floor.

"No, it's not the Kempthorne t-thing..." I stammered. Although, maybe it was the Kempthorne thing, a little bit. "I spoke to a shadow—those ghost-like things that want Kempthorne so badly they keep stalking me on the tube?" Did it sound as insane out loud as it had in my head? "I know why they want him. I think..." And this was where it got difficult. "I think he means to do something stupid, G. He's full of power, like nothing I've ever seen, and I think he means to kill himself to save the rest of us, to restore and reset the balance."

She blinked and the shock on her face thawed a little. "I'll put the kettle on and you're gonna tell me all about it."

It had become clear, fighting Thomas Montgomery was no longer an option, assuming it ever had been. He bristled with power, two-fold mine. If Dom had tried to swing for him, like he'd wanted to in the lab, Montgomery would have roasted him with a glance. So while Dom was in all likelihood rather unhappy with me for taking him out of play, he was, at least, alive.

And so was I. Surprisingly.

"You see," Montgomery continued. We walked the empty corridors of an abandoned facility just like the one he'd recently sacrificed to shake the LOA off his tail and to lure me in close. We'd driven here after ensuring Dom was safe and dropping Penny off at Montgomery's house. "Latents were not made to be used," he said. "We've evolved, and it's time we took our place at the top of the food chain as apex predators."

"Indeed." He appeared to believe my change of heart, for now, but I'd be tested, and soon. Until then, Montgomery was giving me the tour of one of his newer facilities. The man himself brimmed with pride, able to discuss his masterplan with someone who would understand all the layers.

"I'm so glad we could come to this point in both our lives, Alex," he said. "It seemed, for a while, you were going to be as stubborn as your father."

This man, my enemy, was entangled with my past in ways that were still unfolding. Remembering Dom's information regarding the gift of the pen from my mother to Montgomery, I said, "I seem to recall my mother was fond of you."

"Oh yes, a wonderful woman, a visionary really." While my mother had exhibited questionable ethics and morals, she was exceptional when it came to getting what she wanted from others. Dom would call it manipulation. I called it adapting. I'd learned that from her, alongside a deep mistrust of intimacy.

"Such a shame they had to leave us so soon." Montgomery appeared genuine, but the man had multiple layers of meaning in his easy smiles and twinkling eyes. It takes a liar to know a liar. And while he wasn't lying outright, there was a great deal he wasn't telling me.

So here we were, in a shiny new laboratory, yet to be stained by psychic energy. Montgomery explained how he planned to expand his operation beyond Wordsworth to multiple sites across the UK. The UK government made it clear they didn't care what he did with the latents in his care, just so long as Thomas Montgomery got them off the streets. Of course, they also had no idea Montgomery himself was a latent who was out for more blood and power than anyone had realized, including me.

His plans had merit.

I certainly wasn't immune to dreams of absolute power, especially now I'd had my wings clipped by the IRL.

Power was a siren song—one I knew well. And while my privileged life meant I'd been cushioned from the worst most latents experienced in society on a daily basis, I had witnessed it in the likes of Dom's life. What if latents rose up and took the power they'd all been denied? Who was to say that was wrong?

"Your father refused to see the potential in you. At least your mother was more reasonable," Montgomery went on. "From the lackluster latent boy you were to the impressive specimen you are today. She and I spent many an evening discussing your development. Why, I hope you don't mind my saying, I consider you like a son. You were our beginning."

Decades in the public eye meant I knew how to keep my smile, even as the will behind it vanished. "Speaking of family, did Penny voluntarily sign up for your... evolution?"

"Penny, the dear thing. She's one of my more promising acolytes. It will be quite fitting. Your presence here as the alpha experiment, and hers as the gamma." He chuckled, enjoying the big reveal, finally able to share the truth of his life's work with someone who wouldn't throw him in prison.

"What happened to the betas?"

Montgomery laughed softly. "All roads worth taking have potholes along the way."

I thought of all those empty examination tables and the silent screams locked inside them. Some latents hadn't survived his experiments. And nobody had missed them. He really didn't care at all. I wasn't even sure if he was capable of caring. Countless latents had died in the making of his next generation. And many more would die in the days to come, if he wasn't stopped.

Latents were not meant to be gods. No human being was. Unfortunately, that didn't stop some from trying: my mother, Olivia, Montgomery. They'd all manipulated the trick, disturbed the source, stirred up the shadows, and now everything was out of balance.

It had to end.

The balance had to be restored.

"What was your plan for Dom?" I asked. We continued to walk the empty corridor. Lights flicked on ahead of us and blinked out behind.

"Initially, to warn him off—then he became rather persistent, and his sort never do give up, do they. Considering his training and his burgeoning trick, I thought I'd rather put him to use and, of course, use him as leverage over you. I do hope there are no hard feelings between us, Alex." He said all that as though using Dom was reasonable.

"Of course not. I understand. You know, this is all very impressive." I swallowed the acid in my throat. "But I'd really like to see the epicenter of all this. The heart of it all."

"Hm." Montgomery's pace slowed, then stopped. He looked up and studied my face. "How very transparent of you, Alex." He still smiled, but it had thinned, turning sharp.

"I merely want to—"

"Do not take me for a fool, Alexander. You are here, and that is enough for now. But trust must be earned."

I let my fake smile fall away. "You're a liar and a killer but then, so am I. I appreciate what you're undertaking. It's remarkable, really." And that was no lie.

"Well then, from one liar and killer to another, perhaps there may be a seat at my side when the time comes, but I am not of a mind to trust you until you have proven your commitment to the cause. And knowing you, as I do, dear boy, that will not be anytime soon." He smiled, as though he'd delivered good news, and continued on down the corridor.

Briefly, I considered throwing trick at the man, but he'd absorb it and it wouldn't stop the plan he already had in motion.

I had to find the heart of his operation, and as he called my name to follow him through the empty lab, I summoned to mind my murder wall and its map of London. The answer was already there, staring back among the pins and threads, I just had to find it.

28

D^{om}

Our Ravenscourt murder wall was a pathetic echo of Kempthorne's. We had fifteen multi-colored sticky notes, some frayed string, a few photos I'd printed off the Internet, and a whole lot of gaps.

"We can't do this without Kempthorne's brain."

"Pfft." Gina snorted then grabbed a tourist's map of London that had quirky cartoon pictures of the tourist hotspots, like the Tower and the museums, and pinned that to the wall too. "Between us we totally have more smarts than him. He doesn't know *everything*."

He kinda did. He'd made it his life's work to study latents in London and his parents' work. Montgomery had been a huge part of that, a part Kempthorne hadn't always been able to see clearly. But he was there, tangled up with it all somehow.

I tried Kempthorne's phone again—straight to answerphone. I was going to keep trying. He needed to know Montgomery had killed his sister. It was important. More important than maybe anything else we were looking at on our wall. I'd know exactly how important if I went outside and found the knife…

"Montgomery and Kempthorne's mum were close, right?" I asked. "They experimented on Alex for their own gain, and they did it in the study—they flooded him, made him powerful, and that was where it all started. Now, Montgomery is making latents like Alex, but on an industrial scale, using so-called latent prisons like Wordsworth to cherry-pick his candidates." I shuddered at the memories. "He's got other labs all over. He's expanding, and it won't be long before he has an army of pissed off, easily manipulated, power-hungry latents."

"Yeah… we need to stop him before it gets that far."

"The source is out of balance, the shadows are all losing their shit, and we're on our own."

"Except maybe Kempthorne is on the inside trying to figure this out too?"

"Maybe," I said. "Or maybe he's having afternoon tea with Montgomery."

She glared. "You don't really think he's flipped to the dark side?"

"Nah…" I didn't. Did I? No. I knew him. He was slippery and sneaky but he wasn't a bad guy… unless Montgomery had something like the knife to hold over him. But that was outside, in the field. "He's more than capable." I looked out of the window. On some deeper latent level, I could feel the knife's wicked thrum. It wanted to be found, wanted me to pick it up and hear all its secrets, including Kempthorne's. It would probably kill me though, which made a good argument for why not to fuck with it.

"Dom?"

"Huh?"

"I asked if you were okay?"

"Me? Yeah, 'course." I sounded fine, but she knew me too well and her glare didn't ease off. "I dunno... maybe not." I sighed and fell into a chair alongside the long dining table and the quirky map of London. "I've gone a few rounds and I don't know if I can take another knock. Kempthorne—me and him... it was good, yah know?" Her soft, knowing smile made my twisting inside *worse*, not better. "Good like I don't get. I mean, he's Kempthorne, and then there's me? Rough around the edges East End boy? He was gonna take me to dinner." I hiccupped, words choking me. "It wasn't even about the dinner. He bought fish and chips somewhere by the sea and it was the best not-date of my damn life... I don't deserve it."

She snorted and frowned. "That's your arsehole dad talkin'. Kempthorne would be the first to tell you you're awesome. He's a wreck, we all know it, but around you, he's less of a wreck. You're a good guy, Dom. You make *him* good. He's lucky to have you and if he doesn't know that, then he doesn't deserve you. That's why he wants to take you to dinner. Because he cares. Not because you're some curiosity of his."

"I dunno." She was sweet. But did he really care? I'd trusted him. "He drained my trick. There's a line. He crossed it. If he cared at all, he wouldn't have done that—he knows how it fucks with me."

"Except he's Kempthorne, and his way of showing he cares is to do the opposite to the rest of us." She folded her arms and glared at our pitiful wall. "He bought you fish and chips?"

"Yeah. Then we stayed the night at a Premier Inn."

"No way." She spluttered a laugh. "Kempthorne slept at a Premier Inn?"

"I was surprised he didn't burst into flames."

"Was there *just one bed*?" Her eyebrows lifted.

"No." I snorted.

"Please tell me the sex was mind-blowing. For science."

I laughed, which was exactly what she was aiming for. "Christ... Will you stop?"

Her eyes sparkled. "All that repressed sexual angst? I mean, c'mon, he's a beast in bed, right? Ropes and whips. He's definitely into all that."

"We didn't..." Heat warmed my face. "Not then."

She grinned. "But you have! I knew it. Finally, you tapped *that*. The tension between you two has been off-the-charts for months. Even Robin said enough was enough..." She sobered. "Well... anyway... I'm glad. Really. And I know he's a dick, but you two together are... I dunno... It makes me feel like good stuff does happen, yah know? And we really need the good stuff right now. Don't let him push you away, because he will."

I nodded. She made a lot of sense. "Yeah, I know."

"So, where's Kage in this sexy love triangle?"

I narrowed my eyes playfully. She just had to go there. "Not answering his phone. He got a blast of shadow right after trying to arrest us for good ol' U-S-of-A or something. Montgomery said he'd be all right but I don't think we'll be seeing Kage again anytime soon."

"He's pretty *and* complicated. Shame he's evil."

"He's not *evil*. He just got caught up in all this and got burned." I'd try to call him again soon. We had a lot of bad water under the bridge between us, but I didn't want to see him hurt.

My gaze flicked back to a picture of Wordsworth I'd pinned to the murder wall, dragging my memories with it. Robin had marked the old map with all the places the surge had killed latents. I remembered some of them, and grabbing a Sharpie, I dotted our cartoon map with the same, wishing Robin were here to make sure I didn't screw it up. She'd have hidden the biscuits by now, knowing I'd have eaten them all. Christ, I missed her.

The dots didn't all line up, but most did encircle Wordsworth. I stepped back, trying to get an overall feel for what we were in the middle of. Wordsworth was right in the middle. It all came back to that godforsaken shithole.

Wordsworth was close to the source; I'd felt its powerful, rushing beat beneath me when I'd been off-my-head on meds. Wordsworth had its own horrible heartbeat, as though it was alive, like Ravenscourt, but darker.

"I can't shake the feeling Wordsworth means something more in all this," I muttered.

Montgomery had been comfortable there. Comfortable enough to shake my hand and drain me of trick. Comfortable enough to tell me who he was. Max's list had originated there...

Gina sat at the table, grabbed her laptop, and tapped

a few keys. "The building there today isn't the original one," she said, "although it incorporates parts of an older construction. Apparently there was an old hospital on the site. Most of it burned down in the nineties."

"And a plague pit under that?" I snorted, as a joke, hoping to hide how my skin crawled with bad memories.

"No, but... there was an academy there. Oh, shit."

"Wait—not *that* academy?" I leaned over her and took a look at the old 1970s photos. And sure enough, there they all were in their white overcoats. The same picture Kempthorne had had on his murder wall. Gina scrolled down and a picture appeared of the Doctor Kempthornes cutting the ribbon over the doors to the Latent Training Academy.

"Wordsworth is *the* academy," Gina said. "Well... part of it. The site is huge, but the academy was located in the east wing."

"That academy is where it all began, where Montgomery and the Kempthornes levelled up." I tapped the screen. "I knew that hell-hole was bad. I could feel it even before I got thrown in there. Whatever is going to go down, whatever Montgomery is planning, Wordsworth is at the heart of it. It has to be. The whole bloody place is riddled with psychic energy. It's in the walls, the floor... in the fucking air. It nearly drove me crazy. *And* its right over the source. A weak spot." Wordsworth was the center of Montgomery's web. "Gotcha, you bastard."

"Just a thought but, what happens if Montgomery gets Kempthorne there?" Gina asked. "That feels like maybe a really bad thing."

I had that same gut feeling too. What if Wordsworth was like the knife? A dirty artifact, only a solid building, a hundred times bigger? What if it made good latents go bad? What if it turned them into bad gods?

I had to know what Montgomery was really doing. I had to know what Charlotte Kempthorne had seen in the study between Alex and Montgomery that had gotten her killed. And the knife had the answers.

"Gina, I'm about to do something really, really stupid."

"Urm, okay?"

"But first, we need to ask Jordan if the Kempthornes own a gun."

29

D^{om}

"I'm not going to shoot you," Gina said.

We stood in the cold, in the field that rolled away from the back of Ravenscourt House. Mist had closed in, so it felt as though there was just me and Gina and nothing but miles and miles of damp silence. The antique rifle in my hand was a chunk of cold iron and polished wood. The kind of gun these old country estates always had rattling around their cupboards. "You probably won't have to."

"'Probably'?" She looked at the old rifle as though it was a shark about to leap from my hand and swallow her. "I can't."

I needed her to be able to do this. If things went wrong, she was my backup.

"The safety is on. I showed you how to flick it off, you remember?"

"Dom, don't make me do this."

"C'mon... Look. I trust you. You just have to keep it on me and if I lose my shit, pull the trigger."

"What if I kill you?" she whispered.

"You won't. Most untrained shooters deliberately miss. You'll just wing me. It's probably unnecessary anyway." Her eyes shimmered, brimming with tears. She might cry. Or throw up. "Just don't hit me in the balls." I smiled, hoping to see her smile, too, but she didn't.

"Oh my God, Dom! Don't joke!"

I grabbed her hand and shoved the rifle into it. "You've got this. It's gonna be fine. Probably."

"Stop saying 'probably.'" She sniffed. "And I hate you right now."

"Yeah, well, you'll hate me even more if I spiral and blow you and Ravenscourt and half of Surrey into tiny pieces. Trust me."

"I do." She sighed. "Kempthorne will kill me for helping you."

"Not as much as he's gonna kill me... But he isn't here, and that's on him." If he knew what I was about to, he'd drop his Plan C and race out here to stop me. He'd done it before. But not this time. No more rescues. This had to happen.

I plucked my phone from my pocket and hit redial. Straight to answerphone. Again. "Hey... you know that thing you said I should never do? Yeah, I'm doin' it, and it's your fault..." I bit my tongue. What if I died out here? What if these were my last words to him? "Shit. I just... You already have fifteen or something messages from me—some of them pretty er... well, I was pissed off, okay? I'm still pissed at you, you dick. But I want you to know, I guess, that... I don't blame you for pushing me away. It's always worked before, right? You push people away and they get to survive. Well, this is different. I don't want to be anywhere else." *Just with you.* I stopped walking and stood in the long wet grass. The knife was ahead. It called to me, tugging on my chest, on that latent part of me. "I'm about to do the stupid thing and if it all goes wrong, I want you to know, it's not your fault. None of it. You aren't responsible for parents who are dicks, or for a world that would have ruined you if you'd revealed who you were to save an agent who was your friend. I don't think you're a bad guy, Kempthorne—Alex. I just—" The fucking answerphone cut me off.

I puffed out a sigh and left the rest of that sentence in my head.

I just... I think maybe I love you, you pain in the arse.

Yeah, okay. It was a good thing he hadn't answered. It was way too soon to start throwing words like love around. Kempthorne would have laughed anyway.

I dropped my phone into my pocket and peered into the swirling mist. The knife's hot, sickly, beat washed over me like a fever. A few more steps and I'd be standing over it. I glanced back, at Gina holding the gun at her side. She'd kill me for this afterward. If she didn't kill me before.

I threw her a wave and she jerked a single finger back. "*Dickhead!*"

Yeah, she was all right. And probably the best friend I'd ever had. How many friends would shoot you if you asked them to? Or maybe that wasn't a good thing. Shit, I was stalling.

Another step brought me closer to the knife. The long grass hid it, but it was there, throbbing like an open wound. It felt alive. And it was angry. I couldn't blame it. "It's just you and me now, knife."

I knelt, parted the blades of wet grass, and there it was. Rust tinted its blade red. Or maybe that was Robin's blood. I swallowed, trying to moisten my suddenly dry throat. Now I knew what I was dealing with, knew its power, and knew it could fuck me up without even trying, I hesitated. I'd grabbed it before. Used it. But I'd been ignorant then, and desperate. The knife had gone easy on me.

It was different now. I knew what I wanted and the knife knew me.

At least my trick was half drained. I was hoping that meant I couldn't spiral, even if I lost control. But Gina was my backup should that happen.

"Here goes nothing." I breathed in, filled my lungs with wet, misty air, figured it was now or never, and scooped the dirty knife into my hand.

30

Alexander

A thick fog hung over London, drawing night in early. The Aston's headlights barely pierced the gloom as I swung into Wordsworth's parking lot. Streetlights haloed the space, and Wordsworth loomed, all grey concrete and aluminum windows. A shiver tracked down my spine. It always did when I approached the horrible place.

Montgomery had invited me here to review his studies, to show off his grand plans. Since I'd surrendered, giving myself to his cause so long as he kept Dom out of it, Thomas Montgomery had been the epitome of charm. It was all a ruse, of course. He wanted something. Something from me. I'd go along with it as long as he continued to talk. He couldn't know his time was finite.

Or perhaps he did, and he was waiting for me to show my hand.

Either way, it would be over soon.

I opened the car door, about to climb out, when my phone slipped from my pocket and clattered into the Aston's footwell. I'd turned it off, knowing Dom would call, and Gina. Jordan too. The IRL had undoubtedly tried to reach me, the press, Ravenscourt's estate manager, Robin's family with funeral arrangements...

If I turned the phone on, all of that would flood back in.

Wordsworth loomed through the windscreen. Montgomery was already inside, waiting.

Sighing through my nose, I picked up the phone, turned it on, and waited as countless notifications spilled down the screen.

IRL > *Click here to confirm app tracking...*

IRL > *URGENT. Complete these forms...*

Jordan > *The estate manager has asked...*

Dom > *You arsehole...*

Dom > *Pick up your phone...*

Dom > *You fukn drained me, u twat...*

Dom > *Answer the bloody phone or...*

Gina > *Call Dom...*

IRL > *DO NOT REPLY. This message confirms you are now registered...*

Becky (Ldn Tdy) > *Your story is about to break. Call me...*

I dragged a hand down my face and threw the phone onto the passenger seat. Nausea swam in my stomach.

The phone vibrated with every new notification, buzzing on the seat. Messages scrolled up the screen.

Becky (Ldn Tdy) > *It's bad. Tell your side now, Alex…*
Alert > *You have 8 answerphone messages*
Dom > *We need to talk…*
Dom > *Something happened. Call me back. Pls.*
Google Alert > *BREAKING NEWS Billionaire Alexander Kempthorne is a…*

I snorted. "Is a terrible person?" On and on the notifications spilled, until finally it all stopped, and the phone lay silent.

I closed the car door again, shutting myself inside the Aston's quiet bubble, and dropped my head back against the headrest. My life, everything I'd made it, was slipping through my fingers. I couldn't stop it and wasn't sure I wanted to.

Dom had called. Those answerphone messages were from him. *Something happened.* I swallowed, picked up the phone, and dialed the answering service.

"You have eight new messages. To listen to your messages, press one. To save your messages, press two. To delete all, press three. To review deleted messages, press four."

I knew what those messages contained. He'd rant at me, rightly so. Then switch tack. Because he was smart. If I heard his voice, I'd call him back. He'd say something pertinent, something undeniable, and I'd go back to him and nothing would change. I lifted my gaze to Wordsworth and knew…

It had to end.

I could end it.

I hit 3.

"All messages deleted. You have no new messages."

I turned off the phone, slipped it into my pocket, and opened the car door.

There was no going back.

31

D^{om}

Reading an artifact is like swimming in oil. Memories that aren't mine swirl and flow. The oil is thick, heavy, and some of the memories cling, refusing to let go. But they do eventually slip off, leaving an aftertaste behind.

As soon as I picked up the knife, the oil was everywhere, all over me, trying to pour inside. I tasted acid, fire, and pain. Heard a hundred final cries, felt cool tears burn my face. Fear—no, terror crushed me in its grip. I couldn't move, couldn't breathe, couldn't think. I wasn't myself, I'd shattered into countless people, all of them taking their final gasps. I was dying, over and over, cut, stabbed, gutted. Again. And again.

In the field, I went to my knees, heard Gina calling.

But the oil pushed in and over, pouring down my throat, into my eyes.

I'd fucked up.

Kempthorne had warned me.

Don't ever authenticate the knife.

Too late.

I thought I'd have control of it, thought I could do this. I'd been wrong. The knife had me, controlled me. The oil was in my veins, racing toward my heart. The knife burned in my hand. My fingers had clamped around it, locked in steel. That wasn't me, the knife... It wouldn't let go, not until it was done. I heard Max cry out, heard him sob that he didn't want to do this, and then Montgomery's eyes flashed. *"Of course you do. Do it for me, dear boy. It will all be over soon".*

I clamped my free hand to my head, trying to get Montgomery's voice out.

It will all be over soon, dear boy.

My own memories tried to muscle back in, pieces of me fighting to cling on, but the knife uprooted them, implanting itself like a choking weed, growing, filling, spreading.

Alex had warned me...

"Alex... what... no, get off him!"

Yes, that! I reached for Charlotte's memory, but it was snatched away and countless others rushed in to fill the void it left behind. Like whiplashes, they came, one after another, beating me down. Cut, stabbed, gutted, dying a hundred times, a hundred different ways. The terror was hot and cold, wet and dry, it burned me up.

"Dom... oh god, Dom!"

Gina. Fuck. "Get away," I snapped. It must have

worked because whatever she saw on my face made her stumble back through the grass and lift the rifle. Then I was gone again, swimming in oil, choking on it, drowning, dying. Nameless faces, the dead alive again in my head. *Latents... they're all latents.* That thought was mine and it shone like a flame. That was why the knife was different. It had only been used to kill latents. That was what made it powerful, made it deadly.

A sickening wave rolled over me, surged through and under my skin, memories boiling. I heard my cry, felt the damp, muddy earth under my hand, my knees, heard my sobs. But it was just another memory, just another piece of me, tossed about like all the others.

If I didn't control this, it would destroy me, just like Kempthorne had said. I had to be better, I had to be stronger. I was trained for this, flooded for it. The military made sure I could do this. They'd made me for this. Made... just like Kempthorne.

"There's a good boy... down we go."

Yes!

I grabbed at the swimming memory, sank my hands into it so it couldn't slither away.

Thomas Montgomery, fewer lines around his eyes, smiled down at me. "There's a good boy... down we go." Fear burned on my tongue. Excitement too. I was good. This was good. I wanted to please him, this man mother admired. If I could please him, it would make her happy, and I only wanted to please her.

Oh Christ... Alex...

The memory twitched, jerked, pieces shuffling apart and then back together.

Light. So much it was as though the sun itself filled

Ravenscourt. And power. Burning, brilliant power. A river of it, so much—the source—Montgomery's eyes burned, his hands burned, too, where they touched me—touched Alex—touched the source.

"Alex... what? No! Get off him! Get your hands off my brother!" The girl with the golden hair and smiling Labradors. Charlotte Kempthorne. I knew her. I'd been in this moment before, watching through her eyes...

The light shattered. Alex, the boy, screamed.

The knife. Cold in his hand.

"Kill her." Montgomery's words in his ear. Vicious words. Alex didn't want to. But he couldn't stop. *"Kill her. Nobody must know what we have done. Kill her, Alex."*

The blade through her chest. Like butter.

Blood on the blade, blood on his hands. Charlotte grabbed for the table, her hand slipping through coins. Eyes... beautiful eyes. *Why?* those eyes begged.

Alex dropped the knife and the memory stretched thin, threatening to snap. But I clung on, watching... watching Charlotte die, watching Alex stare mutely, unable to help, watching Montgomery lay a hand on his shoulder. "There's a good boy. Nobody must ever know."

Montgomery bent and picked up the knife. His thumb caressed the blade, smearing blood. He looked up —at *me*, not Alex, not Charlotte, but me, now.

I gasped, torn from the knife and its hideous waves of sickening power.

In a field.

I was in a field. On my knees. Wet grass. Cool mud.

Not in the study, not Alex Kempthorne. Me. Dom. Not Charlotte, a knife in the heart—no, not her. I grabbed for my chest, expecting blood. I couldn't breathe

—fuck—*breathe*... My gut heaved and I threw up into the grass. Shivering. Cold. Bruised. Hurt. A hundred killing blows like ghosts crawling all over me.

"Dom... God, Dom..." Gina grabbed my shoulder. "Should I call someone? An ambulance? Something?"

"No," I croaked. "I'm... okay."

The knife lay on the ground. Cold. Quiet. Satisfied. Its burn tingled my hand and up my arm, and my muted trick dripped from my fingertips, sizzling where it fell into the mud.

"You scared the shit out of me! I thought you were dying!"

I spat to the side and rode out the waves of nausea, then turned to see Gina's furious expression. Tears wet her face. Guilt stabbed at my chest, along with a thousand other feelings that weren't mine. "Thanks."

"Now I *want* to shoot you."

I grinned. "I'm glad you didn't."

"You didn't really glow much." She switched the rifle to her left hand and hooked her right arm under mine, helping me to my feet. I rocked and doubled over, catching my breath. I hadn't glowed because I was half drained. Had I been at full strength? The knife would have burned through me, just like Kempthorne had said. I had a feeling neither of us would have withstood the blast. "Are you really all right?" she asked.

"I will be."

"Did you see what you wanted?"

I straightened and tried to fight the tremors off. Gina was looking at the knife. As a non-latent she couldn't feel its power, but she'd seen what it could do, and that glare said she hated the thing as much as I did.

"I need you to take the knife inside the house, bury it in a lead-lined box—ask Jordan, I bet Kempthorne has an agency box somewhere. And hide that bloody thing in a hole."

She nodded. She'd regained some of her color. "And then?" she asked.

"And then we find Kempthorne because he's wrong about everything."

"Really?" She arched an eyebrow.

The memories were sore, bright, and right behind my eyes, trying to blind me. I rubbed at my forehead, massaging what would be one hell of a headache. "He told me ages ago that he needs me because he's too close to it all. And I think he knew... there was something he couldn't see. He believes Montgomery is more powerful than him. But Montgomery's power is stolen. Alexander Kempthorne is a direct conduit to the source. The power Montgomery stole is all Kempthorne's."

"What does that mean?"

I pulled my phone from my pocket and dialed Kempthorne again, fingers trembling. The call went straight to answerphone. "Hey, listen, you need to get away from Montgomery. I read the knife—argue with me later—and I know exactly what happened that night. He took your trick, which is bad enough, but you're not like the rest of us, Kempthorne. You were made to be different..."

I stalled at the sight of a figure lurking in the mist between us and Ravenscourt. A small outline. Someone wearing a hood. A girl, maybe?

"Who's that?" Gina asked.

A sparkling glow radiated from the girl's hands.

"Shit. *Get down!*"

I lunged, tackling Gina to the ground. We sprawled hard. Gina grunted something and then the blast boomed over our heads, raining sparks through the mist. *Shit.* A latent. I reached for my cards, pulled one free, and tried to spill some trick into it, managing a pathetic sparkling sizzle. "Stay down."

Gina, wide-eyed, nodded.

Crouched low, I carved through the grass. Static energy prickled the hairs on my neck. I dropped, and a second later the air above my head boiled with exploding trick. Whoever she was, she was bloody accurate. She had a lot more power than me too. The next time I ducked, she'd aim right at me. I had to get out of the field and find cover, fast. I dug my boots into the soft ground and bolted—a blast sizzled behind me, then another. Trick tingled into my fingers... Dammit... I needed more. It would have to do. I funneled the trick I had through my fingers and into the card and let it fly—then recognized the girl's shocked face.

Penny Montgomery.

32

D^{om}

Luckily for Penny, I was off my game, and my aim skewed right, ending with the card exploding midair. She didn't flinch. Didn't even step away. Just raised her glowing hands, fingers overflowing with trick, and started forward.

I snatched three cards, fanned them in my fingers, and lit them up with spluttering trick. My trick wasn't much more than a tiny flame to her inferno. She hadn't been this boosted before. Montgomery had gotten to her, made her something else in his lab.

I was so screwed.

"Penny, hey... it's me, Dom?" I tried to appear soft, nonthreatening. "Remember?"

She twitched her wrist and trick flew. I ducked. Heat

washed down the back of my neck and blasted the grass somewhere behind me. When I looked up, she was closer, and advancing. The grass she passed through wilted and smoked behind her. In latent terms, she was hot. But not burning up. She'd been flooded, turned into something else. Just like Kempthorne's mother had done with her son, the same as the military had made me, but Penny was next-level.

"Penny, hey... I helped you, remember? You and me, we escaped Olivia—"

Another arc of dazzling trick flew my way. I reeled to the side, stumbling and almost going down. Then the knife released a deep background throb, and Penny's head swivelled toward where it lay hidden in the grass—and Gina crawling toward it.

Penny started after her.

"Oh-fuck-no-you-don't." There was no way she was getting her hands on that knife.

I flung the cards, one-two-three, in quick succession. They blasted close behind her, popping like fireworks. She whirled, lifted both hands, and locked me in her sights.

Power blotted out her eyes, made them pools of gold. The snarl on her face wasn't hers. Not really. She wasn't Penny. Just like with Max, Montgomery had his claws in her. They were all so eager to please him, to follow his orders. He'd sent her here to finish me off. The meaning was clear: Montgomery had no use for me because he had Kempthorne right where he wanted him.

"Stop! Penny!" I ran at her. It was the only chance I had. Get to her, make her see I wasn't the enemy.

Her hands were still raised, her trick bubbling and

boiling in a small star above her head. If she threw it, if it hit me, I'd be dust.

A rifle shot cracked through the quiet. Penny jerked, her right shoulder pitching forward. Her trick collapsed, spilling golden light. She went down to a knee and let out a whimper. I reached for her. She looked up, thrust out a hand, and the next thing I knew I was on my back, blinking into the mist with the smell of melted clothes and sizzling skin filling my nose and lacing my throat. Like Syria. Like when the terrorist-trained latents burned their way through our forces. But the soldier who had fallen this time was me.

As soon as that thought hit, so did the pain. Fiery agony lit up my left side. Still alight, still burning. Fuck, fuck, fuck… The background throb wasn't the knife this time, it was my own body checking out. My trick fizzled pathetically. Even if I'd had enough to wield, my focus was shot, my thoughts swimming again.

Don't pass out—don't pass out.

Penny loomed, her hood shadowing her face. She crouched, cocked her head, and smiled sadly. "Sorry, Dom. Evolve or die. This is how it is now."

33

Alexander

Dom had once said Wordsworth had eyes. And I felt them as the guard frisked me for potential weapons. I'd been here a dozen times before, visiting Olivia, then Dom, but couldn't shake the feeling the old building knew me—the real me.

The guard escorted me to a waiting area set apart from the prison facility. Comfortable chairs and stacks of magazines suggested this was the more public-friendly side of Wordsworth. The name plaque on the door read: *Mr Thomas Montgomery - Latent Studies & Neutralisation.*

I knocked.

"Come. Ah, yes, Alex," Montgomery said from behind his desk, grinning as though this was just another business meeting. The office was the typical masculine type, dark wallpaper, brown carpet, a heavy mahogany desk. This was his space, more so than the house my team had observed him at. Behind him, a large built-in bookshelf held rows of textbooks, including some I instantly recognized as artifacts, and more than one penned by my parents.

"Please sit down."

Ignoring him, I drifted toward a row of framed photographs on the wall. Some photos I'd seen before—men in white coats, austere and self-important—Montgomery among them. One I hadn't seen, and my breath caught at the sight of it. My mother, standing alongside Thomas lounging in a chair. Her hand rested on his shoulder, and they both smiled. Comfortable. Happy. Familiar—more than familiar.

Another photo caught my eye. The Kempthornes cutting the ribbon, opening the academy, dedicated to latent studies. *The* academy. The building in the background was familiar too. Those steps...

Wordsworth.

I should have seen it before, but it had been a long time, and there were parts of my past I deliberately blocked. Like the academy, and my parents' part within it.

It all began with them, with me. The boy who was made.

I straightened my back, pulled on my charming smile, and faced the man who made my skin crawl.

"Sit, Alex." Montgomery lowered himself into his creaking leather chair and gestured at the chair opposite. "Please."

"Why did you ask me here?"

He watched me, searching for something on my face,

some knowledge perhaps. He appeared outwardly relaxed, but he rubbed his forefinger and thumb together on the desk, a nervous tell. "You and I, Alex. You likely don't remember, but we have a *special* relationship."

My gaze dropped to the pen on the desk in front of him, so like my mother's pen. A gift, Dom had said. The photo—my mother's hand on Thomas's arm. My father, absent from much of my past, most of my memories. There... but more a ghost than a solid figure. And then they were both gone. And it was just me and Charlotte and... Thomas.

He smiled back at me now, watching me read the signs, place the pieces of the puzzle together. There was another framed picture on his desk. I reached out and turned it toward me—knowing. And there I was, the same boy from the photograph on my murder wall. A flop of hair I never could tame, a school blazer too big for me, eyes like bottomless pools where people buried their secrets and hoped they never surfaced again. The weight of the past pushed down. I sat on the chair, suddenly needing to.

"She wanted another child after Charlotte. Your father didn't," Montgomery said.

"Because she didn't want a child at all," I said. "She wanted an experiment."

A slight dip in Montgomery's chin. "You were made, from idea to execution." He spread his hands, as though the fault lay elsewhere, not in his lap. "From the moment you were born, your mother was ruthless in her pursuit of knowledge, pursuit of the source, the reason why we all are as we are."

I left the framed photograph of me where it was and

leaned back in the chair. "None of this matters. It's in the past."

"The past is very pertinent, dear boy. It's in the room with us now. It's in your blood. In every breath you take. You were made for one purpose, one reason only." He leaned forward. "To connect with the source, directly."

That couldn't be right. I failed at hiding my surprise. I couldn't connect to the source. It was as mysterious to me as it was to any latent. "What went wrong?"

"Nothing. Nothing at all." He chuckled, enjoying my ignorance. Liking all of this far too much. Why did I get the impression I'd walked into something masquerading as one thing but was something else entirely? Like a trap. The room didn't feel sinister. The artifacts in the glass cabinet weren't powerful. There was nothing dangerous here, besides the man watching me. Always watching, waiting for something...

"Your father could only go so far. I do believe he loved you, despite keeping his distance. When he saw what your mother accomplished? Well, he became something of a liability. They argued. About you, about the academy, about me. He threatened to expose us, and what we'd done to you. She told me—assured me—he wouldn't. He wasn't a latent, so how could he understand the breakthrough as we did? She began to waver..."

I narrowed my eyes on him. "You killed them."

"An unfortunate accident." He smiled as he said it.

I'd known, hadn't I? Known it was no accident. But I'd been a boy, confused, afraid, lost. I'd loved them, even knowing they hadn't loved me—it didn't matter. I'd thought that one day I could have made them love me, eventually. But overnight, they were gone, and my world had changed forever.

Montgomery had killed them.

And that opened up another line between the clues, another pin in my wall. Montgomery had wanted my mother's work, wanted me? He'd probably wanted my father dead long before that fateful plane flight. My mother, though, there had been more between them, not love… but respect. He hadn't wanted to kill her, but had to, to further his own plans.

Montgomery reached beneath his desk, and for a brief second, I thought he meant to go for a gun or something equally asinine, but instead, he placed a battered deck of cards on the desk.

Dom's cards?

But how were they here?

I looked up, fear and anger racing toward my heart. Dom never let the cards out of his sight. Which would only mean one thing. "Hurt him and I'll destroy you, your work, your life—everything."

"Steady on, Alex," he said with a chuckle. "We have an opportunity here, you and I. We can be gods. Together. Imagine it… just for a moment… No more rules, no more laws designed to hobble us, to keep us small and insignificant. We are powerful. We are evolution itself. You and I. I've shown you how far I've come. Latents are strong, we deserve more. We can take it."

I didn't care for any of that. I never had. "You're insane. And this conversation is over." I stood, making a move toward the door.

"Sit down, Alex."

His voice and tone hooked me in, jolting my stride,

tugging on my will. I turned but didn't sit. This room, my past, it crowded in, filling the space, building to a pressure. Dom's cards sat neatly on the desk. Their edges frayed and torn. Every card an orphan. But not the whole deck. I didn't need to count them to know some were missing, and not just the King of Hearts, but others too. He'd used them. Recently fought. And lost some.

He was here. Inside Wordsworth. Montgomery was here. So was I. The academy had begun here. My history was here, woven into these walls. The answers were *all here.*

I wet my lips, breathed in, and took my place back in the chair.

"You can't tell me, dear boy, that the idea of power doesn't seduce you. I know you. We are the same."

I laughed, despite the circumstances. "We're not."

That took some of the humor out of his eyes. He planted a fingertip on his desk. "The fact of the matter is, the new world will happen with or without you, and I'd much prefer you were by my side, where you belong, instead of working against me."

"You would prefer that, yes." I leaned forward. "And if I refuse, you'll hurt Dom?"

"I don't want to hurt the boy. He's quite remarkable—the military are learning how valuable latents can be. They certainly experimented on him in ways even I would be wary of. But he's not you, Alex. Nobody is you." Something repulsive and lustful glinted in his eyes. A hunger so vicious it would consume anything and everything to be sated. A hunger for me.

I'd not feared Montgomery before that moment. But some part of me, some small piece of me, perhaps the boy I'd once been, knew that look and recognized it as dangerous. But more than that, there was an intimacy to him too; it crawled beneath my skin and tried to strike at my own desires. The desire not to be pinned down, not to be used and experimented on, not to have straps around my wrists and my trick manipulated as though I was nothing more than a piece of meat dissected on a plate for Montgomery to chew through. But also the desire to please, to be good, to do the right thing, to be loved.

He'd done it before—I knew, could taste the old fear. He was looking at me now, through me, as though he'd do it again.

The study... Charlotte's shadow... Dom's incessant questions... Montgomery was there? Dom had suggested it, already putting the pieces together. But I'd refused to listen.

Montgomery and the knife.

Fear set my heart racing. I had to get out of this room.

"Well, this discussion has been enlightening." I stood. "And your plans are intriguing—"

"Sit down!"

That pull. That yank on my will, like a dog on a chain. It had me hesitating, despite wanting nothing more than to leave.

"I let you have a life. I allowed you to believe you were free. Until I was ready. But that freedom is over, Alex. You were made for one purpose, and it's time you fulfilled that purpose." He rose to his feet. "You never really escaped, you know."

Power thrummed in the air as a warning, and mine sparked to life, tingling my fingers and urging me to let loose. "I don't know what you and my parents did to me, but I'm not that boy any longer, Montgomery. Don't test me."

"Dear boy." He laughed. "That's exactly what I've been doing." He raised a hand and pooled his squirming black trick in his palm. "You passed."

I summoned my trick, but it came slowly, like honey, reluctant and stubborn. Montgomery smiled, as though I'd done the one thing I shouldn't have, the one thing he knew I would. He smiled, knowing I'd already been caught.

I'd never been free, he'd said.

I'd always been the boy who was made.

"Alex, dear boy, it's better for everyone if you just stop fighting who you were always meant to be. It was always going to end this way." He offered his hand. "It's your destiny."

D^{om}

I didn't need to open my eyes to know I was back in Wordsworth. The place throbbed a sickly beat against the back of my brain and prickled my skin with cold sweat. I remembered voices, the clatter of metal and movement, and now I was here, in a brightly lit space, wrists and ankles bound to the examination table under me.

It was like I'd never left.

Only this time, I hadn't been drugged, not yet. Just abandoned in a curtained-off corner, listening to the air ducts hum and machines blip. Above me, looming like something out of a horror movie, hung an array of tubes bristling with needles at their ends. For harvesting trick.

Panic tried to choke me. My pathetic trick fizzled.

Maybe that was why they hadn't hooked me up. I didn't have much trick left.

I closed my right hand into a fist and yanked on the leather strap. The table rocked, its frame clunking, but the straps held.

Have to get out. Breathe, fucking breathe. My lungs heaved, my head spun. If I didn't chill the fuck out I'd pass out again. *Breathe.*

I tried the strap again. Tried my left arm. *Yank. Yank.* Until my veins stood proud and my whole body trembled, but the damn things still didn't give. I flopped my head back and blinked stinging sweat from my eyes. *Okay. Think.* I couldn't burn my way out; the trick was barely a puff of heat. I couldn't writhe free.

Maybe I could...wriggle? I bucked. The table jolted sideways. I bucked again, and again the table skittered, angling my feet toward the corner of the curtain. Not sure what it was going to accomplish, besides changing my view, I bucked and thrashed, putting all of my weight into it, and must have caught it at a pivot point because the table jolted, tipped, and slammed onto its side, taking me with it. My left arm hit the floor. My teeth snapped together, narrowly missing my tongue.

Okay, so I was on my side, on the floor. I could see beneath the curtains, into other bays with a sea of more table legs.

The curtain divider swayed away as I panted. I puffed at it, shifting it farther away, and got a glimpse of a woman's hand flung limp from the side of another examination table. The nails were chipped. But she wasn't strapped in. And that was bloody important. Another latent? And she wasn't tied.

"Hey," I croaked, coughed, then tried again. "Hey, you."

Machines blipped. The air-con hummed.

"For fuck's sake, wake up!" I puffed again, swinging the curtain, and saw her finger twitch. "Yes. Good. C'mon, wake up." More puffing, and the curtain was swaying now. The woman's hand vanished. Was she awake? Had she gone? "Hey?" Nothing. "Hello?" Bloody hell, if anyone came in now, they'd find me on the floor, and my one shot at escaping would be done for. They'd pump me full of drugs, just like before. That thought made me want to throw up what little I had left in my guts. "Christ, this is bollocks..." I went back to trying to thrash my way out of the bed. "Fucking—arsehole—bastard—twatting —titfaced— "

The curtain swung back and the woman with the half-shaved-half-pink hair cocked her head. "You all right down there, mate?"

Pink! "The-fuck you think?"

She blinked and grinned. "Wow." She leaned over and undid my wrist straps, dumping me face-first on the floor. Then she undid my ankles and rested her arms over her bent knees as I rightened myself into a crouch. She held out her hand. "Cassie. And you're Dom, right?"

I shook it on auto-pilot, feeling clumsy and slow. "You're Renick's inside man—woman." It was then I noticed the needle marks tracking up her bare forearms. Not drugs. The trick harvester. "You're a latent."

"No shit, Sherlock." She hauled me to my feet. "And you're the rich fag's boytoy."

"I—the—what?"

"Sorry." She winced. "Renick's words. You seem a'right." She mock-punched me on the shoulder.

I hissed, and the burn Penny had dealt me blazed to life. My shirt was all singed and stuck to the scabs on my arm. It needed medical attention, but there was no way I could deal with that now. Escape first. I eyed Cassie. Despite the angry red welts, she was coherent, her eyes bright. She'd be drained of trick on the examination table, but she was more alert than me. "Yeah, whatever... You wanna get out of here, Pink?"

Her gaze flicked to the tubes and needles above where my table had been. "Yeah, yeah I do."

Once outside the eerily quiet examination room and walking down a gloomy corridor, it didn't take long to figure out we were beneath Wordsworth. And my joke to Gina about plague pits came back with a vengeance, skittering goose bumps up my arms. London was full of buried secrets, hidden streets, and diverted rivers. That last thought stalled me as we hurried down the corridor. Diverted rivers. I could feel it, I realized. A thrum beneath my feet. Like I'd felt at the destroyed lab. A weak spot, a point at which the source was close. Thousands of years of psychic energy, all funnelling through London, beating London's veins.

"What are you doing?" Cassie snapped.

I'd stopped and spread my hands, soaking up the ambience. Shaking out my hands, I caught up with her and shrugged off her sideways glance. "Nothing."

She didn't feel the same things radiating all-around like I did, so she wasn't an authenticator. Just a latent. Hopefully not an absorber. I'd had enough of those.

Voices bounced down the corridor from somewhere

ahead. We ducked into a dark side room, closed the door to just a slit, and waited for the guards to pass.

"You good?" Cassie asked.

I'd slumped against the wall. My shoulder burned like the bloody thing was still on fire. I shivered, feverish, and thought about throwing up again. I flashed her a fake smile and gave her a thumbs up. "Awesome."

She snorted, opened the door, and stepped into the harsh fluorescent light. "C'mon then, boytoy—"

"Hey, you!"

She whirled toward the voice. I was already halfway out of the room and turned to see two guards reaching for their bright yellow Tasers clipped to their belts. Christ, not Tasers again. If I got hit by one of them it would finish me off.

Cassie swore and something crackled, maybe her trick. I dropped my hands, going for my cards—gone—and ran at the bigger guy on the left. He hadn't expected a charge. He fumbled for the Taser, got it free, and I tackled him in the gut, knocking him against the wall. Plasterboard buckled. The light above flickered. His elbow came down on the back of my neck and a surge of sickness, a cold and horrible darkness, tried to drag me under. I dropped, and he dropped on me. We scrabbled, messy and rough. I grabbed the Taser and, jolting back, fired the prongs into his chest. The big guy's body seized for about three seconds, then cut off.

"Boytoy, c'mon!" Cassie called, already running. She'd somehow dropped and left her guy groaning on the floor, reaching for what looked like a tooth.

Stairs. I spotted them ahead. Stairs were good. Stairs

meant up, and up was away from the surging thrum of power trying to drag me down to it.

"Move!" Cassie barked, then grabbed my hand and yanked. We made it up the stairs, into another bland and disorientating corridor. We stumbled and ran—I mostly stumbled. The bloody place was a maze. Breathless and more lost than ever, we stopped and braced against the wall.

Cassie ran her glare over me. "You about to throw up?"

I rested my forehead on my arm and tried to catch my breath. "I've had a really shit day, okay?" Gulping air, I tried to find some kind of balance, but I was either hurt more than I'd realized, or something else was draining me. My arm tingled where I rested against the wall. Trick leaking *into* me from plasterboard and bricks.

I jerked away.

"What is it?" Cassie moved away, too, eyeing the wall suspiciously.

"Nothing..." Wordsworth was waking up. Literally. And that had to be bad.

"You keep saying that."

"We just need to get out of here." I started forward with a lot more confident strides than I felt. Because the power beneath us wasn't the only thing breathing. Wordsworth was hungry too.

lexander

The source. It flowed and hummed and pulsed, so close I could almost...

"Not yet, dear boy. Not yet."

I opened my eyes—light burned—and squeezed them shut again. Too bright. Everything was too bright.

If I could just... move. Hands held me down. Hands yanked on my trick, the sensation like being pulled inside out. *No... No, not this.*

Don't panic. Do not panic.

Breathe.

I couldn't see—*just the lights.* Couldn't move—*do not panic.*

"This is the beginning of something really quite glorious. I'm so proud of you, Alex. Your mother would be proud too."

I swallowed but my throat was so dry it had almost closed, almost choking me. How... How was I here? I was still in the office, but Montgomery had grabbed my hand, pulled on my trick, dragged me against the desk... John's cards had been there, was John here—"John?"

"Safe." Montgomery's hand folded over mine. And *burned*. Trick pulsed. "Safe, as long as you do everything I say."

I jerked away.

"It will be all right, my boy. Everything will be fine. We will herald a brand-new world."

The source... it flowed like the Thames, deep and bright and so terrible, so full of power, endless power.

It was me.

The source... was *inside* me.

I was the key. I could touch it. I'd touched it before, welcomed it, used it, had it torn from me... In Ravenscourt's study, his hands on me. I'd been... pleased, I'd wanted to help, to make them proud, to please them, have them love me. Mother would have been so proud. But that day in the study, she'd been gone, and just Thomas remained. The man she'd looked up to. I'd wanted to please him for her. He'd had his hands on me then, drawing the source through my veins. But something had happened. Someone... had walked in.

I snapped open my eyes. Thomas Montgomery smiled his friendly smile. "It's going to be—"

I yanked both arms up, jolting Montgomery away. Trick viciously lashed, untethered and wild. "You bastard

—you wretched, slithering leech of a man! You killed my sister!"

His smile cracked and he had the nerve to press one hand to my chest, over my heart, and the other to my waist, as though to hold me down. His hands burned, reigniting old memories, pouring the past over me. He'd done this before. Pinned me down. My trick absorbed—but it wasn't trick, not through me—it was purer, the source. The unfiltered psychic burns of souls, blinding and infinitely powerful. London, her veins alive with history, pulsed all around me, through me. The source had been born beneath London, born as a spark so long ago, but it had grown... with every new psychic blast it had grown and lived and breathed and become something more, something bright and powerful. Something I could touch.

"Alex..." Fear wavered in Montgomery's eyes. "Listen... Control. Do you remember what your mother taught you? It's all about control. Control it now. And give it all to me."

I breathed too fast, each breath sawing through gritted teeth. "Fuck control. And fuck you. You want it? THEN HAVE IT ALL!" I yanked on my trick—the source—and golden fire flooded the room.

36

D^{om}

Something rocked the ground, the wall, even the air. A surge, Kempthorne had called it before. And it was happening again now, an earthquake of trick, bubbling up from below. The walls hummed. Lights flared, hotter, brighter, buzzing as though they were about to blow, and trick surged into my veins, spilling into muscle, every bone. I heard Cassie cry out. My knees hit the corridor floor. Trick flowed through the walls and under me. It was everywhere. Wordsworth rattled and moaned, groaning as though the entire building was coming undone. And then it was gone—cut off. I gasped, choked, gasped again, coming back to myself with a buzzing in my head and trick burning up my veins. Someone's trick, a trick I knew well.

"What the fuck was that?" Cassie wheezed.

"My boyf—my boss."

She rocked back on her heels. "Your what?"

It was Kempthorne. I knew it, felt it, felt him. His trick tingled through me, the touch familiar and warm and bright, and *personal*. He was fired up, maybe burning up, spiraling, about to blow. I had to stop him. "I have to..." I staggered to my feet. "I have to find him." My trick fizzed through my veins, alive and alert and bright and hungry. Hungry for *him*. For us.

"What? Leave him. Let's go." She wobbled to her feet, too, and staggered toward a door that may or may not have been the way out.

"I can't—listen... he's like us, but way more powerful and he doesn't know. The guy who runs this place—you probably met him—M?" She snarled. "Yeah, him. He's going to plug Kempthorne into the source and power-up —for all anyone knows, it'll kill Kempthorne, kill everyone here. And that's probably the best outcome. Kempthorne has so much power he could level London. I can't leave."

"Yeah but, he's just some fag, right?"

What the hell was her problem? "Jesus Christ, no. He's my fucked-up boyfriend who pretends he has every-thing under control but really needs help—*our* help. You seem like a decent person, apart from the raging homo-phobia—which I'll let slide, as you're one of Renick's people. You're a latent. Kempthorne is too—he's one of us. We're all one of us. Don't you get it? We have to help because we're all we have." She looked at me as though I'd lost my mind. "Oh, just fuck off then." I hobbled toward a different door. It could also be the exit, or another way deeper into Wordsworth. My gut told me it was the right way and Cassie's was the wrong way. And that was all I was capable of thinking. My body was on fire, trick bursting my seams, but my head was all messed up, my thoughts muddled, full of memories that weren't mine. Kempthorne on a table, years ago, begging for help. A girl looking up at him, so afraid, so confused— why had he killed her? Christ, it was all too much at once.

Cas appeared at my side, the sight of her bright pink hair oddly calming. I could focus on that and not the nightmares pushing themselves into my head. "Fine, then, Boytoy," she said. "But only because you look like you're about to collapse and I'm not that much of a bitch."

I puffed out a sigh because I *was* about to fall over, and I really needed help, even if it was hers.

She got her hand on the door, gave it a shove open, and froze.

Penny stood on the other side. "I had a feeling you'd get free," she said and slammed her hand into my chest— trick bloomed, hers, mine, I wasn't sure anymore. Whosoever it was, it wouldn't end well. I couldn't hurt her, not even to save myself. I just... couldn't.

Cas brought her arm down in a savage chop, knocking Penny off, and punched Penny in the face.

Penny yelped and reeled. I lunged, got a hand around her throat, and pooled trick into my fingers. "Don't fight me, please don't."

She panted, teeth gritted, blood running between them, eyes ablaze with power. She was the same Penny I'd saved, but twisted, made into something darker.

"He has you under some kind of spell. He's manipulated you, Penny. I know you're good." *Please don't make me hurt you. I can't hurt more people...*

She hissed, her trick bloomed, spilling out around her in an aura of golden light—so much of it, that if I hadn't seen Kempthorne glow like a star, I'd have thought her impossible. I squeezed my fingers and leaned in, trying to stare into her eyes, into her soul, where I knew she was still good. "Don't."

In her left hand, she lifted *the knife.*

Oh fuck.

This was it. I couldn't fight her and the knife. I didn't have it in me.

My thoughts split, half in holding Penny back and half falling into the knife's poisonous siren song. I had to get to Kempthorne, I had to stop Montgomery from draining him, from raising a bloody latent army all bespelled by his decades of manipulation. I had to kill Penny.

No... I squeezed harder. "Please..." I couldn't do this, couldn't take another knock. She wasn't bad, she was just confused. Like Max. Like Annie. They weren't bad people. We'd all been used. "Please, Penny. Christ, please *don't make me do this.*"

Cas tried to intervene by making a grab for the knife, or maybe the knife was whispering to her too. "No, don't fuckin' touch it!"

Power jolted through Penny—a thousand volts lit me up. I flew backward, into a fleeting, second of weightlessness, then hit a wall, knocking the air out of me. I slid to the floor, trick dancing over me. By the time I shook the fog from my head, Penny had Cas by the neck, had lifted her off the floor. Red welts bubbled on Cas's neck. Cas tried to pry her hands off and kicked at the air. I couldn't stop this... I saw it all unfold and didn't have it in me... Too many ghosts swirled in my head, too many wrongs.

The gunshot was so loud and so sharp, it slapped my wavering consciousness back together. Penny dropped. And Cas stood gasping, gulping air, rubbing at her neck.

The man striding down the corridor, gun in hand, long coat flaring, was like someone out of a Hollywood dream—the prick.

Kage lowered his gun and knelt by my side. Amber eyes so bloody fine. "You all right? Can you walk?"

I blinked at him. "How..."

"Gina called me."

Gina was here too... She knelt beside Penny's motionless body, checking for a pulse. Penny was dead. Kage never missed, and the hole in her head made it pretty bloody obvious she wasn't surviving him. Few latents did.

"You fucking killed her," I growled.

Kage glowered. "She was about to kill that woman and you."

"No, I had her—I was getting through."

"You didn't. You want to believe that. But you didn't have her, Dom." Kage reached for my arm. I pulled away and clambered to my feet. He straightened, lowered his gun in front of him, and nodded at Gina. "There's no time for this. The IRL has agents infiltrating the prison as we speak, and if they find you, they'll take you with the rest of the latents."

"The IRL? What? What the fuck did you do, Kage?"

"What should have been done in the beginning. Called the professionals."

I shook a sizzle of trick from my hand. "The IRL can't even spell professional."

"Do you want to stand there and argue or get out of here?"

"Fuck you." I started down the corridor, still shaking excess trick off my hands. The bloody stuff wouldn't let go. At least the storm in my head had cleared. "I have to find Kempthorne."

"*Thanks for saving my life, Kage,*" he drawled in a terrible attempt at my English accent.

I whirled on him. "You didn't save my life. You killed a kid."

"I killed a dangerous latent."

I held his stare, and knew... if it came to it, he'd kill me too. And maybe that was a good thing, maybe he was right. Look where we were. In a building brimming with trick, with latents about to blow, potentially killing hundreds, maybe thousands, blowing a hole in London a mile wide.

Penny lay dead. Another dead latent by Montgomery's hands. My anger toward Kage spluttered and died.

Maybe, just maybe, he'd been right.

I heard Cas ask Gina, "They know each other?"

"Oh yeah," Gina replied.

"Hey, thanks, mate," Cas called. "That bitch was burnin' me up. You saved my life, bro."

Kage flashed her a small grin, and I'd never wanted to punch him in the face more. "D'you know the way out?" I asked him, drawing his gaze back to me.

"Yeah, it's—"

"Then take Cas and Gina and get the hell out of here.

Get everyone out—the whole place is unstable." I was moving again, moving fast. I shoved through a door, into a stairwell, and started to climb.

"What about Kempthorne?" Kage asked, climbing close behind me.

I swallowed, stopped on a step, and turned to meet Kage's glare again. He already had a smoking gun in his hands. He'd kill Kempthorne in a heartbeat. "Kempthorne is mine. If you go near him, I will burn your bloody heart right out of your chest."

He rose onto my step, meeting me eye to eye. "I know, Dom. I'm trying to help."

"Like you helped Penny?"

"You see good where there isn't any." He backed off and swore under his breath, then nodded at the girls. "Let's get you out of here."

Gina squeezed my shoulder. "Go save the boss, Dom."

I nodded, swallowed the stupid lump in my throat, and split off from them at the top of the stairwell. Trick sizzled the air, its smell like hot electrical wires. *Find Kempthorne. Stop Montgomery.* Nothing else mattered. Flicking my hands out, I spilled trick into my fingers and reached into the latent part of me that knew things I didn't—like where its other half was. Wordsworth hummed and trembled, its walls either about to funnel trick right from the source or blow apart.

I was out of options and time.

A pull in my chest tugged me onward. Kempthorne was close. And hurting. Fuck. I was going to kill Montgomery. And I had just the thing to do it.

From my back pocket, I eased the dirty knife free, using my sleeve to shield some of its horrible throb. The psychic resonance squirmed in my mind, desperate to take control.

I spilled trick down its blade. "Not yet, hold on," I told it. It would have its feast. Thomas Montgomery, the bastard, was about to get a taste of his own vicious poison.

37

Alexander

The source bubbled through London's cracks, rising in my latent sight like molten lava, and pooled beneath Wordsworth, from where it climbed through every brick, every timber, touching the past with every inch, stirring up all its nightmares, bringing the building to life. This was what I'd been made for. A boy, a tool, a creature, flooded and pushed to my limits, until I could open up and swallow the source inside. My mother's experiment, Montgomery's dream, and, I suspected, my father's fear.

I lay on the desk like an offering. Every inch of my skin blazed, every breath scorched my lungs. I'd stopped trying to fight it—and fight him. It was too late for that. Montgomery's hands holding me down were a part of me now, like the man was a part of me, as he'd always been.

Because this had happened before. I remembered. Wished I didn't. Ravenscourt's study. He'd pulled the source through my body and mind, or tried to, but my sister had intervened. And I'd killed her for it.

Kill her… Nobody must know.

The source swelled, burning through my heart, through me. I might have screamed, if the trick hadn't burned all the air in my lungs. Montgomery stood over me, back arched, head thrown back, absorbing all of it, all of me, and still taking more. Perhaps it would kill him. Perhaps it would kill us all.

The air burned with trick. The walls rippled.

Men weren't meant to be gods.

The boy who was made.

The man who had failed.

Me.

London trembled. Old streets moaned, foundations cracked. God, I couldn't contain it. It was all going to fall because of me. Millions of people would die. And for what? Montgomery's need to have more and more power?

I could stop it, I had to. Had to stop the source. Stop what I'd started.

Stop.

I closed my hands into fists.

Stop.

Gritted my teeth.

Stop.

It was too much, too bright, too fast, and it felt so good to welcome it and let go, to let it take me, to let Montgomery have it. But good was bad. It didn't make any sense, nothing did anymore. I was losing control, if I hadn't already, and that was very, very bad.

Stop.

The source swirled—spiraling through me like water down a drain. If it didn't stop, it would burn me up. I wasn't ready to die. Not when I'd found something—someone who could keep me afloat. Dom... with his deep, chuckling laugh. The way he looked at me, desire so open on his face it was a wonder the whole world didn't know, a wonder how I'd been such a fool to resist for so long. How he'd kicked his boots up on my desk and fallen asleep there, so hopeless, so beguiling. Dom, who was everything I was not. Brave, strong, brilliant, and good. My opposite.

Stop.

I choked the source back, tried to smother it, to push it down, but the source kept flowing around and through me, pulled by Montgomery. I wasn't enough, too small, too insignificant. I couldn't do this alone.

"Yes, dear boy, give it to me. Give it all to me!" Montgomery laughed, and it sounded like thunder, as though all of Wordsworth's agony laughed with him.

Disappointment.

Limited.

Failure.

Mother had been right.

In the end, what had I been good for?

"Get your hands off my man, you son of a bitch!"

Dom.

He stood in the doorway, surrounded by rippling, boiling shadows. They flocked around him, beating against the light pouring off me, shoving against the source in oily waves, and Dom was there, knife in hand, *the knife.* Brilliant with trick—brilliant and alive, and fierce, and *everything*. My heart swelled, even as the source burned through it, slowly reducing it to ash.

Montgomery plucked his hand from my chest and his horrible, filthy trick withdrew inside him, some of the source falling away with the broken connection.

Shadows howled, filling the room with thunder and darkness. Montgomery blazed and lifted his free hand, still feeding, still gorging on me, on the source, but distracted. Powerful. He was—I was... powerful. So were the shadows.

I dropped my head back and knew how this ended.

The shadows didn't want me, they never had. They wanted power. They wanted balance. They wanted what was theirs. They didn't want the boy, they wanted what he'd been made into.

I closed my eyes, sighed, and let go of my control.

38

D^{om}

Shadows had boiled out of the walls, the floors, pushed from Wordsworth's psychic stains by the source bubbling up from under my feet. But I hadn't been their target. They'd surged ahead, spilling around me, leading the way straight to Montgomery's office. I knew why when the door flew open under their wave.

Light and heat and power—I'd felt it before, but this was a thousand times more. The source. It rolled in waves from Kempthorne, sprawled on his back on Montgomery's desk. Montgomery stood over him, a monster of a man, bloated with power, his hands fused to Kempthorne's chest.

"Get your hands off my man, you son of a bitch!"

Montgomery jerked his head up and flung a hand

out, slicing through the shadows toward me. It should have hit, but I did the opposite of everything my training had taught me—I shut my trick down, going dark.

Ravenous shadows lunged, blocking Montgomery's strike, and then they devoured it.

And they didn't stop there.

Montgomery's immense power surged, drawing on more and more, pulling it out of Kempthorne. The shadows pushed in, buffeting me, through me, pouring from all of Wordsworth's corners and cracks. So many, as though the night sky had come alive and funneled into this one room.

They raged like a storm, light and dark surged and clashed, spinning, lashing. And inside it all, at the eye of the storm, lay Kempthorne. Eyes closed. Lips parted.

He's not dead.

He's not.

I pushed into the storm, into the howling wind and bitter taste of hot dust and crackling power. Montgomery roared and his trick—the source—flared and the shadows exploded into ash. And the storm vanished, leaving a void of stunned silence. I stood on one side of Kempthorne's motionless body with Montgomery on the other, his left hand still on Kempthorne's chest.

The knife, hidden behind my back, throbbed its ugly beat in my head. But the knife and I knew each other now. Knew each other's secrets. It knew a killer when it saw one.

Montgomery chuckled and the chuckle sounded like mountains moving. **"Oh, dear boy... you are nothing but a tiny speck."** His warped, power-laden voice rolled through the walls and floor, rumbling Wordsworth's foundations.

He's not dead.

He's not.

I couldn't look, didn't want to see Alex's grey face—blue lips, the way his expensive shirt was all burned and askew, his chest weeping blood—didn't want to know. "What have you done to him?"

Montgomery's chuckle rumbled like thunder. An aura of energy rippled around him. His eyes glowed their gold-flecked darkness. **"Alexander has fulfilled his purpose. A destiny his mother and I mapped for him."** He plucked his hand free of Kempthorne's chest, jerking Kempthorne's lifeless body. **"Few can say the same."**

The knife whispered its terrible desires, and I needed no encouragement. But there wasn't much time. I couldn't miss, it had to be fast.

Montgomery smiled—at me, at Kempthorne—he smiled as though he didn't have a care in the world, like he was happy. **"The world will finally fear me. Fear *us*, John. As it should have from the beginning."**

"Yeah, about that *us* part. Your army kind of cleared out. The IRL wasn't so useless after all. Who knew? It's just you, mate."

"Lies," he snarled.

I shrugged. "Yah see, they got wind of your little side project. The labs, the prisoners you all fucked with? Yeah, they've taken it all. The surge you just pulled out of the ground? It didn't get to your latents, not like you hoped. You're an army of one."

His god-awful glow faded and spluttered, revealing more of the old lines on his face and the worry they'd pinched into. **"One god is enough!"** He flung a thread of blinding, overpowered trick. White light and heat scorched through the air where I'd been standing.

I dashed behind him, hooked an arm around his throat, and plunged the knife into his back—straight into his heart. The knife went in clean, went in deep, so smooth... like butter.

He bucked, mouth opening, gasp slipping free. "That's for Charlotte Kempthorne, you bitch," I snarled. I twisted the knife, leaning into it, grinding the blade against bone. He spluttered, the sound wet. "And that's for Alex." He shuddered, staggered, but I held fast, clutching him close and making sure he stayed upright so he could see how the shadows swelled again, pouring back in. "Well done, you're the brightest, most powerful latent alive. But not for long. I hope the shadows make it slow—"

And right on cue, they struck.

A tidal wave of darkness crested.

I shoved Montgomery against the desk and released the knife, leaving it stuck in his back.

"No, no!" He pulled on his vast well of power to protect himself.

The shadows poured over him, into him, drowning him in darkness. I hid my trick, hid it deep, hid it far away, made myself small and insignificant.

The shadows howled around Montgomery. He staggered, reeling, trying to summon more and more trick to protect himself, but the shadows spiraled around him, drinking everything he gave, gorging themselves on the trick he'd stolen—restoring what they'd lost.

I stumbled against the desk. As the roaring went on

and the wind tore over me, I ran a hand up Kempthorne's chest, feeling for warmth, for his breathing, for a heartbeat. For some sign he wasn't dead. *Cold... so fucking cold.* "C'mon..." I cupped his face, turned his head toward me. Dark eyelashes lay closed. Cold sweat or maybe tears had wet his face. "You're not a hero, remember?"

I searched for his pulse at his neck, fingers trembling. The shadows raged and howled, and Montgomery's screams rose. I didn't care about him, or them, just the man I'd come to love slipping away from me. I couldn't feel a pulse. Nothing. Shock choked me. "No, fuck you!" I propped a knee on the edge of the desk, climbed up, straddled him, pressed my lips to his, and *breathed*. "You don't die here." Again, I sealed my lips over his and *breathed*.

It wasn't enough.

I was losing him.

"Jesus..." I clutched his face and pressed my forehead to his. *"Please, come back."*

What had he said? Something about friction resonance and harmony and focus or some shit? He'd had his hands on me, he'd healed me. He'd healed Kage. If he could do it, so could I. But he was a direct link to the source, he was always different, always fucking amazing. And I was just me. Just some kid from the East End who could throw a few playing cards and burn shit.

I pressed my hand to his bare chest, where Montgomery's touch had burned his shirt away and scorched his skin. What the fuck was I supposed to do? Panic laced my tongue with acid, made my chest burn. He lay there, and I was losing my fucking mind...

Trick suddenly pooled into my fingers, as though it

had its own will, and poured *under* his skin. Something else he'd said, some niggling memory, something about us being important—it hooked into my panic, yanked it out and cleared my head. He'd stood in front of his murder wall and clasped his hands together and he'd said we were important. Us. Together. Him and me. His trick and mine. We worked, we flowed. Opposites attract. We had balance.

I pushed trick into him. The shadows raged and howled, tearing through Montgomery's well of stolen power. But I'd begun to draw on the trick too. Ice spilled down my back, their attention turning toward me. I didn't care. I had to bring him back. To do something. I sealed my lips over his again—*breathe*—as though I could breathe my own life into him, share some latent part of me and bring him back. I pushed more trick in, let it spill free and wind itself around his heart. Make it beat again.

Balance.

Push and pull.

Restore.

Breathe.

"Breathe, you arsehole." Lightheaded—the maelstrom spun my thoughts, whipping me up with it. Trick flowed like it had done when we were locked together. Gold trick flowed, making him glitter. "Breathe!"

The shadows exploded, snapping the air and vanishing. A psychic blast knocked me sideways, ringing through my skull, almost knocking me out cold. Wordsworth trembled, the walls groaned, and the hideous building sighed its last psychic breath.

Breathe.

My trick spluttered. So did my heart.

It was over. It had to be over. I glanced at the floor to where a husk of an old man lay dead.

Montgomery.

I should have felt something, anything, but there was nothing because under me, Kempthorne didn't move.

He wasn't coming back.

I couldn't... think, couldn't breathe, I'd given it all to him. Everything I had in me, I'd pushed it into him. And he was still dead.

Something vast and hungry split me open, the horrible sensation of grief, of knowing it was over. I'd never see his sly smile, or bat that stupid flop of hair away from his eyes, or listen to his wicked little laugh, or hear him threaten someone in his icy voice. I'd never hear him stumble over something silly and small, like making breakfast, because he was Alexander Kempthorne and he had no idea how the real world worked. And now he never would.

"Hello..." he croaked.

I lifted my head. Glacial eyes tried to focus on my face. He blinked, once, twice, quickly. "Do you mind getting off? It's just, you're rather heavy and I'm—"

"*Fuck*." I crouched over him and peered into his blue eyes. He blinked. One of his dark eyebrows lifted.

The bastard's mouth ticked.

"Fuck," I said again, then kissed him.

39

1 *week later.*
Alexander

I set my phone down and sighed. So many messages, so many people pulling me in all directions, when the one who I really wanted to pull me wasn't here at all. The empty shelves of Cecil Court's basement and my non-existent trick weren't helping my gloomy mood. Of course, hiding in the basement wasn't going to solve anything.

The newspapers spread across my desk declared *Latent Catastrophe at Wordsworth*. Other headlines such as *Lock Up Latents, More Restrictions Needed*, caught my eye.

My name was all over the press—I'd even made the BBC news. *London Billionaire at the Heart of Latent Plot to Overthrow Government*, and around and around it went. *IRL Praised for its Part in Foiling Latent Takeover. Latents*

Saved! Wordsworth Condemned. That praise should have been Dom's. He'd been the one to meet with Doris, to suggest she dig deeper into Montgomery, to point the IRL in the right direction.

The only reason I hadn't been arrested was because nobody had witnessed me do anything illegal, but the paramedics had wheeled me out looking grey and half dead, so that made me guilty by association. The photos were everywhere too.

I rubbed at my forehead. This wasn't ever going away. I was going to be hounded forever. Perhaps I could leave the country? Go somewhere where my name was just a name, not synonymous with my parents' ambitions to create an all-powerful latent.

I sighed. I almost wished for those days when being gay would shock everyone. I was no longer London's most intriguing and eligible bachelor. However, I was—according to the *Daily Mail—London's Latent Billionaire Supervillain.*

Wonderful.

Laughter bubbled down the stairs. Gina and another female voice. The shop had been closed since Robin had... left us. Kempthorne & Co was defunct; the agency's operating license had been revoked. My taxes had been hard at work paying for the IRL to screw me every way they could. Having a registered latent track down unregistered latents was a conflict of interest. As for handling artifacts? Well, the empty shelves were proof of what the IRL thought of that.

The only good thing to come out of all this was Dom, or should have been. But after Wordsworth, he'd sat beside my hospital bed, too quiet, too thoughtful, and then had left. And I hadn't seen him since. Seven days. He hadn't called. I'd checked my messages, even the ones I'd gotten rid of—through un-deleting them. I'd listened to several from him from before Montgomery had tried to make himself a god, most of them angry rants, but one... One had stolen my voice and my heart.

"I'm about to do the stupid thing and if it all goes wrong, I want you to know, it's not your fault. None of it. You aren't responsible for parents who are dicks, or for a world that would have ruined you if you'd revealed who you were to save an agent who was your friend. I don't think you're a bad guy, Kempthorne—Alex. I just—"

He'd had no idea how much I'd needed to hear those words. *Not my fault.*

The world thought me dark and villainous, and for the longest time, I would have agreed. Montgomery had... well, he'd seeded himself deeper inside me than I'd realized.

"You gonna hide down here forever?" Gina approached with a mug of tea and set it down on the spread of newspapers on my desk. She noticed the headlines and frowned.

"I am considering it, yes."

"They don't know you. It's just sensational shit to sell more papers."

I lifted my eyebrows. Did she know me? She smiled back. Perhaps she did. We hadn't talked about... anything. I didn't have a job for her anymore. Could I pay her to be my friend? Was I that desperate?

"So..." she said, dragging the word out. "I know Dom's favorite restaurant."

"And?"

Her frown turned to frustration. "And... aren't you and him supposed to be going to dinner?"

"Oh! Yes." If he ever came back. "You do?"

"Come upstairs?" She smiled. "There's someone here."

She left and a little while later, the voices started up again. I plucked the coin from my pocket and set it down on my desk. If it thrummed, I didn't feel it. If it was still an artifact, I wouldn't know. My trick had burned out of me. Or rather, I'd pushed it out of me. Given it all to Montgomery, so the shadows would rip him apart. Balance restored.

Leaving the coin on my desk, I grabbed my tea and headed upstairs. Gina and I had pushed the bookshelves against the wall and brought in a few colorful patchwork chesterfield sofas, making a living room in what had been the shop.

A woman with cropped pink hair was sprawled on one of those colorful sofas. She wore a white and grey hooded top, tightly fitting jeans, and heavy unlaced boots. On seeing me, she got to her feet. "Hi, we 'aven't met, but I know you, Mister K. I'm Cassie. I helped your boyto—boyfriend in Wordsworth."

Her accent was thick east London, all brash cockney. I must have frowned because Gina frowned back, then lifted her eyebrows, urging me to speak.

"Thank you for helping him."

Cassie's smile twitched. She dropped back onto the sofa and leaned forward. "I wanted to thank him—make sure he's okay, yah know? He was in a bad way in that place. But Gina said he's not here?"

"Not for a few days." A week and… eight hours. I perched on the arm of the opposite sofa and cradled my tea on my thigh. Her top had shifted up her arm, exposing her wrists and the track marks there. I might have thought the pale welts left over from drug abuse, if I hadn't known she'd been kept in Wordsworth. Those marks made her a latent. Was she really here for Dom, or for something else?

"I er… well, anyway… thanks for the tea." She smiled at Gina and got to her feet. Her eyes, a startling green, not unlike Robin's, fixed on me. "It's funny, right… Shit happens. People go missing. Some die. Things change. Sometimes for the better."

"I'm sure." Funny? No.

She held my gaze. And the accent, the fact she'd helped Dom from inside Wordsworth… I understood who her *people* were—Charles Renick. She was trying to tell me how his disappearance had made things better for her and other latents in the East End.

She started to leave but stopped at my side, thrust her hands into her pockets, and turned her head, catching my eye. "Just er… you know… Keep doin' what you're doin' Mister K. Some of us 'preciate it."

I nodded. She winked. And we were both on the same page. She lifted her hood and opened the shop door. The old bell tinkled. "Fuckin' 'ell, Boytoy," she said to someone outside. "You're a bitch to find."

Cassie stepped aside and Dom—frozen, as though she'd caught him loitering on the doorstep—frowned at her. "Hi, Pink. And don't call me that."

She punched him in the shoulder, leaned in, and whispered something. His eyes darted to me.

Something electric and powerful sang through my veins. *He came back.*

Then after shaking Dom by the shoulder, Cassie left—she was quite the character, that one.

Dom stepped into the shop. He closed the door behind him, the bell tinkled, and then it was just the three of us. He wore heavy boots, too, loose dark blue jeans, and a V-neck sweater that appeared to be a size too small by the way it hugged his torso.

I didn't recall everything that had happened in Wordsworth, but I did remember his weight, his mouth on mine, and the desperate need to get back to him, to find his light in the dark.

He cleared his throat. "Hey."

I'd been staring and focused on my mug of tea—now cold—instead.

Just hey. Not a word. Not a call. Nothing. Just hey.

"You wanna cuppa?" Gina asked, already scooting off up the stairs without waiting for his answer, no doubt making herself scarce for our benefit.

"The shop looks good." Dom drifted through the living room, admiring its new furniture and layout.

"Nobody wants to buy books from a dangerous latent and his cohorts." The words came out a lot sharper sounding than I'd meant them.

He winced and turned. "Sorry."

I wasn't even sure what he was saying sorry for. Sorry for not being here, sorry for the shop, sorry for my life having crumbled around me? Bloody hell, I hadn't realized quite how much it all hurt. It was all necessary, and inevitable, but that didn't make it any less painful. "The agency is dead," I said, and he winced again, and before he could say something soft that might crack me open, I added, "So there's no reason for you to stay. I'll have to let Gina go, as well, of course. I'll rent the shop out. Cecil Court fetches prime rental rates—"

He crossed the floor in two strides and for a breathless second, I thought he meant to kiss me, but something stopped him. He stood so close his trick tingled my skin—my chest, where he'd had his hand and poured his life into me. I didn't breathe, didn't move.

I didn't recall everything, but I knew what he'd done. He'd saved me, brought me back, and the depth of my gratitude was almost overwhelming. That and something else, something as powerful and bright as trick, something born of the heart that a man like me had no right to feel. Something like love.

"If that's what you want?" he said.

"What I want?"

"To fire me and Gina?"

"What choice do I have?"

"There's always a choice." His lips did that little smile that won me over every time.

I sighed, wished I could hold my head up, laugh about all this and brush it under a rug like Alexander Kempthorne would have, but too much had changed. I wasn't that Alexander Kempthorne anymore. "I'm afraid I really don't know what to do."

His smile bloomed, dazzling and bright. He flopped onto the sofa behind him, instantly at home, as though he'd never left. "What would Robin do?" he asked.

What *would* Robin do? I looked around us, at the chaos that was now my life. A bookstore, full of books with nobody to buy them. An agency nobody wanted to hire. Staff, friends who relied on me. "Tell me to get a cleaner."

He snorted. "C'mon... this is you." He rolled a hand. "Billionaire supervillain."

Oh dear. "You've been reading the headlines."

He chuckled, and looking like he did, sprawled there for the taking, it was a good thing Gina was upstairs or I might have knelt over him and—

"Tea?" Gina reappeared with a tray of tea and biscuits. "Note there are two Jammie Dodgers each. Dom, no stealing." She set the tray down on the coffee table and plonked herself next to Dom.

"Pfft, it's the custard creams I'll fight you for," he said.

"I thought you didn't like custard creams? Wait... *No*." She gasped. "It was you! Robin was right!"

"And him." Dom nodded at me as I took a seat on the sofa opposite. "The sly bastard. Nobody ever suspects him. Robin's hoard of biscuits didn't stand a chance."

Gina laughed and Dom reached behind her, trying to sneak a biscuit from her unguarded plate. She grabbed his wrist. "Drop it or die."

I watched the pair of them jostle and laugh ad my heart constricted. The thought of this ending was almost unbearable.

This couldn't be the end of us. The agency was dead, yes. But Kempthorne & Co had helped people. Helped latents. We didn't need the IRL's stamp of approval to continue that work. There were plenty of latents still out there, still needing assistance. The military still had its claws in Dom and could yank him back at any moment, the outcome of which would be devastating for Dom, and the wider world—considering his *classified* potential. If anything, the world was a worse place now than ever before. My Cecil Court misfits could make a difference. *We* could make a difference. *'Keep doin' what you're doin','* Cassie had said, and she had a good point. Wordsworth was gone, Montgomery was dead, the shadows had fallen quiet, but latents were still the same. Our lives continued to be controlled. The source still flowed, content for now, but for how long? There would be more battles to fight. My trick would return. This wasn't the end.

"I have an idea." I dunked my biscuit in my tea. The pair of them stopped their pretend bickering and levelled their stares on me. I needed Gina's enthusiasm and intelligence for what came next, needed Dom's strength and clarity to keep me focused. I needed the pair of them like a latent needed an artifact. They made me better, and they could make others better too. "And I believe you'll like it."

40

D^{om}

We talked. For hours—Kempthorne, Gina, and me—about what we could make of the new and improved Kempthorne & Co. An agency that didn't detain latents, didn't police them. We were going to *help* them. The details still needed thrashing out, and it was close to midnight by the time we'd gotten that far. Gina yawned and took herself off to bed, leaving me and Kempthorne in Cecil Court's new, comfy lounge.

He had that windswept and slightly mad appearance about him—all his edges were frayed, his hair loose, his shirt askew, and his brilliant mind thinking up how to make the world a better place. He was talking now, about hiring someone new, someone with their finger to the pulse of what it was like to be a latent on the ground. Not me, I was ex-military, and not him, because he was Alexander Kempthorne, billionaire latent bad guy. We needed fresh blood. He waffled, and I half listened; the rest of me was watching how the shop's soft lighting made his skin glow, just a little bit, not with trick—it was just him. Like this, unhinged, radiating passion.

My thoughts fell back to seeing him on Montgomery's desk, and knowing he'd died there. He'd died and I'd lost the only thing in my whole life that had mattered.

He'd stopped talking. "You're not listening."

"I am..." I'd already kicked off my boots hours ago, but I deliberately sprawled all of myself across the sofa now, with my head propped on a hand.

His gaze travelled the length of me and snapped back to my face. "Then what did I just ask?"

I had no idea. "How some of your expensive whiskey is a great idea right now?"

"That's not—" He cut himself off, his gaze wandering again, pooling heat down low.

All that fervor and passion in him switched tack. His body language changed, smoothed, and he leaned back in his sofa, kicked his shoes off, and rested an ankle on his knee. "You're right. It's late. We should take a break."

Oh, the sly git. No, a break was not what I wanted at all. And he knew it. He laid his arm along the back of the sofa, inviting me over without saying a word. Christ, he was hot on his new multi-colored sofa, oozing fuck-me vibes. The suspicious bulge in his trousers suggested other parts of him were interested too. That was why he'd leaned back, to let me get a good look at what he was offering. We weren't drunk this time, or coming down off a bender, like we had been before. This was all us, as it should be.

His eyes burned with lust. If he'd had his trick, he would have glowed with it. I'd been hoping to tempt him over to my side, but there was no way I could resist him reclining, waiting for the inevitable.

"Come here," he growled.

I stretched my arms over my head and rolled onto my back, knowing my shirt rode up, exposing some middle. "Maybe I will—maybe later."

He *moved*—suddenly bracing over me, his eyes fierce, mouth pressed into a serious line. I began to say something sassy, but his lips on mine stole the words. He kissed hard, thrust his tongue in, and my head emptied of everything but the hard press of his hip, the taste of tea and something gingery on my lips, the rasp of his stubble rubbing mine. He rolled his hips, grinding in and over me, and my moan slipped free. He was ablaze, hot and fast, everywhere at once, hand and mouth and tongue, teeth and fingers.

He shoved my T-shirt up and flicked my nipple. I bucked, swore, realized he had hold of my wrists over my head and groaned for more. His tongue swirled, travelling downward, dipping between my abs, down... With his free hand, he popped my jeans button open and in seconds had my erection in his grip. Shivers ran from head to toe. He let my wrists go and pulled my cock between his lips. I garbled some nonsense, mostly fucks —a lot of fucks—and thrust my hands into his hair. Wet, firm, sucking, the roll of his tongue, his left hand on my pec, right holding my thighs open, and I was caught, a hundred percent his.

Pleasure tightened, coiling like a spring. Jesus... I garbled some more noises, then a breathless, "Wait..."

He lifted off, eyes questioning.

Like this, lips pink, eyes glazed, he was too bloody gorgeous. "We don't need to rush," I said. "I'm not going anywhere."

He looked away as though I'd pricked some nerve. Shit, what had I said? I touched his chin, drawing him back. "What is it?"

"Nothing." All gruff and short. He swallowed, then found my gaze again and attacked, grabbing my jaw, grinding against my cock. His lips sizzled against mine and he mumbled, "Where did you go for a week?"

I breathed, panted... so bloody aroused the words got stuck in my throat. "... Home."

"The East End?"

"No... somewhere else. My mum's... she's in witness protection—I can't tell you where."

He let go and seemed to realize he was holding me down and demanding answers. He straightened, propped himself on an arm, braced over me again. "Why?"

"The cops, they think it's best if my dad's people don't get to her—"

"No, why did you go home?"

I shuffled onto my elbows. How much should I say? The truth, probably. "I er..." Well, this was a mood killer. "Sex first, then the Q and A?" Maybe he'd forget he'd asked about my home by the time we'd fucked ourselves boneless.

"I..." He cleared the gravel in his voice and sighed. "You frightened me." His gaze skipped sideways, then out into the shop to focus somewhere far away.

Christ... I shifted up, wriggling out from under him, and when he straightened, sitting up again, trying hard to avoid my glare, I planted my knees either side of his, straddling his thighs, trapping him on the couch.

He dropped his head back and managed a small smile. "Comfortable?"

"Nah." I slipped my hand behind his head to cradle the back of his neck and kissed him, slowly—just a gentle sweep of the tongue across his lips. He opened and met the kiss as though afraid of it. "Idiot," I mumbled.

"Me?" His eyes widened.

"Both of us." I grabbed his shirt in a fist. "You scared me too. That's why I left. I... with what happened, I scared *myself*. You fucking died, Kempthorne." I'd been straddling him when he'd died too, a bit like this, but less upright, and less comfortable, with a storm of shadows howling and his last breaths leaking out of him. The memories tried to muscle their way in—his lifeless body under me, my lips on his, trying to breathe into an empty shell.

"Will you call me Alex?" he said, all soft and vulnerable.

I kissed him again, kissed him harder, rougher. Because he'd made me so fucking afraid. "I don't scare easily, Alex," I whispered.

"Neither do I."

"You died, and I couldn't handle it, okay? So I went home to reset."

A dark eyebrow arched and his mouth twitched. "To your mum?"

"Fuck off." The kiss was harder again, sharper, full of tongue and teeth. His cock pulsed where it was trapped between us.

He clutched at my hair and pulled me off, the both of us ragged and breathless. "Did you talk to her about me?" His eyes flashed.

"What do you think?"

"What did you say?"

"That I almost lost someone I… care for."

"And?"

"Christ, can we not talk about my mum right now and fuck first?" To emphasize my point, I ground my cock against his navel and felt his cock twitch in response.

I don't know how he did it, but his hand dropped to my back and he bucked, flipping me down, my back on the couch, and with a swift jerk of his trousers fly, his silky-smooth dick brushed against my exposed belly at the same time as his fingers dove inside my pants and sank under my balls.

"Oh Jesus…" I clutched at his arse, still infuriatingly hidden inside trousers. There were too many clothes between, and way too much fumbling. I needed him naked. Now.

"I am going to fuck you, John," he growled, pinning me under his glare. "But I want an answer."

"This is emotional blackmail." I laughed, then choked on the laugh when his fingers cupped my balls and squeezed. I growled. "You know, Alex, if you want a piece of my arse"—I clutched at his backside and pulled us so tightly together that his hand got trapped against my cock and his—"you gotta play nice."

He swore in the queen's English, making me laugh some more, but soon sobered. "After you left, I thought I'd committed some heinous act. I was sure you weren't coming back. You didn't call. I tried to call you, but—"

"I lost my phone in Ravenscourt's field. Haven't had time to—" His kiss went through me like an electric shock. I grabbed at his hair and pulled him back. There was that fear again. Fear that he'd lost me. And I knew that fear well, having felt it open up a hole in the ground and swallow me down. "Alex, I'm not going anywhere. Okay?"

"All right."

He didn't believe me because his whole life was full of people who left and didn't come back. I planned to change that. Starting now. "No more talk. We're both idiots. Fuck me into this sofa."

"Yes." He smiled his true, Alex smile. And then he scuttled down and his mouth sealed over my cock and all the bad thoughts fluttered away. All but one. I hadn't only gone home. I hadn't only been away because my love for him and having him almost die had scared me shitless. I'd gone to the Docklands, gone to Kage, to check he was all right, to talk about Penny, but what I'd found there had scared me too. The apartment door had been shattered, the apartment trashed—blood on the shining tiles, blood on the kitchen units, broken glass, bullet holes, and a note. A bloodstained note in the trash. Thrown there for me because he knew I'd look.

Don't come for me.

Don't do the right thing.
It's what I deserve.
~ K

Shadows of London continues in #4 Truth or Dare. Read on for an excerpt. Buy now.

TRUTH OR DARE EXCERPT

Alexander

The bell above Cecil Court's front door tinkled, signaling Dom's arrival. He stomped into the shop, trailing clumps of slushy snow.

"Boots!" Gina scolded from somewhere behind me in Cecil Court's new-look lounge.

He grumbled, turned, and spent the next five minutes picking off wet gloves and trying to pry off his boots without leaving more puddles on the old shop's freshly stripped and varnished floorboards. "Sorry I'm late. I don't know why the tube doesn't bloody run when it snows. It's not like it's snowing *underground*."

"You posh West Enders are shit in the snow," Cassie, the newest member of the team, said in her cockney twang. A moment later, a coin plunked into the swear jar. Most of the time she pre-paid at the beginning of the day by slotting five pounds through the jar's lid and proceeded to bring a whole array of animated and colorful words into Cecil Court. The jar had been her idea.

"I resent being called a West Ender, thanks, *Pink*." Dom smiled and my heart flip-flopped in my chest. I'd tried to ignore the general furor and focus on the business accounts Gina had printed off for me, but as with anything John Domenici related, the moment he appeared, I could think of little else.

Dom shrugged off his coat and sauntered toward the Victorian fireplace we'd recently discovered while redecorating the shop into something more like a home—a home with a lot of shelves. And books. After warming his hands over the fire, he sensed my gaze and glanced up. His smile thawed, growing.

"Hey." He dropped into the sofa beside me, thigh touching mine. He smelled of the cold air and road salt. Color had nipped at his cheeks and his dark-lashed eyes shone. It had been almost a month since Wordsworth and Montgomery, since I'd died and Dom had dragged me back by sheer stubbornness, and whatever this was between us burned brighter and hotter than any fire.

"What yah doin'?" He peeked at the documents on the coffee table.

"Trying to concentrate."

"Oh." His hand slid up my thigh. "Really?" Fingers dug in, reminding me of exactly how he'd dug them in last night, and the night before that. He reclined, hand shifting to my back, and a little of his trick spilled in, tingling, familiar, and warm.

"How was our lovely IRL friend, Doris Worthington?" I asked. He'd been summoned there for the typical monthly competency tests.

"I passed, ruining her day."

I smirked at that. "Good for you."

"Fuck, yeah," Cassie blurted. A moment later: *clink.*

"Or you could just ease up on the swearing," Gina suggested.

"Not bloody likely."

I leaned back and spread my arm along the back of the sofa, behind Dom, at the same time as glancing at Gina. She had her head bent close to Cassie's as they went over some marketing initiative that Gina had thought up. A way to advertise our endeavor as latent-friendly, and less like the other agencies, which only wanted to throw latents in prison, or worse. Cassie had been with us a week and was still finding her place. My instinct said she was right for us, but a niggling tickle at the back of my mind warned me that there was more to her being here than wanting to help latents and get paid, while getting out of the East End.

"She'll be all right," Dom said softly. He liked her. Even if she did shock him as much as the rest of us.

"Yes, I think so."

The shining sparkle in his eyes lost some of its luster. "Listen... I need to tell you something."

"The reason you wanted to meet me here?"

He'd called on his way to the IRL processing center and left a message to make sure I waited for him at the shop. He'd be back for ten a.m., and we needed to talk.

"Detective Diaz called for you, Dom," Gina said. "He sent an email? Said he was waiting on your go. I guess you know what he means?"

"Yeah, thanks." Dom caught my eye, then shifted forward on the sofa and rubbed his hands together. He was on his feet next and drifting back toward the fire. Restless. Anxious. Why? "Okay, so... Cas, this probably won't mean much to you, but you're here so... you need to know."

His gaze clipped me, moving quickly on. "A few weeks back... I dropped by Kage's place." He stared at Gina, skipping me altogether.

Ah.

A few weeks ago. When he hadn't called me, when he'd vanished... He'd gone to see Kage. "And what did the American have to say?"

"Wait, who's Kage?" Cassie asked.

"The guy who shot the girl to save you and Dom," Gina offered, as a quick explanation.

"Oh, *him*," she purred. "The badass supermodel American, that one."

Dom found the ceiling fascinating, Gina gulped, and I discovered I'd quite like a whiskey.

There was a lot more to it than Kage having saved Dom when I couldn't. Such as how he'd drugged Dom, stalked him, reported on him to his superiors, and how he'd cuffed him, hellbent on kidnapping him for the Latent Observation Agency, the American version of our IRL, but with guns, and teeth. He had also slept with Dom, and for a while, they'd been... close. So close, I'd saved Kage's life for Dom, a decision that continued to circle back around and bite me on the arse.

I got to my feet.

"Wait—where are you going?" Dom asked.

"Getting a drink." I climbed the stairs, all the way to the top, anger building with every step. It wasn't a lot to ask that Kage Mitchell not feature in our lives, was it? I disliked the man, mostly because he was in love with Dom, but also because he shot latents for a living. I should have shoved him out of a window long ago.

I retrieved a bottle of whiskey and three glasses—all I could fit in my fingers—and carried them back downstairs to find the three of them seated on the sofas, heads bent together, muttering in hushed tones, no doubt bringing Cassie up to speed on Kage and Dom's history.

If I had nothing to worry about, why wouldn't Dom meet my gaze? What had happened in that week? He said he'd gone home to his mother's. Perhaps he had. For a day. Perhaps he spent the rest of the time with Kage?

I poured three drinks, grabbed a mug, and poured mine. Jealousy was an ugly emotion. Hideously unfair and irrational. I'd never thought of myself as the jealous type. Until now.

"Well? What did you talk about during the week you vanished and visited Kage?" The weather? How Kage wanted me dead? And how, now that Montgomery was out of the way, I was probably next on his hit list?

My tone was barbed and Dom narrowed his eyes, disliking it, and me. "He wasn't there. But this was." He tossed a slip of creased, stained paper onto the coffee table.

"Oh God. Is that blood?" Gina picked it up, turned ashen, and passed it to Cassie.

Maybe it was a suicide note? One could hope. *Good Lord, I'm a horrible person.*

"The apartment was trashed. He'd been taken—by force. I found bullet holes, and Detective Diaz found casings. There was enough there for the Met to open a MISPER file."

So dramatic, so American, so Kage.

"Jesus, Alex," Dom growled, reading my unguarded face. "I know you don't like him, but he could be dead."

"How terrible."

Now all three of them stared. I pinched my lips together. This was why I struggled to keep friends or maintain relationships.

Cassie handed me the note.

Don't come for me.

Don't do the right thing.

It's what I deserve.

~ K

Telling them the note was meant for Dom to go chasing after Kage, because that was exactly what Kage Mitchell, an FBI-trained psychoanalyst, would do, would not endear me to any of them. So I kept my thoughts to myself and dropped the note. "The Met will find him."

"But they haven't. It's been weeks. Diaz's email... He says there's chatter among the LOA that one of their agents has been kidnapped on UK soil." Dom hesitated. "They're looking at you, Kempthorne, because Kage had orders to procure you. You were his last target."

"*Procure* me?" And I was the one in the wrong? "Excuse me." I couldn't participate in this conversation without digging myself a hole to climb into. I took my mug of whiskey back upstairs.

"Alex?" Dom called up.

"Carry on... I have nothing to add."

He jogged up the stairs, and by the time I'd made it to my loft, he breezed in a step behind me and slammed the door. "Don't be a dick about this."

He didn't see my flinch because I kept it inside and

hid it by sipping whiskey. "What do you want me to say?" I thunked the mug down, spilling whiskey on the table, and sneered at it instead of Dom. "The man works for the LOA. We aren't the only people he's crossed. He likely has many enemies. He made his thoughts regarding you and I very clear. This is not our problem." I turned and found Dom standing very still, his jaw locked and his hand clenched at his side. Did he care that much for Kage? "The Met will deal with this."

"You just don't want to help."

"No, frankly, I don't."

His brow furrowed. "I don't know what I thought... Maybe that you'd help me? Something has happened to him. He was one of us."

"He *betrayed* us."

"He had to."

I didn't understand why we were arguing about Kage Mitchell. I had enough to battle with without pulling the American back in. Or maybe it was because Dom couldn't let him go? I leaned against the table and clamped my hands around its edges, holding myself rigid. Dom had that look on his face, the soft expression, the one I couldn't guard against or say no to. I'd do anything for him and the more I held his gaze, the more the hardness around my heart melted away. "What do you want?"

"Your help."

"Do you want me to find him?"

"Yes... You have connections. I just... Look." He gestured at the air, grasping for an explanation. "It's not what you think. Okay? I don't... There's nothing between us. I just can't let this go. It's not right."

"Can't let *him* go."

He stilled, frowned, then snorted a laugh and sauntered up to me. I didn't move but, slouched as I was, I had to lift my chin to meet his smoldering eyes. He knew he'd won. "I didn't think you'd be the jealous type," he purred.

"Neither did I." I didn't want to be *that* kind of man. Hadn't expected to feel helpless in all of this. If he knew how much I cared for him, wanted him to be mine, nobody else's, he wouldn't tease. This—him—us—it was all new. Like walking on thin ice. One crack, one wrong step, and I'd shatter everything.

Dom's firm, warm hands eased around my waist. "Would you just trust me?"

I straightened, parting my knees, slotting him between my thighs, where I'd discovered he felt so right.

I did trust him, more than anyone. So much it was terrifying. Because he had no idea how he held my heart in his rough hands, where it could so easily be crushed. His mouth teased mine, breaths mingling. "I barely know who I am around you," I told him, and meant it. This was all new. My whole world had crumbled around us. *I* was new.

"Is that a yes?" He nuzzled my neck, breaths fluttering warm against my skin, each one a tease that soared through me, gradually breaking me down and filling me. Well, parts of me. How could I say no?

"I'll pull some strings."

Shadows of London continues in #4 Truth or Dare. Buy from Amazon today.

ABOUT THE AUTHOR

Born to wolves, Rainbow Award Winner Ariana Nash only ventures from the Cornish moors when the moon is fat and the night alive with myths and legends. She captures those myths in glass jars and returning home, weaves them into stories filled with forbidden desires, fantasy realms, and wicked delights.

Sign up to her newsletter and get a free ebook here: https://www.subscribepage.com/silk-steel